Drew wasn't sure  him

He did know hg.
Not here in the ol
his physical rea ed
against him had tting
the snow.

He wanted to stop time with the feel of her in his arms. He glanced down at her, dark lashes forming half circles on her pale cheeks, her mouth parted around shallow breaths.

"Are you all right?" he asked automatically.

She surprised him by sliding her arms around his chest. The heat melded their skin together. Her hair tickled his nose with every breath. Her sleek curves unfolded against him so he could feel the length of her soft thighs, the way she fitted into the curve of his body.

His pulse began to race, rebelling wildly against his best intentions. And they were the very best. Just useless against the feel of her in his arms. A familiar burning started inside, a reaction that was going toe-to-toe with his discipline.

For the first time, he was losing sight of his job, rapidly forgetting that he had to protect her. Instead he was reacting like a man to a very beautiful woman.

Dear Reader,

I'm fascinated by the people who dedicate their lives to national security and defense. These caring people possess such courage of heart—whether they serve at home or abroad, in peace or adversity. The sheer fact they live their lives in such diverse settings and circumstances for the benefit of others speaks to the nobility of the human spirit.

That's the idea that gave life to the Excelsior Agency.

I fell in love with this world of covert operations back in 2005, when I wrote *In the Cold* (Harlequin Signature Select Spotlight November 2005), and I am beyond thrilled to have the freedom to revisit Excelsior again in *Her Last Protector*. Mirie and Drew are people who understand the meaning of loyalty, each in their unique circumstances and in their own ways. While their goals may seem worlds apart (countries, actually!), together they learn that honor does not come without sacrifice, everything worthy is worth fighting for and love conquers all.

Ordinary people. Extraordinary romance.

Harlequin Superromance is the place to enjoy stories set in circumstances where love will endure. I hope you enjoy Mirie and Drew's love story. Visit me at www.jeanielegendre.com.

Peace and blessings,

Jeanie London

JEANIE LONDON

—

Her Last Protector

HARLEQUIN®SUPER ROMANCE®

Recycling programs
for this product may
not exist in your area.

ISBN-13: 978-0-373-60827-0

HER LAST PROTECTOR

Copyright © 2014 by Jeanie LeGendre

This edition published by arrangement with Harlequin Books S.A.

For questions and comments about the quality of this book, please contact us at CustomerService@Harlequin.com.

Printed in U.S.A.

ABOUT THE AUTHOR

Jeanie London writes romance because she believes in happily-ever-afters. Not the "love conquers all" kind, but the "we love each other, so we can conquer anything" kind. Jeanie is the winner of many prestigious writing awards, including multiple *RT Book Reviews* Reviewers' Choice and National Readers' Choice Awards. She lives in sunny Florida with her own romance-hero husband, their beautiful daughters and a menagerie of strays.

Books by Jeanie London

HARLEQUIN SUPERROMANCE

HARLEQUIN BLAZE

*Falling Inn Bed...

HARLEQUIN SIGNATURE SELECT SPOTLIGHT

Other titles by this author available in ebook format.

To everyone who defends this wonderful country
I call home.

Your dedication reminds us all that we gain nothing
through apathy. And your courage sets the standard.
You are appreciated. May God bless you all.

CHAPTER ONE

"Drei Timko," a voice barked.

Drew responded to the name as if it were his own. In the ways that mattered, the name was his. The man once known as Drew Canady had become a ghost from another lifetime. A life so long gone, he had almost forgotten. *Almost.* Not quite.

Turning, he watched the grizzled old man muscle through the crowd, broad shoulders forging a path through the mourners, face split with a gaptoothed grin. The logger, a man named Vlas, had befriended Drew back when he had been a stranger among strangers in this mountain village of Alba Luncă.

"You guard the princess as closely as you once guarded a lighthearted girl." Vlas clapped Drew on the back.

Drew glanced at the woman walking behind the casket cart—graceful and dressed head to toe in white, from the fur *ushanka* on her head to the hiking boots on her feet. She looked appropriately austere for a funeral, colorless but for the flushed cheeks and wisps of caramel-colored hair lifting on the wind, her expression as brittle as the weather.

"That's what they pay me to do." His breath clashed with the morning air in a frigid burst.

Princess Mirela of Ninsele hadn't been that light-hearted girl for a very long time.

Not since the years before his princess had come out of hiding. One minute she had been the girl he'd been hired to protect, a girl who loved to run barefoot through the meadows in spring.

Now she was the ruler of this mountain kingdom, and a very desirable woman. When he looked at her, he didn't see Princess Mirela, last royal of the House of Selskala. He saw past the woman who engaged the media with intelligence and grace, who handled foreign diplomats skillfully and didn't retreat when facing revolutionaries and thugs who would bully her to sidestep justice. He didn't see the woman the media had nicknamed "Mirie of Alba Luncă," a princess who had long hidden among commoners.

Drew saw only the laughing woman he had devoted so many years to protecting.

The woman who rarely made an appearance anymore.

He didn't share the thought with Vlas, who had once been a friend. Long ago, he and the old logger had stood around the bonfire in the square, sharing opinions and flasks of *făţată*. Now they trudged uphill in an early-morning funeral procession. Nearly a mile of icy dirt road. In minus-twelve degree weather. The people of Alba Luncă were Spartans.

At least Drew wasn't carrying the casket or digging the grave in frozen earth. He had retreated far enough to assess the procession perimeter but still had his eyes on his target. He had been in lockstep with Mirie for more than fifteen years. "The princess seems pleased to be back," Vlas said.

Drew wouldn't go that far. Mirie was burying her nanny, the woman who had saved her life during a coup when the royal family was executed. Geta Bobescue had hidden the eight-year-old princess in this obscure village. With the help of a retired royal guard, she protected Mirie during the decade-long civil war and prepared her for the day the dictator was overthrown. That day had come six years ago. Mirie had been plucked from Alba Luncă and taken to the capital city of Briere to rule her kingdom.

She hadn't been back since.

Geta's funeral was a bittersweet reason to return. This visit also posed an unnecessary risk. But Mirie hadn't considered the risk to herself enough reason to forsake the task of burying her nanny.

Fortunately this funeral procession wasn't a fast-moving train. It wound through the village slowly, people adhering to the crowd like filings on a magnet with each shop they passed, each house and alley. This parade of mourners was intent, like Mirie, upon honoring its dead. And enjoying the charity meal that would come after the burial. That was tradition.

Drew scanned each newcomer and kept a watch on the rooftops, balconies and doorways, assessing potential threats. He needed to get a lock on everyone who ventured near Mirie.

The Ninsele Royal Protection Guard, known as the NRPG, was the branch of military charged with the princess's protection. Right now guards were posted throughout the village, but once the procession moved beyond the gate, the terrain would be nearly impossible to secure. Drew would be the first line of defense. He was always the first line of defense.

"Her Royal Highness tried to return before Geta died, but it wasn't possible," he said. Not with all the preparations to host representatives from the European Commission, who would be arriving in Ninsele in a matter of weeks.

A historic first step that was attracting global attention.

"Geta was at peace. She called the priest and received absolution and the Eucharist. She didn't expect the princess to return even for the funeral." Vlas withdrew an envelope from his coat pocket. "This is why I chased you down. And *this*." His face split into another grin as he pulled out a leather flask.

Drew accepted the envelope, which had been addressed in a shaky scrawl with the princess's formal title. Slipping the envelope into the pocket inside his coat's lining, he asked, "You want me to deliver this letter to Her Royal Highness?"

"Eventually. When you think she is strong enough to be reminded of the past and her losses. Deathbed request." Vlas took a deep swig after uncorking the flask. "Geta worried about the girl. She told me you would know when best to pass along her words. Give the girl time to grieve."

Drew scanned the crowd around Mirie again, ready to intervene at any sign of a threat. People were keeping their distance, which made his job easier.

The envelope was sealed. Geta would never burden Mirie without good reason. No one knew better how deeply the loss of her family had affected the young princess.

Drew wished he could allow the contents to remain private, but that wasn't his choice. "Anything else I need to know?"

"Secrets, Drei? That girl was Geta's only secret." Vlas motioned to Drew with the flask. "Go on. It'll warm you up. She'll be safe. We protect her as we always have."

The villagers had done that. In the past when the princess's existence had been fodder for conspiracy theorists, the people of Alba Luncă had claimed her as their own. Of course they hadn't known she was a princess. Back then she had simply been a military officer's daughter orphaned in the coup. That explanation justified the privileges and protection Mirie had enjoyed growing up in a rural village—the additional tutors, the bodyguard.

No one had questioned the facts then, and no one remembered them now. Mirie belonged to Alba Luncă. Period. A princess had lived among commoners. She belonged to these people now even more than she had then. No wonder the paparazzi never left her alone. Mirie's story had captured the imaginations of a world that wanted to believe in happy endings.

Drew was determined to make sure Mirie got hers.

"As much as I'd like to accept your hospitality, my friend, I'll have to pass," he said. "I'll make sure she gets this letter at the best possible time."

There would be no good time. Mirie was barely twenty-five years old. She had royal obligation to a country violently split in its regard for the monarchy. Her days were filled with duty as she worked with the Crown Council to win the support of the European Commission to become an acceding country into the European Union and provide Ninsele with a future.

Whether the people wanted that future or not.

Many didn't, but in a life filled with enemies, the one foe that had gotten close was the one Drew couldn't fight.

Time.

He glanced at Mirie again, her hand resting on the

casket as if she didn't want her nanny to be alone. Her head was bowed low beneath the fur *ushanka,* and Drew could tell she was fighting back tears. He wished she'd had the chance to come back and say goodbye one last time.

She might be surrounded by people every moment of every day. Ministers and military officers. People who served. People who clung. People who schemed. People who wanted her to succeed. People who wanted her dead.

But her last connection to family lay in that casket.

Drew understood why Geta had been worried. He also knew why she had wanted him to decide when to turn over the letter. She had faith in his ability to protect Mirie—from physical as well as emotional threats. Protecting Mirie was his job.

One of them, anyway.

But no one in Ninsele knew about his other job. Never once during all these years had Drew given anyone a reason to suspect he wasn't exactly who he claimed to be.

Drei Timko, Romanian close-protection guard.

No one had any idea that he was actually Drew Canady, a sleeper operative for Excelsior, a United States national security agency.

"You will cast down the branches to mark her passing. You who were loved by her as a granddaughter would be."

Grateful for this honor, Mirie accepted an armful of fir branches from the village elder council that stood as ceremonial guard around the grave containing Bunică's casket.

Grandmother.

Geta Bobescue may not have been blood related, but she had become many things to Mirie during their years together. Protector. Confidant. Mentor. Savior in so many ways. Bunică had helped Mirie make sense of the senseless tragedy that had upended her life and helped her find strength. It had been there as promised, buried deep inside. But above all, Bunică had been a last flicker of love when all other flames had sputtered out.

Now she was gone, too.

"Peace, my beloved Bunică," Mirie whispered.

She tossed the branches. They scattered over the casket with the springy sound of living flora. But they were no longer alive. Cut from the tree of life, they would soon grow brittle and dry and wither to dust.

Such was life.

Kneeling, Mirie reached into the pit and broke away a clump of frozen dirt. She tossed a fistful into the grave.

"Godspeed, Bunică. Take our leave now and rest."

You will be missed, she added silently as the priest reached for the hoe.

The church bell tolled, a hollow sound that echoed

over snow-tipped trees covering mountain peaks in every direction. Mirie retreated as a group of young men came to fill the grave.

The tolling filtered through her as if she stood naked in the wind. She had learned restraint through the years, but she had also learned that the past was a ghost and the future beyond her grasp. *Right now* was all she had. If she could only endure *this* moment, she would find her strength again, even though her insides felt frail. As if the wind might sweep away all ability to feel and she would never know anything but weakness again.

And loneliness.

Bunică was free of this life. Bunică of the quick hugs and practical wisdom, who brooked no disobedience or rebellion, yet understood the need for kindness and confidence. Only Bunică's belief in Mirie had helped her learn to believe in herself.

This simple, solid woman, who had been chosen by Mirie's grandfather to rear her beloved Papa, had lived all the stories with her lost family. Bunică had witnessed the first steps and last breaths of two generations. Weddings and coronations. Life and laughter. Fear and murder. How many moments and memories had not yet been told, tiny minutes in the lives of Mirie's family that were now being buried in this grave?

The church bell withered to silence. The priest gave a blessing, and the women gathered to sing the burial song. Mirie joined the circle and raised her voice in a melody that rained sorrow down the mountain.

The song might have been beautiful but for the sadness. And she remembered this feeling, heartache that wrung every ounce of her strength as if her insides were made of sponge.

But she couldn't take Bunică from this mountain. Nor could she leave any part of herself here. She had already given away everything, kept only what she needed to survive.

When the song faded to silence, the feeling lingered, loss cast on the wind, across frosty trees, rebounding through her.

Mirie might never see this place again.

Alba Luncă had been home when she had needed one most. When she had been robbed of love and identity, she had found joy again running through the dirt streets of the village, through leaf-strewn forests, over sunlit meadows.

This place had become everything to her. Shelter. Safety. Solace. But hope most of all. Mirie had learned life would go on here, like it or not. Whether that life was joyous or miserable was a choice that was hers to make and hers alone.

She had clung to that knowledge during these past six years, knowing life in all its simplicity was exactly where she had left it—in the mountains with Bunică. The knowledge had given her strength during never-ending council sessions, consolation when the palace she had been born in felt like an alien planet. Alba Luncă had given her purpose. She worked for Ninsele, fought to preserve a way of life she believed in.

Stay in the present, she reminded herself. *Just focus on this moment.*

The mourners began to move and whisper. It was time to leave. Perhaps forever.

Inhaling deeply, Mirie memorized the taste of the sharp wind in her lungs, of spruce and snow, of hope when all had felt hopeless, of life that filled her with possibilities the way the wind whistled through trees and filled this valley.

There was a path nearby that led to a hidden grove with a spring and a waterfall, one of the many secret places of this harsh yet heavenly country. Secret from strangers, at any rate. Teenagers had long ago designated the place as a rendezvous point. Mirie had kissed her first boyfriend there after escaping from her bodyguard.

Of course she had been caught long before youthful exploration had much of a chance to heat up. She had never been able to lose her tail for long.

That thought only made her sigh.

The fresh earth over Bunică's grave looked like a dirty scar marring the snowy ground, but even in death Bunică's nearness made Mirie long for that simpler time. She could not tear herself away even though she could hear people retreating. Bunică was her connection to Alba Luncă, to her life of eventual peace after everyone she loved had been taken.

Mama, Papa, Alexi, Petre, Stefan...

There had been only Bunică. This tiny mountain village. And these people.

A slight touch on her arm brought her back to the moment.

Drei.

He was there as he always was. The man who had long ago replaced Bunică as Mirie's protector, such a constant presence he had practically vanished. How could she notice her shadow or be surprised by the sight of her reflection in a mirror?

He was a blond bear of a man, hard from every angle—big body, chiseled expression, gemstone eyes. But his gaze was soft now as he watched her with eyes so startlingly green they seemed out of place on a granite face. He waited for her cue, an exchange that had become as natural as breathing to them.

She inclined her head, and he led her away.

They rounded the front of the church, following the procession that was fast losing its formation and reverent demeanor. People joined friends and family for the walk back to the village. They greeted each other. Someone laughed.

Mirie followed with Drei a step behind, feeling the wind sting, more bitter somehow as they left the churchyard. Once these people would have welcomed her easily among them. The women would have ordered her to refill buckets from the well and the men would have asked her to fetch glasses of *țuică*. Now they had receded from her as silently as snow in the spring.

She was no longer the girl they had known. More important, she no longer felt like that girl. And that knowledge made her mood grow as leaden as the clouds that promised snow.

"The storm's coming," she said.

Drei glanced up. "Are you thinking about going back early?"

She nodded.

"What about the charity? The priest is behind us. He'll expect you to say something to kick off the celebration."

Mirie met his gaze, as green as the meadows for those few glorious weeks during summer. She could think of nothing she would rather do less right now than celebrate. "We may risk getting snowed in."

There were no plows to clear the roads. Trans-Alps highways did not traverse the gorges of these steep passes. Not close enough for convenience, anyway. Not until Mirie could find some way of bridging the distance between opposing parties and get a majority to agree on what Ninsele's future looked like.

If she ever got everyone to agree.

Drei only nodded. He would do whatever she

decided, no matter how much effort it cost to rearrange their plans. But Mirie glanced into the storm clouds and knew she would have to take her chances. Tradition must be upheld. She may feel like a stranger right now, but her quick exit would be noticed. She was a conversation piece. Alba Luncă would tell tales of the princess who had hidden among them for generations to come.

She would leave no one disappointed with Bunică's send-off. Especially since she wouldn't be back to host the series of charity meals that would commemorate Bunică's passing for the next year. Mirie would rely on others to host those. Today she would honor the woman who had given her life.

"We'll cross our fing—" She broke off when she saw Drei.

He cocked his head to the side, his grip tightening on her elbow, bringing them to a sudden stop. Mirie knew he was receiving a report through his earpiece. Then he was in motion, pulling her hard against him, his arms like a vise as he spun her around.

"Go, go, go!" he yelled over his shoulder at the villagers. "We have gunfire. Get to the village. Quickly."

Chaos erupted among those who had been nearest the grave site. Plaintive demands and fearful questions discharged into confusion. But none drowned out the sudden growl of an engine in the distance, unseen, yet swelling quickly, churning through the mountain stillness like the roar of an avalanche.

"The village," Drei commanded. "Not the church. Get safely behind the gates."

People started running, shouting, "To the village. To the village."

"Quickly, Your Royal Highness," Drei hissed while spurring her into a run.

Toward the church.

The priest broke away, vestments whipping around him as he bolted in the opposite direction. "I will sound the alarm."

"Get the people to the gates, Father!" Drei shouted.

But the priest followed them to the church, following *her* when he should have been running in the opposite direction.

She tried to keep up with Drei, but the way he surrounded her with his big body kept her blind and off balance. His thighs rammed into the backs of hers with each step, forcing her to keep his pace and nearly sweeping her off her feet as he slammed into the churchyard gate, throwing it open.

The church steps proved her undoing, and she stumbled. Drei lifted her against him as though she weighed no more than air and dragged her up the remaining steps and across the threshold.

He spun around with practiced skill, using the building to shield her as he pulled open the door.

And in that instant, she glimpsed the priest flying through the open gate, and a military transport helicopter riding low just above the treetops, armed men bulging from the open sides.

Powerful engines reverberated through the gorge, the rhythmic *swoop-swoop-swoop* of the blades, the grumbling heartbeat of a conveyance that carried death. The sound was deafening, yet not loud enough to drown out the eruption of gunfire that stunned the morning.

Drei dragged her inside and pulled the door shut, but not before Mirie heard the familiar thuds of bullets pounding flesh.

No warning bells would sound the alarm in Alba Luncă today.

CHAPTER TWO

"Is Her Royal Highness to safety?" General Bog-danovich demanded over the audio device. *"Secure her. Repeat. Secure her. We've eliminated three of the enemy on the road, but a team of six has entered the churchyard. We're surrounding the perimeter, but we're drawing fire from the copter."*

Drew could not respond. The doors of the church slammed open as if on cue, and footsteps pounded over stone.

Mirie stared up from beneath her hat, features drawn and eyes wide. She had pulled on her courage as she might her coat, but he saw the fear in her tight expression, in the dilation of pupils turning blue-gray eyes almost black.

He questioned her without words, and she inclined her head, confirming she was unharmed and functioning. She knew the drill, and she was no longer a terrified eight-year-old.

Drew reevaluated, unsure if they could make the escape route undetected. Their pursuers appeared to be well-funded paramilitaries, seizing the opportunity to eliminate the last royal of the House of Selskala, who had made herself an easy target for the first time in six years.

Raising his pistol, he cased the stairwell before leading Mirie down the steps to the crypt. There were no windows down here, only the dank cold of frozen ground. They moved quickly, sound buffered by stone. But the impenetrable dark finally forced him to lower his pistol and feel his way with a hand along the wall.

Their attackers would break into pairs. One team would head into the loft that ran along the back of the church and the bell tower. Another team would make its way to the sacristy and vesting room, which would lead them here to the crypt entry. The remaining team would canvass the nave with the rows of pews and alcoves of small side altars.

"Major Timko," General Bogdanovich demanded in his ear. *"Sit-rep. Is Her Royal Highness alive?"*

The general wouldn't be getting a situation report any time soon, so Drew tapped once against the audio device.

Affirmative.

She was alive for the moment, anyway.

Mirie pressed against his back, following the drill they had practiced time and again to prepare for this emergency situation.

She needed to pace her breathing, but he could risk no warning. Their feet echoed, the sound amplified by the quiet.

Doors led to mausoleums and a chapel, and an escape route that had been excavated during World War I. Drew could make out the faint glow of the sanctuary lamp in the distance, coming from the second door on the right.

His pistol scratched stone, a noise that made Mirie gasp. He pressed his fingers against her lips, and her soft mouth yielded beneath his touch. Her eyes widened, a flash of white in the darkness. Drew wasn't sure if he had surprised her, or if she was reacting to the low exchange of conversation that filtered down the stairs, but his fingers tingled as he drew his hand away.

Drew pulled her through the second doorway as the voices erupted again, louder this time, nearer. Luck was with them, though. The sanctuary lamp illuminated the obstacle course of furnishings. Chairs. Candle stands. Icons.

The entrance to the tunnel was concealed behind the tabernacle, recessed into the wall behind the altar. But Drew couldn't enter the passage yet, couldn't risk any noise that would jeopardize the only escape route they had. They needed to hide until he had a lock on the enemy's location.

He considered whether they should make a run for the mausoleums. Then Mirie motioned him to the altar, and he learned there were more secrets to this chapel than even he'd known.

The marble altar had a decoration of inlaid mosaic tiles, which turned out to conceal a panel to a hideaway.

Slipping the pistol into his waistband, Drew helped Mirie inside, ensuring that every inch of white fur was hidden. He backed away to shut the panel, but Mirie grasped at his coat, urging him down beside her. The last thing he saw was light slicing beyond the door, and then he was on his knees, curling around her.

She began to shake. Drew could feel her against him, as she struggled to control her chattering teeth. Tightening his arms around her, he held her close until he could almost feel the slim outline of her body through the outerwear already making him sweat.

This was when normal people came unglued, lost their heads and did something stupid that led them to get caught. People who weren't trained to handle the time-bomb pressure of managing fear and waiting to see if luck was with them or if life would get ugly.

Mirie had already witnessed more ugliness than most people. Her family had been slain in military-style executions while she had hidden beneath mock flooring. She had been spared one horror, only to live another, with her nanny's hands pressed over her face to contain her screams and spare her the brutality of her family's last minutes of life.

Boots scuffed over rough stone so close that Mirie inhaled an audible breath. Drew tightened his arms around her and maneuvered his face until he could press his cheek against hers, share the warmth of his skin, use their nearness as distraction.

His heart throbbed dully in his chest, his entire body an insane tangle of nerves and awareness. For two people who had spent every minute of every day together for so many years, for two people who knew so much about each other's lives and intimate habits, they really knew nothing about each other.

Mirie didn't know his true identity.

And Drew had no idea she would feel as if she belonged in his arms.

"Hovno!" A gravelly voice spat out the curse.

A Czech or Slovak curse, and a clue to the identity of their enemy.

The footsteps marked the perimeter of the room. Drew could make out the path, hear the intruder searching behind the chairs that ran the periphery of the chapel beneath the icons adorning the walls in all their Orthodox glory.

The resurrection of Christ.

The Blessed Mother.

Michael the archangel.

A buffet of saints, all of whom Drew sincerely hoped were praying for their escape right now.

Mirie shuddered, but Drew pressed his lips to her cool cheek, the only reassurance he could offer as seconds ticked by, each one stretching into another, protracted and tense. He inhaled fur from her *ushanka* until he was forced to knock the hat from her head with his chin before he sneezed.

Then he was treated to the full impact of her hair, a crisp, clean scent that filtered through his consciousness, made him aware of each strand against his skin.

"Any luck?" the Slovak speaker asked.

Definitely Slovak. They were near the gate.

"Bah!" another voice ground out, sounding like cigarette smoke over gravel. "They did not come down here."

"You break that news to Ratko."

A gruff snort, and the sound of retreating footsteps. Drew filed away that name and hoped the NRPG might neutralize the threat so they could ride out the danger in this hideaway. Could they be so lucky?

But one exchange over the audio transmitter reminded him that Ninsele's resources were no match for well-funded paramilitaries. The effects of a decade-long civil war would be felt for a long time.

"Incoming, General."

"Secure the village gate," General Bogdanovich shot back.

"Roger that."

Then silence.

Drew was out of choices. He couldn't lie in wait until the church was surrounded or a villager tortured into revealing the church's escape route. He had to protect Mirie until the NRPG had a lock on this situation or could spirit her to safety. He could make no other choice, take no chances with Mirie's life.

THE METAL DOOR snapped into place with a gunshot crack that echoed forever. Mirie's heart pounded in time with the sound, so hard that her chest ached from the rapid-fire beat and her ears throbbed with a steady *tat-tat-tat-tat-tat* like automatic gunfire. She couldn't tell if the sound was real or some adrenaline-fueled trick of her imagination.

The memory of gunfire from long ago.

Sinking against the wall, she felt every muscle turn to liquid and her strength drain away.

Drei's attention was on sealing the door, so their pursuers wouldn't follow. From inside the chapel, the decorated metal panel was a showcase for the gold tabernacle with its locked door and keyhole concealed in an apostle's pocket.

The panel concealed a spring-hinged door.

By the time he turned around, Mirie had gotten a hold of herself. With a hand on her arm, he led her into the narrow tunnel, barely high enough for her to stand upright. Drei was forced to hunch over, and kept a step ahead of her as the passage wasn't wide enough to walk abreast.

Only after they had traveled a distance did he dare switch on a light. The red beam gleamed on rough-hewn walls as he whispered, "Talk to me, Your Royal Highness. How are you holding up?"

Her staccato heartbeat and the stale air suffocated her. She swallowed back a cry when her fingers sank into some sticky substance on the wall.

A spider's web? Sweet Lord. If only the remnants of a web and the creature within were the worst of her troubles....

"I'm okay." A lie.

She was bone-cold and shaking. Retrieving the glove in her pocket, she slipped her fingers inside and willed away thoughts of the men with rounds of ammunition strapped to their vests and the sound of gunfire outside.

Tat-tat-tat-tat-tat.

Drei didn't reply. She could barely see his face, only the pinpoint beam of light that sliced through the endless darkness.

"Frightened," she finally admitted. "Worried about the villagers." And so, so guilty because she had been advised not to make this trip.

"The general has secured the gate and called for reinforcements." Drei's deep whisper embraced the dark, soothed with its tone. He liked this answer much better than the first one she had given. "He and his unit will capture these thugs."

"You think they're criminals?" That surprised her. Why would criminals bother with an attack when they could all too easily cross Ninsele's borders— one more problem that hadn't yet been solved?

"They're thugs no matter who finances them."

Ah, Mirie understood. Of course they were after *her*. Why else would anyone bother this sleepy village? And Drei would take any attempt against her personally.

She should never have risked leaving Briere, no matter how much she had wanted to be here for Bunică. Her selfish decision would impact everyone now because the NRPG could not deploy aircraft to pursue their attackers. The nearest air base was at the country's western border and it belonged to Hungary. And Ninsele didn't need the bad press. Not now. Not so close to the arrival of the European Commission's representatives. Would they call off the talks, fearing for their safety? Had she just sabotaged all the progress they'd made toward the stabilization plan?

Was it any wonder she was struggling to breathe?

"The people expected a meal with a princess," she said. "A celebration of a life lived with love."

Was it really so much to ask for the princess they had treated as their own to speak at a funeral?

"They'll have tales to tell their kids," Drei said. "And they will celebrate life. Geta's memorial and their own escape. The meal is already prepared."

If they escaped. Mirie prayed he was right, appreciated his effort to reassure her.

But words and kindness couldn't take away the guilt. She was responsible for her selfish choice to leave the safety of the royal compound. Now people were running for safety and fleeing armed paramilitaries.

How many would be killed like the priest?

"The general will make inquiries," Drei continued, clearly determined to reassure her. "We'll know by the time we get back to Briere. Who knows? Maybe some group will claim responsibility and save us the trouble of a search."

"You hope."

That made his gaze soften just a bit.

"I do."

They both knew the trouble with assassins and revolutionaries was that they usually didn't want to be identified. Secrecy gave them power. A terrorist cell would claim responsibility immediately and whip the media into a frenzy to frighten people.

"Let's keep moving." Drei locked his fingers around her wrist and guided her hand around his waist. His touch was solid, a reminder against worrying about things they could not control. Drawing her close, he pointed the red beam of his flashlight into the darkness.

Mirie kept pace beside him, concealed by his broad chest, chiding herself for her weakness. She had known the risks when deciding to make this journey. Yet she had hoped for the best, had felt she deserved to make this trip. She had survived when her family had not. She had a purpose to fulfill, an obligation. And she asked nothing in return. Only a chance to bury the woman who had loved her like a grandmother.

"How did you know about the altar?" Drei asked.

"Bunică was always afraid I would be discovered and instructed me how to escape."

"She was wise." He wanted to distract her. Her protector in body and spirit. Always.

But he couldn't protect her from the truth.

"Has the general confirmed any casualties?" Innocent people had become targets. People guilty of no more than burying their dead, of lingering to get close to a princess.

Anyone who came near her was at risk.

She was poison.

Mirie could imagine the funeral procession in the wake of her escape, people frantic and screaming for their lives as they raced down the road for the gate, some whose steps would have been slowed by age or infirmity.

Had they stood any chance of reaching safety?

"Your Royal Highness." Drei stretched out the syllables, a stern warning. "The general knows his duty. And the potential risks. He brought only his best men. They will secure the situation. Trust that much, at least."

He knew her so well. She forgot that most of the time.

"I do." But the cost of even one life was one that could never be calculated.

There were no answers in the passage that curved tightly in upon itself. The footing was treacherous. Drei moved along awkwardly, using the wall to brace himself. He kept her locked against him, steadied her as the floor descended sharply.

Mirie had known of the passage, but had never traveled it. The exit was far from the village, a place one might be able to escape through gorges that sliced a path toward the northern border. The secret of the passage was held tightly by only a few on the elder council, passed down through generations to those trusted with the villagers' safety.

"You knew of this passage but not the altar?" she asked.

"I've spent a lot of years formulating escape routes in case we needed them. I'm sure Geta wanted you to have escape options even from me."

He was right. Bunică had witnessed the effects of trusting the wrong people. But Mirie had to trust Drei. Otherwise, how could she function?

"Then it's good we work together," she said calmly, when she felt anything but. "You know where this passage leads?"

"The general vicinity."

"Think we'll be able to escape?"

"Yes."

"Would you tell me if the answer was no?" She felt the motion as he slanted his head, as though peering down at her.

"No." He gave a short laugh.

Under normal circumstances, his answer would have annoyed her, but the sound of that one humorless laugh stuck, a thought to divert the other sounds in her head.

Tat-tat-tat-tat-tat.

He seemed not to feel the brutal cold while her adrenaline seeped away in slow degrees. She couldn't be sure how long they walked, but not much time had passed since she'd said her farewell to Bunică. Forcing herself to focus, Mirie put one foot in front of the other despite her quaking knees and chattering teeth.

Drei must have noticed her struggle because he brought them to another stop. Handing her the light, he opened his coat to forage through his inner pockets.

He withdrew a thick square wrapped in crackling plastic. With a few quick gestures, he shook out a weather poncho made of thin waterproof canvas.

"Wear this." His voice was gentle as he drew the white outerwear around her and pulled a hood up over her head, hat and all. "It'll help with the cold."

"You travel prepared."

"That's what you pay me to do."

Such a simple reply, yet not so simple. He had known there might be danger because she had left her secured palace, a glittering shell that housed the golden egg.

"Any better?" he asked.

She nodded, appreciating his precautions and his concern.

The tunnel began an ascent. Gravity and ice conspired to make each step more difficult. There were no handholds, and she was finally forced to cling to Drei, who anchored himself against the rough wall, a bulwark always, shifting his balance to secure her, his arm locked tight, his grip strong yet gentle.

And when they finally reached the end of the passage, they found a half-rotted wooden portal shaped like a manhole cover. The exit had long ago been concealed beneath snow and forest debris, making an icy, dirty blotch that didn't budge when Drei put his weight to it.

He shut off the light. "I need you to step back, Your Royal Highness. This mess may collapse. I don't want you far, though."

"I can hold the light."

"I have to see what's out there, and this wood is disintegrating. I start loosening this ice, and the mountain might fall in."

Mirie retreated just far enough to watch Drei work.

He tested the wood, used a knife to coax away debris so he might see outside.

Mirie gasped when the crack of ice startled the quiet. Suddenly thin light penetrated the darkness. He slipped some sort of slim instrument through the hole—a mirror?—and must have been satisfied with what he had seen because he pulled out another weather poncho like her own, camouflage to blend in with the snow-covered terrain.

This man was such a blessing in her life. Had she ever even told him how grateful she was for all his careful attention?

Probably not. She barely noticed him at all. Took his presence for granted. An oversight she would have to change immediately.

"I'll stay within earshot, but if you hear gunfire, you head back the way we came," he said, business-like. "Just stay inside the passage until the general makes contact."

He withdrew his audio transmitter, then with cal-loused fingertips, he tilted her head to the side. She could feel the warmth of his skin as he slipped his hand beneath her hat and brushed aside her hair. He wedged the tiny device in her ear, his touch soft, warm, so alive.

For the moment, anyway. They both knew if she heard gunfire, he was dead. That would be the only reason Drei wouldn't return to her, and without him, her chances of making it out of this passage alive weren't good.

"We're out of range now. But if you make it back into the church, you'll be in contact with the gen-eral. Got it?"

She nodded.

"Stay hidden."

Then he crawled through the opening and vanished.

Mirie could hear the rustling of branches and tree limbs, his boots crunching through the snow. Then all sounds faded, leaving only silence to drown out the noise of her thoughts, solitude to distract her from the memory of the attackers in the helicopter, a fat-bellied fly skimming pristine white treetops and old Vlas running from automatic gunfire on creaky legs.

Tat-tat-tat-tat-tat.

When she could no longer resist the lure of the light, she eased toward the exit, listening for any sound from outside, adrenaline making each breath come hard in her chest. She peered through the broken slat and took in the surroundings.

From the village these trees sloped steeply up the mountain, always covered in snow, so beautiful, like a scene in a child's globe. One turn of the wrist and glittery snowflakes sprinkled down upon a tiny village.

Ninsoare. Her country had been named for the snowy peaks that defined the land.

What Mirie saw now was more desolate than magical. Wind gusting so hard it whistled like an emergency siren. She had known the storm was coming, and here it was, recalling the last time she had been forced to flee into these mountains. So many years should have dimmed the memory, drowned out the sounds of screams and tears and murder.

Tat-tat-tat-tat-tat.

It had been snowing then, too.

CHAPTER THREE

"Damn," Drew said aloud, not bothering to rein in his frustration.

The tracks were fresh, and the snow came down so hard and fast, he had almost missed them. Inspecting the ruts, he followed the trail until determining that four snowmobiles had passed along this ridge. Probably not more than ten minutes ago.

Given the altitude and climate conditions, Drew was willing to bet no sports enthusiast would be up here snowmobiling for kicks. No, he was looking at a second group of thugs patrolling points of egress. The terrain was difficult, essentially ineffective for launching a surprise attack on a funeral procession. Most likely these snowmobiles had carried scouts searching for the missing princess.

Did they know about the tunnel? Would they be back?

These were the only questions that interested Drew right now. And who was behind these well-organized thugs? Were they Slovakian, too? Drew didn't have a clue and knew General Bogdanovich likely wouldn't, either.

"Damn, damn, damn."

Gusting wind drowned out his frustration. Heading back to the tunnel, he used a branch to sweep away his tracks. Not that anything would be visible for long with this storm, but his boots were doing a helluva job marking his trail. He would have to assume the snowmobiles would be back, but with any luck the storm might slow them down a little.

It was certainly deterring him, and his options were narrowing by the second. He couldn't use his two-way radio to contact the general. He would be lucky if he could transmit over a mile in these conditions, and couldn't risk an intercepted transmission anywhere close to these snowmobile tracks.

As near as he could tell, the snowmobiles had headed in the most direct route back to civilization, which left him with the next problem—Mirie wouldn't last long in this weather. They had dressed for a funeral, not for prolonged exposure to the elements, and she had already been fighting the effects of shock when he'd left her. He needed to get her safe and warm because he didn't see any alternative but riding out the time it took the general to secure the area and retrieve them. Drew needed an alternate plan B.

Shoving up his coat sleeve, he glanced at his watch and made out the compass display. Visibility was getting crappier by the second. There was a place where they might hole up safely, but he would have to get Mirie there, and that wouldn't be easy. The terrain was tough in good weather. Of course the storm would complicate travel for the enemy, too. That much was a plus.

Drew trudged back, unhappy with his choices. He hadn't been gone five minutes total, but after crawling back inside the tunnel, he took in the sight of Mirie, *safe,* like a punch to the gut.

She still stood with her arms wrapped tightly across her chest, as if trying to fold in on herself to contain warmth. But Drew knew by one glimpse of her lovely face that she struggled. She would hide it. She would strap on her courage like Kevlar, but she was struggling hard right now. He could see it in the raw edges of her expression, the haunted eyes she lifted to his, the shuddering breath that echoed between them.

He had to get her to safety.

"Any problems?" he asked.

She shook her head, sending wisps of hair dragging along the fur collar, but she didn't reply.

She couldn't. Not without revealing her chattering teeth.

Crossing the distance between them with a few strides, Drew yanked off his own gloves and dug into his pocket.

"Any word from the general?" he asked.

She shook her head again. He hadn't expected a transmission, but Mirie could use a distraction. He found the package of heat packs. They were small, the perfect size to fit inside a glove or a boot. He had hoped to conserve their few supplies, since these heat packs only had a short life span. Six minutes tops. She couldn't wait.

Not optimum since she hadn't been outside yet. She watched him curiously as he worked the packet to create a chemical reaction that activated the heat.

"Put this inside your glove." He handed her the first, then went to work on the next. "It'll help."

She did as instructed and gave a small smile. "S-so what's the plan?"

"How are you holding up?"

"Fine." Her teeth let out an audible chatter and she rolled her eyes. "Freezing to death, b-but that's because I'm standing around waiting to get shot."

Drew eyed her narrowly and made the decision. "If you can handle a bit of a hike, then we should go for it. I'm not much for standing around waiting to get shot, either."

That brought a smile to her lips, which hadn't yet turned blue. A good sign.

"The village?" she asked.

"Not yet."

She didn't ask for details, didn't want them. Mirie understood limitations better than most people. What did details matter right now when she couldn't do anything to help?

He knew what her answer would be.

His own hands were warmer, so after giving her the second packet, he pressed his fingers to her chin. Her eyes widened in surprise, but she followed his urging and tilted her face to the side. Her skin was chilled and smooth beneath his touch, not waxen or stiff. No outward indication that her body temperature was dropping low enough to concern him. Yet.

Tucking the stray hairs into her hat, he withdrew the audio transmitter. "Thanks for hanging on to this for me."

"Glad I didn't need it."

"Me, too." He let his fingers trail from her face, forced his gaze to her gloved hands. "Any better?"

"Much. Do you want to use them, too?"

"You hang on to them. They can be reactivated with boiling water." Which would require fire and a pot. There was definitely plenty of snow around to melt. Drew would save the rest of the heat packets for the other end of their hike to hold her over while he got a fire going. Hopefully they would be enough.

"Ready?" he asked.

"Rather dodge the bullets than wait for them."

He liked that about her. Even as a young girl, she'd always been up for a challenge.

Drew surveyed the area again before he helped her out of the tunnel. Their path was clear and the snow fell steadily, no worse than before.

This was luck, and he would take all he could get. He shoveled debris against the hole to conceal their exit, trusting the snow to finish up the job. Using his belt, he created a leash of sorts to connect them, and then retrieved the branch he had used to cover his tracks.

He had to keep a close eye on his compass. This forbidding gorge wasn't on the radar for people making their way through the mountains since it led to one of the highest peaks in the region. Not even sports enthusiasts appreciated this gorge, which was nearly impossible to descend without rappelling gear, and the narrow width made it hardly worth the effort. But there was shelter there, and a safe place to hide Mirie.

Drew had found it for exactly that reason. He had been trained by the man who had held the post of close-protection guard for two Ninselan kings. The man had been old, but he had taught Drew that the most important rule for protecting royals, was to know all the good hiding places.

Oskar would be rolling over in his grave right now because Drew hadn't known about the altar. Or maybe Oskar was getting a good laugh, since he had probably been the one who had told Geta about the hideaway in the first place.

His former mentor had once delighted in sending Drew out to find the cleverest hiding places he could come up with. Then Oskar would shoot holes in every one.

He had liked the cave in the gorge, though.

He had shot holes in it, of course—too far away, too tough to access, not enough natural resources—but had also conceded that it would be a damned good hiding place if one could get to it.

Drew watched Mirie for outward signs of exhaustion. She trudged along with her head bowed against the weather, the weather cloak snapping around her as the winds picked up.

Their luck had held until now, but Drew finally abandoned the effort to cover their trail. Instead he motioned Mirie to grab the other side of the branch. Together they lifted it high enough to create a sort of windshield to block the falling snow and give him some visibility.

He couldn't miss the outcroppings that would signal the entrance of the gorge. They were close. He could sense it even though he hadn't been in these mountains in six years. And when they finally came upon it, Drew very nearly stumbled in. The snow concealed the sharp slope, and he took a step into nothingness. His feet shot out from underneath him and the branch went flying, jerked from Mirie's grip. She gasped his name, and he would have dragged her over with him, if not for the tree limbs he managed to catch himself on.

"Grab the branches," he shouted. "We have to climb down."

Unfortunately, climbing down also meant dislodging snow. The snow seeped into the hood of his poncho like frigid fingers of ice. And they had to keep climbing until he could locate the cave ledge, which ran a good seven meters along the ridge. He had a strong sense of how far down it was, and when he caught the edge of it with his boots, he was relieved to discover that they had come down practically in the middle.

"Step down, but don't let go of those branches," he instructed Mirie.

She clung to the boughs until he cleared the cave access, digging and kicking through hard-packed snow. When he could finally scramble inside, he used a laser for a cursory check of the interior, relieved to find the cave was empty and dry.

"Come on." He helped Mirie disentangle herself from the branches and crawl safely across the ledge.

The access was low, and he crawled in behind her, paying attention to her movements, looking for signs of exposure.

She seemed to be moving normally as she sank back on her haunches and asked, "How on earth did you find this place?"

"Dumb luck." Drew directed the light so he could see her face. "Everything wet has to come off right now."

She nodded, her skin translucent, her lips pale. She was freezing. He reached for her hand, tugged off first one glove then the other before digging through his pockets for the last of the heat packets.

"Wet clothes off first. Then activate these. They'll help until I get a fire going." He searched her gaze. "Understand?"

"Yes."

Drew headed outside to search for spruce branches his boot knife could handle. Mirie had called him prepared, but he wasn't. He carried basic survival items necessary in these mountains and a few extras—training from growing up on a lot of acreage with several generations of Canadys.

"Drew boy, you never know what to expect. Life's always throwing surprises at you, so be prepared," his great-grandfather had told him back in his other life.

That early training had come in handy in the Marines Special Forces and as an agent stationed in a mountainous region, and Drew didn't take long to shave the branches into kindling he could light with the fire striker he kept on his key ring. The sap from the spruce would burn despite the wet wood.

He returned to find Mirie sitting with her back against the wall. She had removed only her hat and cloak and was fumbling with her boots. Even in the dark, he could see that her pants were wet all the way to midthigh. Her eyes were heavy-lidded, her efforts sluggish. Her body temperature was dropping, and he had to get this fire going fast.

"Get those clothes off," he barked more harshly than he'd intended. "Unless you want my help."

She growled impatiently in reply and tugged off a boot with what appeared to be monumental effort.

Drew set down the kindling, ditched his outerwear and fished out the remaining weather cloak.

"Wrap this around you. I'll have the fire going soon."

They were deep enough into the gorge that the smoke should dissipate before reaching the top of the ridge. The storm should be grounding any aircraft. Even that transport copter. He was risking a fire regardless. If he didn't get Mirie thawed out, he wouldn't have a princess to keep safe until the NRPG came after them.

The fire took some coaxing, repeated efforts with wet branches that would only burn because of the sap.

"You doing okay?" he asked, prompting Mirie while he willed the flames to ignite. They needed heat and light fast.

Only when he had coaxed a small blaze to steady life did he dare turn his attention away. "Come on. Get warm."

"Okay," Mirie said, but made no move to get up. So Drew went to her and found her fists still wrapped around the heat packets. Her boots were off, but she hadn't even removed the cloak from the packaging.

"Let me help." He made quick work of the poncho, then began the exquisite torture of helping her undress.

"I can do it." She resisted as he peeled a sock away.

"I know," he said mildly, massaging her slim foot between his fire-warmed hands, feeling the smooth skin, watching her reaction. "But humor me. How does that feel? Any pain?"

She shook her head, but he didn't believe her and shifted to view her foot in the firelight. Her skin was red and icy.

"We can handle frostnip, Your Royal Highness. Let's get these wet pants off. Trust me, you'll feel better."

She struggled to keep her eyes open, and made a few fumbling efforts to unfasten her waistband.

Drew couldn't wait. He moved in to help, and she didn't resist this time, which told him everything he needed to know about her condition. He unfastened the hook, then worked the pants over her hips, dragging her thermals along for the ride. She made several halfhearted attempts to assist by lifting her hips, but Drew barely noticed. Not when his fingers brushed her sleek skin as he peeled away the fabric, revealing a barely there thong and never-ending pale legs.

His breath galvanized in his chest at the sight of her nearly naked from the waist down, and ended that particular torture fast by draping the cloak over her middle.

With a hand behind her shoulder, he urged her to lean forward. "The coat now."

"Okay, okay." She swatted at his hands.

Her impatience should have been a good sign, but he knew Mirie. She would have to be unconscious to accept help without resistance. And sure enough, she leaned forward and practically melted into his arms, boneless. Suddenly, he was overwhelmed by *her,* the feel of her body against him, the scent of her with his every sharp breath, the awareness of her bare legs so pale in the firelight.

Only knowledge of her weakness helped him focus on survival right now. Her collar was as wet as his own, so he tortured himself by dragging the shirt over her head, exposing the swell of her breasts and the sleek terrain of bare skin, her hair falling around her shoulders.

"Come on. Let's get you closer to the fire. You'll warm up. I promise."

She only nodded, her teeth chattering audibly, so he sat back on his haunches and lifted her against him. Dragging the cloak around her, he carried her to the fire. She curled up in the warm glow, and he watched her, unsure how much of her sleepiness was exposure or shock.

He made quick work of his own wet clothes. Everything had to go. Thermals. Shirt. Pants. The lining of his coat was in fairly decent shape, so he kept that on. Mirie might not care now, but she would come back to life when she warmed up. He didn't want their relationship to get weird. He counted on the professionalism between them. A lot.

After setting up a blockade of stripped branches at the cave's entrance, he was content that they would be alerted to any disturbance. Then he went back to the fire.

Mirie was still curled in a pathetic ball, her teeth rattling louder than the crackling fire.

No, he hadn't been adequately prepared, no matter what she thought. Not when all he had to protect her was a poncho and a small fire and himself. Not when all he could do was sit down beside her and say, "Let me in."

He pulled her into his arms and curled his body around hers. She sighed, nestling against the meager warmth he offered, resting her head against his shoulder, burying her face in his throat. He dragged the cloak around them, tucked her fingers into his armpits and willed himself with every fiber of his considerable self-control *not* to react to the feel of this near-naked woman in his arms. No other woman would test him this way, only *this* woman. But he would not react.

Even if it killed him.

And with the feel of her soft curves against him, the scent of her hair filtering through him with every breath he took, Drew thought it probably would.

They had come to Alba Luncă for a funeral.

SUFFOCATING DARKNESS, THE kind with the blackest shadows, was where fear liked to hide.

The soft voice that sang such sweet songs, the voice that brought love to life during those scary, drowsy moments before sleep, was suddenly ragged and hysterical, almost unrecognizable through the fear.

Even in Mirie's worst nightmares, all the terrors Stefan and Petre said hid in the shadowy places under her bed had never hinted at this sort of fear that made her want to bury her head beneath the blankets and never come out. Not ever.

This was fear like she had never imagined.

How could she have? Her life was filled with laughter. The soft voice of her mama tinkled with laughter and scattered worries like the courtyard fountain splashed water on the tiles.

She had never, ever heard anyone scream with such fear.

That fear paralyzed Mirie, made her eyes squeeze shut and her hands shake. Choked her. No, that was Nanny, smothering her with knotted old fingers and a bony chest. Nanny's hissing voice shushed Mirie in the darkness, demanded silence, but Mirie was sure she would never make a sound again, not with Mama's hysterical pleas in her ears. Desperate, agonized screams.

"Not my babies. Not my babies."

Tat-tat-tat-tat-tat.

Then silence.

MIRIE AWOKE. FOR a stunning moment, all she could see was red. Red so violently bright, swelling and dripping, as if the world had erupted in a geyser of blood.

With the breath locked tight in her chest, reality receded, and no matter how hard she tried to grasp it, there was distance between the scene before her eyes and the awareness in her head. She could only feel the rapid-fire thudding of her heart, ready to erupt in another geyser of blood.

Tat-tat-tat-tat-tat.

Her heart throbbed so hard it hurt, trapped with the breath in her chest, a weight crushing everything inside her, pressure so great she would die because she couldn't breathe.

But there was no death here. *No!*

One word finally penetrated her awareness, and the vision faded, bleaching the memory to dusty shades of gunmetal and smoke. The way she felt inside.

There was no impending eruption, just the pounding of blood in her ears.

And a long-ago nightmare.

Mirie drew a shuddering breath that dispelled the pressure the tiniest bit. She remembered.

Bunică. Men with guns. The dead priest.

And Drei. She felt his strong body tight around her, his arms holding her securely, the cloying warmth of heat and skin.

The pounding of another heartbeat beneath her cheek. Only his heart beat solid and steady, as if wanting to set the example for her own, reminding her not to panic.

But calm seemed beyond grasp, even though she was so much warmer now. There was no gunfire in the crackling quiet. Nothing to fear in Drei's arms.

His face rested on the top of her head, so heavy her neck arched beneath the weight. Given the pace of his breathing, she thought he might be dozing.

She would do nothing to disturb him or this moment. Not until she had regained control of herself. The nightmares were no stranger. But she had not had one in a long time. She shouldn't be surprised to have one now, back in this place of so many memories. A place where she had once had a life.

A life Mirie had once dreamed of, simple, intimate, but filled with so much love.

She should feel something for the loss, shouldn't she?

She was wrapped nearly naked in a man's arms. Such an occurrence hadn't happened since her high-school boyfriend. She remembered the strong warmth of a man's arms, the intimacy of skin against skin.

Shouldn't she feel something?

Gratitude. Embarrassment. Awkwardness. *Something*.

Nothing.

A twig snapped, sending sparks raining over the

flames, a swelling of light that made the surrounding darkness darker. Two people in a cave buried beneath a mountain of snow. They could be the only two people alive in the world. They could die here and who would find them before they withered to ash and bone?

Thanks to the media, many would notice her passing, but none would really care. Mirie didn't even know if Drei would be missed. She had seen no evidence of a life in all these years they'd been together. *She* was his work, and his life it seemed.

Her heartbeat wouldn't slow down. Her thoughts raced with what-might-have-beens and what-could-never-bes. Mirie had no patience for self-indulgence. Maybe the adrenaline that had fueled the nightmare had sparked this overwhelming loneliness, or maybe it was simply because Drei held her in his arms.

A man and woman mimicking intimacy.

She willed herself to calm down, but couldn't grasp the edges of this panic. She was a woman who could lie in a man's arms, surrounded in the warm cocoon of his hard body, smooth and settled with years of muscle, so unlike the boy in her memory. She remembered.

Drei held her like a man comfortable with a woman in his arms. Not too eager. Not overly impressed. Just easy.

But she only felt alone.

She didn't want to be this woman, to pass from

her life as Bunică had, only with many more years ahead, trudging through day after day, enduring, existing, knowing only duty, and obligation, and emptiness, feeling dead inside.

Until death claimed her for real.

Tat-tat-tat-tat-tat.

The fire sputtered, and Mirie stiffened at the sound. Drei exhaled heavily, a man who didn't want to be disturbed, but who was attuned to her slightest motion, even in sleep.

Definitely asleep.

His breath fluttered against her ear, a slight burst of warmth she may not have noticed except for the way it caressed such sensitive skin. A velvet touch that reached down deep inside and drew the faintest reply.

A tingle low in her belly.

An echo of something she had forgotten.

She leaned into Drei, not wanting to disturb him yet desperate to know if the sensation was real or her imagination.

That one tiny feeling accomplished what she hadn't been able to do on her own. Her breathing finally slowed, her pulse stilled, as if every fiber of her focused.

Drei's breaths came soft and even, as solid as the man himself. But she felt nothing, heard only the crackling fire. Mirie held her breath and leaned in a bit more....

There it was again. A tingle that made her insides hum, a fragile tremor as if someplace deep inside her yawned, shrugging off a long sleep.

More like a coma, actually, but not death.

Not death.

CHAPTER FOUR

DREW WASN'T SURE what awoke him, but he damned sure shouldn't have been sleeping. The struggle to control his physical reaction to the feel of Mirie pressed against him had worn him out more than battling the snow.

He had wanted to stop time with the feel of her in his arms. But something was off with her. He sensed it, knew it was probably what had awoken him. He didn't think she was asleep. Her body was too tense, too aware.

Scanning the shadows for any sign of a threat, he found the cave as he had left it, trusted his years of training to alert him to an intrusion. The fire was holding up, so he hadn't been out for long.

Shifting against the wall, he glanced down at her, dark lashes forming half circles on her pale cheeks, her mouth parted around shallow breaths.

"Are you all right?" he asked automatically.

His voice intruded on the quiet, but her only reply was to nod. She surprised him by sliding her arms around his chest. Repositioning herself, she relaxed a little, but her breath hitched in her throat, an unexpected sound.

Frowning into her hair, Drew resisted the need to interrogate her. She was warm, so any threat of hypothermia was gone. She'd had a tough day, but she would deal with her losses, wouldn't let him see her fear. That much he knew. If hanging on to him made her feel better right now, then he would find some way to cope.

Not by sleeping.

No, he had to remain stone-cold sober to this assault on his senses. The heat melded their skin together. Her hair tickled his nose with every breath. Her sleek curves unfolded against him so he could feel the length of her soft thighs, the way she fitted into the curve of his body.

She exhaled a sigh, and her mouth shuddered against his skin, soft and yielding. His pulse began to race, rebelling wildly against his best intentions. And they were the very best. Just useless against the feel of her in his arms. A familiar burning started inside, a reaction that was going toe to toe with his discipline.

Drew was having a tough day, too.

He would take armed assassins over facing down this humiliating lack of self-control.

Mirie had no idea she was playing with fire—and not the blaze making this icy cavern habitable, either. And he didn't want to deal with the consequences of her realizing just how fragile his restraint was around her. He couldn't afford any change that might jeopardize their relationship. He was her close-protection guard and a U.S. sleeper operative.

Not a man.

So with his jaw clenched tight, he forced himself to focus on making out the cave entrance beyond the firelight, the gray light from the storm beyond. He deliberated how to fashion a makeshift pan to melt snow. They would need water soon, and frozen snow was no option to quench thirst.

But how could he concentrate on anything but the way her breasts molded to his chest, the swelling softness pressed full against him? The skimpy fabric of her bra was no protection.

When she stretched against him, his pulse galvanized. He wanted to thrust off the cloak binding them together. Heightened awareness was making him read so much more into the moment than was possible.

Lust was making him lose his mind. And this was an argument not to ignore his needs the way he too often did. He was a man in the intimate employ of a woman he wanted but couldn't have. Of course normal relationships were out even if he had wanted one—that was not the life he had chosen—but he never lacked for companionship when he was off duty, taking the occasional leave. They didn't happen often, but he always tried to make the most of them when they did.

But if he had seen to his own needs, he might be able to resist Mirie now. She sought warmth and comfort, lying here in the arms of someone she should be able to trust, an entirely natural response to their situation. And he should be worthy of her trust. He should shut down reactions that were inappropriate at best, forbidden at worst.

Torture either way.

But Drew's best intentions meant nothing when Mirie nestled still closer, nestled her face in the hollow of his throat. Not an accidental action, but an intentional one, an inquisitive one that ignited fire in its wake.

One purposeful touch, and the whole world shifted.

The boundaries that had long established their relationship dissolved as she leaned into him, a slight arch of her back that pressed her breasts against his chest and brought her mouth in line with the sensitive skin beneath his ear.

Her breaths came soft and warm against his skin, smooth, silken sighs. Had she noticed the way his every muscle had fossilized? Did she suspect that one touch would shatter his willpower into a million brittle pieces and litter this cave with his best intentions?

Drew didn't know. He only knew his arms ached with the effort of holding her already. He couldn't push her away or pull her close, because in this moment he was paralyzed by her vulnerability.

And his need.

HE TASTED MALE. Mirie wasn't sure why she was so sure what *male* tasted like, since she had only tasted one man, and the actual details of long-ago teenage rendezvous had faded in the haze of years. Drei's skin was the texture of rough velvet, faintly stubbled and redolent with a hint of sweat.

She was so aware of him, of the way his body surrounded hers, generously shared his heat. His strength beckoned her to stretch out against him, melt over the ridges and hollows of his hard muscles. She liked the solidness of him.

He was a man, not a boy.

Loneliness faded beneath this. She felt no embarrassment to be nearly naked in his arms, only awareness of him in a way she had never been before.

The feeling made perfect sense.

Drei felt right because he was right. The *only* person she could trust.

She had never thought of him as anything but her shadow. He was a fact of life that she had long ago accepted. He was always there and always had been.

She had never considered him as a man.

She'd been a child when he'd shown up. But that had been so long ago. A lifetime. Right now he was a man, and quite a handsome one with his gemstone

eyes and chiseled strength. And not so old, either
What had once seemed ancient to a girl was nothing
to the woman. Ten years. A decade on the rosary or
all of God's commandments.

How had she missed this? She had looked at him
for years, but had never actually seen him until this
very moment.

Arching her body lightly, just enough for her thigh
to settle a little deeper between his, she tested the
feel of her skin against the textured hardness of his,
half-afraid he would stop her and demand to know
what she was about.

But even worry left her feeling more alive than
she had in so long. As the seconds passed, emptiness yielded to daring. It was easy to be bold in this
moment. They might be dragged from this cave and
shot, their bodies tossed into the gorge. They might
slip into a calm death from exposure, locked together
forever because the spring thaw never touched these
peaks.

This man may yet give his life for her.

Perhaps they would survive, and the general and
his men would collect them. They would remind her
unnecessarily that the risks she took involved others
by default. They would return her to the royal compound, and life would go on, never-ending commit-
ments that blurred days into loneliness. Her whole
existence strung along by tiny triumphs after hard-
won accomplishments that were never good enough.

One step forward. Two back. Ninety-nine to go.

Once inside her glittering shell, she would return to looking at Drei but never really seeing him.

How could she not have seen him?

He lay so still around her, he might have been carved from marble.... No, nothing as refined. Stone, she decided. Craggy and rugged and enduring like these mountains.

And she couldn't stop touching him. That faint vibration she felt inside urged her to greater boldness, to see if a fire could be stoked from a single flame.

She nestled her face in the valley between his neck and shoulder, inhaled the scent that made him *him*. She liked the whimsical thought and shifted again. Just enough so her breasts lifted from his chest, a slight motion that grazed sensitive tips against wiry chest hairs.

The heat low in her belly flared as Drei's hands locked hard around her waist. Mirie gasped, a sound that startled the quiet as she was hoisted off his lap as easily as he might have removed a pet.

"Your Royal Highness." He used her title as her name, his tone a warning that she had crossed a line. He forcibly scooted backward as if she had become an ember that burned him.

Mirie stared at him across the blaze-soaked distance. She found the bright green of his eyes indistinguishable by firelight, found herself pierced by the reproach in his expression. And something else…

"What do you fear from me, Drei?" she asked, surprised.

"What are you doing?" A demand.

"I was…testing."

He arched a quizzical eyebrow. "Testing what? I'm still breathing, Your Royal Highness."

His indignation made her bristle. Or maybe it was the title that did. She had a name. He knew it.

Was it so wrong to want to be a woman? For one stolen moment, she wanted to think of nothing but what it felt like to feel again, to respond and to care. She already responded as a woman because she felt hurt by his withdrawal.

He dropped back into a crouch, a defensive stance, as though she were Eve with the apple. The muscles in his thighs bulged with the motion, drew her attention to the way he moved, so easy with his nakedness.

How had she never truly seen this man in all these years they had been together? She must have been blind.

The firelight cast his body in gold, his long legs, his narrow hips, the vee of his waist that spread into that chest that had provided shelter against the storm raging outside.

The storm raging inside.

Reason told her to retreat, but Mirie couldn't stop.

Not when retreat meant the spark inside would smolder to ash.

"You protect me." Her voice wavered. She could be so weak.

Placing her hands over her heart, she stood her ground. "Protect me from this loneliness. Right here. Pretend I am only a woman who wants a man."

"You're a princess."

His retort stung. Always the voice of reason.

"I'm a woman, too."

And she could not lose this feeling that made her feel alive. To be like Bunică. Her family. Mirie did not want to live her life as one ready for the grave.

She feared that fate worse than men with guns.

"Please." The word broke, not a demand but a plea.

Drei's expression was unreadable, but his gaze pierced her as if he'd plunged a hand through her heart. She resisted the urge to shrink before him with her selfish demands.

Then she noticed his hands. They were balled into fists at his sides, tense-knuckled and desperate almost. Not because he didn't want her, she realized.

Because he did?

There was much about this man she didn't understand, had never taken the time to learn. But Mirie recognized the chiseled angle of his jaw, as though he ground his teeth to meal inside his mouth.

And foolish, foolish woman she was, so naive and self-absorbed, she had ignored the most obvious sign of all. Running her gaze down the muscled terrain of his body... Her breath hitched at the sight of him in his arousal, concealed by his stance, but such proof of his want.

He was a professional, and an honorable man.

But she had no such honor and simply couldn't bring herself to stop.

Swaying toward him, Mirie felt her motion as though her body had turned to liquid, warmed by the flames. Not of the crackling fire, but the fire Drei had created inside her. Reaching out, she ran her fingers lightly along his thighs, savored the shock that visibly rocked him on contact.

"Drei, please." Another plea.

His growl ripped through the quiet, a sound of the purest frustration. But Mirie knew, even as his arms shot around her with whipcord strength, that he couldn't deny her.

He sprang up with the physicality of a man well-trained, and pulled her to her knees along with him. One swift move brought her into hard contact with his body.

She gasped as he locked her against him, arm a vise around her waist that anchored her close until suddenly all she could see was him. His broad shoulders blocked out the firelight. She could feel every ridge and hollow of his chest, the hot arousal that branded her belly, the steely thighs that braced her upright.

She had no chance to react before he speared a hand into her hair, coaxed her head back to tilt her face to his.

And his mouth came down on hers.

Time stopped. Her heartbeat simply paused. Somewhere inside she recognized how she had provoked him, but his kiss tasted of a need that shocked her, a hungry man.

Mirie couldn't think past her surprise, not when his need became hers, catching her in an upsurge the way the fire sucked in the surrounding air.

She sighed against his mouth, her lips yielding eagerly. Their tongues tangled in discovery. And she was so grateful she had pushed, so glad he had given in.

Winding her arms around him, she ran her hands down his back, thrilled when he trembled beneath her touch. He was no longer Drei, but a strong, handsome man making her body hum with his kisses. Yet he was still Drei, a man who had always been there, a man she could trust with her needs.

Mirie felt comfortable with him, able to abandon herself to this haze of sensation that stole her breath, made her bold and eager and heedless of the consequences.

But not so her protector.

"You better be sure about this, Your Royal Highness," he whispered against her lips. "There's no turning back."

She could practically feel the battle raging inside him, the tension in the body against her, even though his words might let her go.

Gently nibbling his upper lip, she teased his skin into her mouth, determined to win him to her side. He should forget who he was because she was no longer Mirie. She would shed the limitations of rank and duty to become a nameless woman who savored the moment with no inhibitions. A woman able to forget everything that normally dictated her life.

For one stolen moment, she would be only a woman.

"I have never been more sure," she admitted. "Let this moment be ours, Drei. Just this one."

He didn't believe her. She could see doubt all over his face. Maybe she was a fool to believe her own words. Or naive.

But Mirie didn't care because she *felt*.

Drei coaxed her head back to expose her throat. Deliberation carved stern lines in his handsome face as he considered her as if she were some tempting morsel he wasn't sure whether to resist or devour.

Her chest rose and fell on a sharp breath, the anticipation making her body vibrate.

Had she ever felt so alive?

Her answer came when Drei nibbled his way along her jaw, lingered in that valley below her ear with his warm breath and teasing tongue, such an unexpectedly sensitive place.

Never.

His mouth traveled freely, as though he had waited forever for the privilege to explore and was determined to savor every inch of her. Fire filtered down into her very deepest places until an ache throbbed low in her belly, and she gasped when he flipped down her bra with a quick move that sent her breasts tumbling out as a feast for his devouring.

And he devoured with exquisite tenderness. His stubbled cheeks teased her skin. His tongue tested a peak that tightened eagerly. His strong hands lifted her breast so he could draw the tip into his mouth with a soft pull.

Mirie gasped and her whole being trembled with a prayer that he would not stop.

He didn't.

Acquainting himself with her responses, Drei coaxed the fire inside her to feverish life. Until her body grew molten and she clung to him.

But he held her securely, raking his firm grip down her ribs as he lifted his head to catch her mouth with his again. Her excitement spiraled in response to his need when he ground his hips greedily against her, a dare to frighten her off, maybe, or an invitation to accept the challenge.

Mirie touched him with an urgency she had never known before. She dragged her palms down his back, over the tight curve of his bottom as she pressed him close, determined to explore every inch. She rode the length of his arousal and caught the sound of his excitement with her kiss, trembled against him as his hard body shuddered with need.

She wanted to make him feel the way she did, but he was the one in control. She found herself suddenly on her back, tangled in the weather cloak, as he maneuvered between her legs. Not to make love to her with his body, but to pleasure her with his mouth.

And she could only glance up at this familiar stranger and tremble in anticipation, for he touched her in ways so intimate that she grew dazed with desire, and could only reach out and hang on to his strong shoulders, as her thighs trembled and silken moans slid from her lips unbidden.

And only when her body pulsed and she was wet with her own pleasure did Drei cease his tender assault. He pulled her into his arms and forced her legs wide so she could straddle his lap, leaving her mouth poised perfectly to kiss him.

She did.

Mirie tasted her pleasure on his mouth, the strength of his hunger, the need that stunned her with its intensity. How could he be invisible to her one moment, then in an instant, the world revolved around their kiss, as if she would die right there if he stopped touching her?

When Drei joined her with an upward thrust, his growl was a desperate sound that reverberated through the cave, through *her,* and Mirie understood that while she had made love before, she had never made love with a man.

And there was a vast world of difference.

THE FIRE HAD burned dangerously low. Drew needed to get up and add more kindling before he wound up back outside stripping sappy branches. A part of him was relieved for the task. He was tempted to sit here forever, his back propped against a frigid stone wall, his butt numb from the frigid stone floor.

Life should stop right now, so he could die a happy man. He didn't know what had just happened between him and Mirie, but he sure as hell knew it wasn't smart.

He had a mission, and so did she. Two different missions to two different countries. Hers by blood; his by oath. This, whatever *this* was, would only complicate their work.

He could control his imagination. He could distract himself with other women. He could even feel noble about sacrificing his life to protect Mirie's journey from childhood to royal duty. He had always told himself the fantasy would be better than the reality anyway, that he'd had the better part.

But he no longer had that excuse.

Reality was far beyond the fantasy. There had been no way he could have known how he would feel inside her, with her body melting around him, pulsing with pleasure as if her mouth had been formed to fit only his. As if her every curve had been formed to align just perfectly with him. As if her sighs had been tuned to his exact frequency.

As if inside her was the only place he should be.

He had never known that feeling before. Discontent had sent him fleeing family and home when he had been younger. It was what had kept him chasing thrills with Special Forces, what had allowed him to dismiss his identity for a mission as a sleeper agent.

He had never known *right*.

Until Mirie.

"Drei?" Even her voice was an assault on his senses, a sultry tone that caressed the quiet like mist.

"Mmm-hmm." He wasn't up to coherent responses yet, not with his blood still slugging through his veins like lava and his thoughts racing with what he had known all along.

Giving in to *this* was not smart.

"How do you do it?" She let her head roll back against his shoulder, so she could peer up.

"Define *it*." Good. He'd shoved two words out. Of course his voice sounded like gravel over broken glass.

"Live in the shadows. Live a half life." She exhaled another breathy sigh that had such power over him. "I don't know what else to call *it*."

He was so not up to philosophical questions right now. Not when the simple feel of her hair trailing down his arm felt monumental, as if their sex had only scratched the surface of years of lusting and when he recovered he was going to be a whole lot hungrier than before.

He dragged his gaze to hers, buying himself time because he couldn't wrap his brain around anything beyond the arms she draped tightly around him, as though he were her anchor.

"Half life?" Two more words and an inflection that made them a question. He was making progress.

Her lips tucked at the corners as she considered him, looking thoughtful. He could see the sprinkling of freckles across her nose and cheeks even in this light. Those freckles were the bane of her existence. Once she hadn't noticed them, but with the constant media attention now, she spent time in front of the mirror trying to conceal, blend or beat those freckles into submission.

She would be mortified he'd noticed.

He thought freckles suited her and hoped she never found a way to cover them. They were a reminder of the free-spirited girl she had once been, a girl who had danced through the meadows and splashed through streams.

The girl who had grown up to be a woman bold enough to make love to him.

"You guard me," she finally said. "You live with me. Your schedule is my schedule. You don't leave my life to go live your own. I don't know anything about your upbringing or your family, and I can count on one hand how many times you have taken a vacation since Oskar died. That leaves you with a day off here and there and then only when I'm entertaining dignitaries in my glittering shell, with the royal guard and media smothering me."

"Glittering shell?" He knew what she meant.

"The compound." She waved a dismissive hand. "That doesn't seem like much of a life to me. So, a half life."

He nodded, considering.

She waited, and shivered.

"I need to deal with the fire." He found the words to seize an opportunity for escape. Only the knowledge that they might freeze to death spurred him to get up off his ass and back to reality. There was another part of him that felt he would be okay with freezing to death as long as Mirie was in his arms.

But she complied and untangled her naked self and scooted back against the wall. Her skin gleamed pale in the failing firelight, and his crotch danced a little jig at the sight she made with her long legs stretched out before her, her hair threading around the swell of her lovely breasts.

Christ, he was in trouble here.

That thought was unavoidable as he used the last of the kindling. He'd be heading outside again soon. He should plunge himself into the snow while he was out there. He didn't think even the blizzard would cool him off.

He coaxed more of the sappy kindling to life with the glowing embers, carefully stoking the fire back while he considered Mirie's words.

And the stab of pride at her opinion of him.

He had a life even though she couldn't see it. He served his country and carried out his mission objective. He had only sacrificed the normal life he had never been much interested in anyway, for a much more noble cause.

Like Mirie herself, although she had been born to her cause. But she didn't see his life from his perspective, and she didn't sound as if she was all that content with her own.

Loneliness was eating away at her bit by bit.

He wasn't surprised.

"I guess from your perspective it doesn't seem like much of a life." Distance helped him get a grip.

"Sounds a lot like my life." She finally pulled on the cloak to cover her exquisite nakedness.

He snorted while tucking a branch deep into the embers.

"What?" she asked.

"I thought the same thing."

He hadn't meant the admission as an invitation, but she took it as one. Suddenly, she was covering the small distance between them, kneeling before the growing fire, stretching out her hands to embrace the heat.

Drew only heaved an inward sigh. He wanted her

to warm herself, wished her nearness didn't test him and her discontent didn't add to his defenselessness against her.

She saw only how he trailed after her around the clock, not living a life that would fit anyone's description of normal. Because she didn't live a normal life, either. She had once run through these mountains, flirting with the boys, giving her virginity to the one she had allowed to catch her.

Now she gave herself to the only man within her grasp to stave off the grief of her losses. What a waste.

"You've been working on a miracle," he said, hoping to lend her perspective. And some encouragement, which she didn't hear enough as far as Drew was concerned. "Once the government stabilizes and the economy shows some improvement, you'll get back to a normal life again. Then, so will I."

She faced him with a scowl. "By the time this political situation stabilizes, I'll be ready for the grave like Bunică."

"Your Royal Highness," he chided.

To his surprise, she scooted toward him, coming up full against him and wrapping her arms around his waist. "Drei, call me by my name."

Her breasts pressed against his back, and for a man who'd just spent himself in a big way, Drew's body was on red alert again before he had a chance to suck in a breath.

He was in such trouble here. The very thought of her name on his lips collided with the memory of his body inside her, and he found himself clutching the stick hard enough that the damned thing broke. Wet wood. Go figure.

But it was the anchor he needed to resist turning around and grabbing her, pulling her against him and going for round two. There'd been no contact with the general. It was just the two of them, stranded here, alone.

She was upset. He got that. He also understood her isolation. He saw her life up close. He lived it. His own wasn't much better except for the occasional furloughs. But unless they got back to normal between them, this "interlude" could only cost them. And cost big.

They were protector and the princess he'd been hired to protect. Period.

"Princess Mirela of Ninsele."

"Drei." She strung out his name on a long melodic syllable that reminded him of her earlier song.

Had it only been hours since the funeral?

The world had shifted since then.

"Mirela Selskala," he tried again, earning only a huff of exasperation.

Then she surprised him by sinking backward, pulling him off balance and dragging him with her.

Suddenly they were tangled together in the weather cloak, too close to the fire, and Drew was forced to roll over and take her with him. She seized the advantage and twisted in his arms until she straddled him.

And Drew was already so far gone he didn't resist. *Couldn't.* Not when she lifted her mouth to his again in an unspoken demand and laughed that silken laughter that he never heard anymore, hadn't realized how much he missed.

The last thing in the world Drew should do right now was give in. The absolute last. He'd do better to put the pistol in his mouth and pull the trigger.

But when she rocked her hips, swaying until she had his reawakening erection trapped between her smooth thighs, he could only ride out the motion and try to hide that she was about to shake loose any possibility of resistance.

But she already knew because she sighed softly and swayed erotically, opening herself to him, and he finally gave in. Arching his hips, he found her softness, and thrust home with her name spilling from his lips.

"Mirie."

CHAPTER FIVE

MIRIE HAD ONLY wanted a moment, had asked for *right now.* By definition that meant their interlude in the cave wouldn't last forever, yet when Drei tugged on the harness she wore and asked, "Ready?" she wanted to shake her head with an emphatic *no.*

A strange sense of panic took hold now that they were dressed again. She wasn't ready to leave, wasn't ready to face the aftermath of her choices.

And she wasn't ready to end her time with Drei.

Not when she had felt more alive during these fantasy hours together than she had in a very long time.

"Yes," she said. *No!*

He only nodded, so terribly distant.

She couldn't read his mood. The handsome face that had been hungry with arousal and so alive with pleasure had solidified into an expression that should have been familiar.

In some ways it was. She recognized the features, but had never understood that the impassive facade was a mask. She had glimpsed the real him today.

The intimacy they shared made him a familiar stranger. The difference was striking enough to unsettle her. As she had dressed, she felt uncertain, as if somehow putting on clothes together had been more monumental than taking them off. Her nerves were playing games with her, making her thin-skinned after too many conflicting emotions, too many memories in a short span of time. The memories alone had always unsettled her.

But all was well now. Or should have been.

General Bogdanovich had made contact. The attackers had long since escaped, and when the storm eased up enough for travel, her close-protection unit had arrived to retrieve her. They were above on the ridge. They'd sent down dry clothing and gear so she could safely make the ascent.

Mirie should be relieved the threat was over, and grateful to be alive. But when she looked at Drei, securing his own harness with the hands that had just held her, pleasured her, she felt a pang of...*something,* and her breath hitched in her throat at the physical intensity of the sensation.

He glanced up. The hard lines of his face softened, and she could see past the mask. His eyes caressed her as if he might never see her again. She glimpsed longing, and regret.

For one instant, Mirie thought he would reach out and touch her. An acknowledgment of what had passed between them, the caring, the comfort, the contentment. But he didn't. He said unnecessarily, "They're waiting above."

He didn't bother extinguishing the fire. There wasn't much life left in the flames anymore, just enough to light their way as they left this place of shelter and unexpected escape.

Nerves were definitely making her thin-skinned and moody. Emotion swelled in her chest as they stepped out onto the ledge.

The path was lit with emergency lanterns to mark their way, a path that ascended straight up from the ledge. From this vantage point, Mirie marveled that they had made the descent successfully at all. Surely she would never have made it had fear and a storm not driven them to desperation.

Drei braced her close as he secured her to the rappel lines, his expression shadowed by the artificial light, his motions perfunctory. Could he so easily forget the way they had found comfort together? It shouldn't matter, but it did. She wasn't sure what she had expected after breaching the boundaries of their relationship so completely. Maybe that was the problem. She had acted impulsively, and he had been forced to react to her. There had been no thought. She *had* felt, and hadn't been willing to let that feeling go.

She considered this while clinging to the rappel line one-handed. The line lifted her off the ground, and she used her feet to maneuver the branches, twisting them out of her way to avoid the snow dislodged with each step.

The climb was steep even with assistance from

above, but Mirie felt no weariness, only awareness of Drei a few feet behind her. He steadied her with an occasional hand on her bottom. He helped her shove aside branches to spare her the trouble when he could. He would have caught her had she fallen.

He protected her. That much was the same.

Then the climb was over. There were men handling the equipment on the ledge, their bodies harnessed around tree trunks to provide the leverage to work the lines. She could see them well before the general reached for her hands to drag her up the remaining distance.

And Mirie left behind her emotions in that snowy gorge, put her own mask back on. "Thank you, General. Gentlemen," she said, as she gained her footing.

There were quiet greetings, but Mirie was left to the company of the general as the unit of armed men worked to bring up Drei safely.

General Bogdanovich was minister of security with the NRPG under his command. He draped a blanket around her shoulders, and Mirie quietly endured his inspection as she stared into the face dominated by a bushy mustache that overcompensated for a head of thinning brown hair.

"Thank God you're all right," he said.

She felt the same way about him. "What of the villagers? You said there were injuries. How serious?"

"Scrapes and falls in the rush to get to the village

mostly. No casualties—yet. The priest is in critical condition. The *poliţie* transported him to the hospital."

But he wasn't dead yet. Mirie's eyes fluttered shut, and she inclined her head. The nearest hospital was forty minutes away in the best of weather, and the storm had not yet spent itself.

God, please, please, please... "Will we be able to contain the fallout?"

"We can brief tomorrow, Your Royal Highness," he said curtly. "The only thing that matters now is that you're safe."

Which told Mirie everything she needed to know.

She had brought this situation upon everyone.

She felt responsible for the consequences, for the potential consequences and for undermining the efforts of people who had worked so hard on behalf of the Ninselan people.

On her behalf.

And when Drei surfaced over the ledge, his gaze sought and found hers immediately, and she felt his glance along with the memory of him wrapped around her. *Inside her.*

Her longtime protector quickly took charge of her again. He forced her to drink, then eat a few bites of a protein bar while the soldiers dismantled the gear. After speaking privately with General Bogdanovich, Drei instructed her on their destination and settled her behind him on the snowmobile for the trek back to civilization.

But it wasn't until their convoy had departed, as Mirie sat with her arms tight around Drei's waist and cheek pressed to his back, wishing they could curl up and doze off together as they had earlier, that Mirie realized her *right now* might not be so simple after all. Not when the man she had looked past forever was no longer invisible.

"Welcome back, Your Royal Highness."

Mirie accepted the coffee cup from her private assistant. "Relieved to be back."

That much was true.

She set the folder on the desk. The business she had missed since leaving for Alba Luncă could wait a little longer. She took a fortifying sip of the coffee and glanced at Drei. He stood inside the doorway, his usual post while inside her office. His black uniform helped a giant of a man blend into the woodwork no matter where they were.

He wasn't blending this morning, which had everything to do with the fact that she knew what he looked like beneath the blazer, turtleneck and pants. Mirie took another hot swallow. The past twenty-four hours had taken a toll. Most especially on her senses.

"Why are you still hanging on to that newspaper?" she asked her assistant.

Helena Avadoni exhaled a sigh that said more than

words ever could. A petite powerhouse of energy and organizational skill, she oversaw every detail of life from names of visiting dignitaries during events to spare panty hose if Mirie happened to snag her nylons on a chair leg.

"Are you ready?" Helena asked.

Mirie held out her hand and, bracing herself, scanned the bold headline that read:

Luca of Whitefish.

The headline was an obvious play on her own media nickname. "And so it begins."

The story summed up the claim of a man named Luca Vadim, who had arrived in Ninsele from a town in the northwestern United States, asserting he was the product of an affair between a Ninselan envoy and the late king.

The article claimed Luca Vadim had heard reports of Mirie's assassination and worried that if the throne was suddenly vacant, Ninsele might be plunged into another civil war. He'd come forward as a public service.

"A public service," Mirie said aloud. "Really?"

Silence was her only reply. Both Helena and Drei knew the drill. This wasn't the first time an imposter had come out of nowhere to claim a blood tie to the throne.

Mirie herself had set the precedent to inspire these copycats. After years in hiding, she'd resurfaced with enough political support to oust the dictator.

But she'd been backed by royal supporters, and her first item of business had been proving her identity through DNA testing.

Drei opened the office door, and both the general and Georghe entered. Mirie left her desk to greet them.

"You haven't slept." She recognized the signs.

"Like anyone sleeps around here." Georghe kissed her cheek.

Forcing a smile, she felt the weight of her choices even though Georghe was too kind to point out the obvious.

The chancellor of the Crown Cabinet was one of the most caring people Mirie had ever known. His inconspicuous competency was the reason he had survived the dictatorship when most civilian staffers had been executed or exiled.

The dictator had recognized Georghe's function within the government and had believed he could control the mild-mannered man. Georghe had played the part, working behind the scenes to ease the peoples' plight in so many ways and ultimately providing Mirie with the necessary support to overthrow the dictator once she had reached the age of majority.

"Come, come." Georghe motioned to the chairs. "We have a lot to discuss and some decisions to make."

Business as usual. "Pour yourselves some coffee, gentlemen."

After visiting the sideboard, Georghe and the general sat in front of the desk.

"I'm not surprised by Vadim's attempt to capitalize on the attack," Mirie said. "But what's this about an assassination? Who reported I was assassinated? I thought we didn't announce that I would be attending the funeral as a safety precaution."

"That was the problem," Georghe explained. "Since we didn't issue a press release, no legitimate media were invited. You can thank the paparazzi for the false reports. They camp at our gates, so they followed when you left the compound."

"Not only were those idiots broadcasting the locations of our units, but they jeopardized everyone's safety," the general complained. "There were reporters and video cameras cornering villagers as they tried to get through the gate. I had to sacrifice a unit to get the situation under control."

Wonderful. The consequences of leaving Briere just kept breeding, like mold. Mirie set the cup aside. It would take more than coffee to make her feel better this morning. "Losing that unit impeded your efforts, General?"

"We might have been able to bring in a few more of your attackers alive if I hadn't needed to divide my forces." He scowled blackly. "The paparazzi were a distraction, and we let them know that loud and clear."

Georghe gave a disgusted snort. "So I've heard,

thank you. My office was flooded with complaints about your infractions against free speech and the public's right to know before you even picked up Her Royal Highness. Did you really have to instruct your men to destroy the van's satellite equipment? We were faxed a bill for its replacement."

"They're lucky I didn't take them into custody. I would have if I'd had the manpower. That won't happen again. Since they can't be trusted to use discretion during a crisis, they won't be allowed near Her Royal Highness. I want to assign a unit to keep them away from our gates."

Mirie wasn't sure she understood the point of redirecting their limited manpower. "I don't leave except to go to church."

"Exactly. That's your Sunday routine, and these vultures need repetition to get the point. We'll create a perimeter around the church to keep the paparazzi at a distance. Georghe can write up one of his diplomatic letters informing these media outlets they've lost their privileges."

Georghe exhaled a low whistle. "I like it. We'll hold the paparazzi accountable, protect the public and let the legitimate press know we're taking action so the paparazzi won't stumble on breaking news again. A show of good faith."

Helena scribbled some notes while the general raised his coffee cup in a mock salute.

"Now can we get to business?" Georghe asked.

"I want to hear what we've learned about these attackers."

The general glanced at Drei. "We believe the transport copter continued through the mountains out of Hungarian airspace. They may have grounded the aircraft. We don't know. The Hungarians' radar didn't yield anything, but they did offer to review surveillance tapes from their military base and a private airstrip in the region."

"Do you think they'll find anything?" Mirie asked.

"The attackers would have to be idiots to go anywhere close to civilization. Drei thinks they headed to Ukraine, using the mountains as cover for their escape."

For the same reasons he had used them to escape with her. Spotty satellite coverage. Terrain that limited radio frequency. Was it any wonder Ninsele couldn't get a lock on her own borders?

The military had been dismantled and replaced with paid thugs during the authoritarian regime, so the general had been rebuilding their armed forces ever since Mirie's return. Unfortunately, rebuilding cost money the treasury didn't have at the moment.

"Do you think the attack was a protest of the upcoming talks?" Mirie had to ask.

"If so, no one has claimed responsibility," Georghe said. "Not yet, anyway."

"We do have several corpses, so we haven't hit a dead end," the general went on. "The medical examiner is working to identify them now. Hopefully they'll provide some leads."

Georghe glanced at Mirie, his expression neutral. He would never say, "I told you so," but he wasn't happy. He glanced at Drei, and then said, "I'm sure you'll come up with something soon. Her Royal Highness is home safely, which is what matters most."

Mirie sighed. "Let's discuss damage control for my newest half sibling, shall we?"

Georghe briefed her on Vadim, an American attorney who claimed to have been born out of wedlock during the first years of her parents' marriage.

"A first child," she said. "We haven't had one of those before. And an American. That's new, too."

No one replied. Dealing with these claims was always awkward. Her father couldn't defend himself against the charges and no one wanted to offend Mirie by impugning his moral conduct.

She kept the lead. "Do we know when Vadim was born?"

Georghe shuffled through some paperwork. "I've got his entry papers. June 29, 1980."

Mirie mentally calculated. "My mother would have been pregnant with Alexi."

No response.

"Do we know yet if my father even visited America during—" more calculations "—October of '79 or thereabouts?"

Georghe didn't bother looking back at his papers. "His Majesty visited Washington, D.C., for several weeks the year the honorary consulate opened. The time frame works."

"And the alleged mother. She was in our employ?"

"That checks, too. An envoy named Ileana Vadim. A Ninselan citizen. She put in her notice in late 1981, and I couldn't find any documentation that she ever returned to Ninsele. I've got my staff trying to track her down now."

She nodded. "So Luca Vadim has done his homework."

Silence. Mirie didn't really need a reply. Everyone around the table was likely thinking the same thing.

Jus sanguinis. Salic law.

She may be in charge right now. She may eventually give birth to a son who could grow up to be king, but she would never be queen. Primogeniture decreed that only males could rule.

She couldn't change that law even if she had been so inclined. Until she could negotiate consensus on the government structure, such a move would be seen as self-serving and could potentially deepen the rift between the opposing factions that had only tentatively been bridged since the civil war.

"Vadim is an attorney," she said. "His most likely move will be to take his claim to court and sue for the right to the throne as the only living male heir."

"He'd have to establish paternity," Georghe said.

"He won't," Mirie said firmly. "Not through legal means, anyway. But if he continues to use the media, he will cast doubt on my right to negotiate with the European Commission. Enough doubt, and he may give the representatives one more reason to delay the talks."

The very last thing they needed was to make the process of hosting representatives from the European Commission more complex. Like the Western Balkans that endured years of civil war, Ninsele had to be stabilized before it could formally become an acceding country with the commission's support.

Global attention would turn to Ninsele during these historic talks. All these years of work would finally culminate with the inception of this plan.

A plan that would offer Ninsele a future.

This had been her father's dream. This was the only logical course to move into the twenty-first century.

Mirie glanced around the room. These were her closest advisers, her family now.

Her one decision had begun a chain reaction she couldn't have foreseen. She understood that, but she'd risked opening the door all the same. It wasn't enough that innocent people had been in harm's way, might even have died because of her. Now she had undermined everything these caring people had been working toward for so long.

All signs had pointed against her making the trip

to Alba Luncă. The risk to her safety. The fact that they were preparing for the visiting European Commission representatives. Even the weather.

Yet Mirie hadn't listened. She had refused to believe that her presence at her nanny's funeral was too much to ask when she devoted every minute of every day to duty.

Why? To honor Bunică, who wasn't alive to care?

Or had Mirie needed to return once more to the place where her life had once been simple? Had she been so desperate to escape her glittering shell that she seized an excuse to leave?

Or had she risked everything because she was so empty that she had sought any distraction from her loneliness? *So* desperate that she had begged a man to make love to her just to feel life flow through her veins again?

Mirie shrank inside at the thought of how weak she'd been. She'd caused such havoc with her needs.

And everyone had done what she'd asked whether they'd agreed or not.

Even Drei. Another *why*. Why had he made love to her? Out of pity? Kindness? The man had never expressed an interest in her or pursued her in any way. Yet she'd asked something so personal of him, and he'd indulged her.

She felt crushed beneath the weight of responsibility. Swiveling her chair, she stared out the paned windows that ran the length of the eastern wall. The landscape was thinly blanketed in snow beneath the bright morning sun. Mirie could easily remember what the lawns looked like lush with spring, when the trees flowered in full bloom.

Exactly the way the world had been the last time she had played with her brothers out there. Some rough-and-tumble tag game where they had chased one another like maniacs. Not Alexi. He was the oldest and had taken his role as crown prince so seriously. He would have grown to be a compassionate man.

If he'd lived. If he'd ruled after their father. If the dictator had never come and the civil war never happened.

If, if, if.

Just like Mirie's choices, some things couldn't be taken back.

CHAPTER SIX

DREW LOGGED OFF the computer and sank back in the chair. He ran a hand over bleary eyes and glanced at the wall clock. Digital numbers stared at him in the electronic glow of the security station. Two-fourteen. He could feel the lateness of the hour in the air and in his aching muscles.

But sleep hadn't been on his radar in the days since their return to Briere. Falling asleep meant emptying his head, which left the memory of making love with Mirie to move in until he could practically feel her every touch, hear her every sigh.

So he spent his nights working or roaming the royal compound in an exercise from long ago, walking escape routes. He checked the hidden crawl space Geta had used when the royal family was murdered. He looked for others he may have missed like the altar in Alba Luncă's church.

He did his best to think like Oskar.

And distract himself from obsessing about Mirie.

Was she lying in bed remembering, too?

Jesus. No way was he heading back to his suite tonight until he was tired enough to pass out when his head hit the pillow. Instead, he spun around and headed back to the security station, deciding to check for any word on who might have funded the attack. Then, maybe, he could log a few hours of sleep.

"Any news yet, Major?" the night-shift commander asked.

Drew technically wasn't an officer with the NRPG, but the men had to call him something. "We'll see."

"Maybe that's good news. At least you haven't hit another dead end for certain."

"You got that right." The last thing Drew needed was another brick wall in his way.

The medical examiner had identified the dead attackers. All Slovaks, which corroborated the language lead. Ratko was still a mystery. It was sort of like tracking a Robert in the United States.

But Drew had traced these men to separate mercenary outfits. Guns for hire. None had known affiliations with any factions opposing the unification and stabilization plan or any ties to the United States or Luca Vadim.

None had any connection to Ninsele, period, beyond being gunned down in the mountains near the northern border and breathing their last breaths here.

The money trail had been another bust. After wasting too much time tracking circuitous routes to accounts belonging to the dead mercenaries, he'd come up with several large cash deposits. And couldn't get dead men to talk.

The money was bugging Drew. Even if Luca Vadim had the kind of resources to fund these mercenaries, which nothing in his public record indicated he did, hiring mercenaries from outfits in this part of the world seemed a stretch for a guy who'd been raised in Whitefish, Montana.

Vadim was a U.S. citizen, and Drew knew better than anyone how the United States conducted business. Either Vadim had coordinated this raid, which revealed some military skill from a man who didn't have a military background, or someone with that skill was bankrolling him. If there was a connection between Vadim and the attack on Mirie, they had to find it.

Tonight the general had flown to Ukraine to track a lead on the transport copter. Drew was waiting to hear from him, which was driving home one of Drew's biggest frustrations—cooling his heels to let the NRPG work. Ninsele's military had come a long way, but it still wasn't much to speak of. Not compared with Drew's agency. Excelsior could dig deeper with its global network of contacts and produce something tangible.

Something that might safeguard Mirie.

But the very nature of Drew's assignment meant Excelsior contacted him when they wanted his help, and not vice versa.

Drew wouldn't complain, though. The best part about his cover was that he was expected to investigate threats against Mirie, which went a long way toward dealing with his impatience.

He checked his email queries, checked the fax, checked his phone. Nothing. And sitting in the station wasn't proving any more constructive than walking the halls, so Drew shoved away from the desk, got up and scanned the wall of surveillance monitors, looking for a distraction.

Audiovisual cameras made it impossible to travel unobserved through the compound. All the high-tech monitoring had been compliments of the former dictator, who had been one paranoid bastard. Understandably so, since half of Ninsele had staged a coup to oust him. The other half… Well, it turned out that even the men in his employ had been scheming behind his back. Dictators weren't known for inspiring much loyalty, which, Drew supposed, was the downside of being a bully.

There was always a bigger one.

If Mirie's family had been half as paranoid, they might be alive today.

Three guards monitored the live feed around the clock. Armed guards patrolled the compound, communicating via radio. The audio feed in the private suites was typically muted, but kept active in the public access areas.

Offices. Delivery routes. The palace grounds where daily tours were conducted.

But the entire compound locked down at dusk with

no access except through a monitored gatehouse. The security station was quiet save for the blips and bleeps of equipment and the hum of the climate-controlled system as it cycled on.

Drew scanned the monitors until he spotted the guard posted outside Mirie's suite. Not all her rooms were monitored, only the access points. He didn't expect to find any movement at this time of night, but in the next monitor, a glimpse of motion caught his eye.

Mirie.

The sight of her took his breath away. She was a silent, pale vision standing on her balcony with her hair and long robe floating around her on the wind.

The fact that she was only an image on a surveillance monitor didn't make a damned bit of difference. One glimpse of her leveled him with memories yet again.

"How long has she been out there?" Drew asked.

The guard glanced down at the digital feed running in the corner of the display. "Eighteen minutes, Major."

Too long to be outside in minus-two degrees Celsius wearing a bathrobe.

"Thanks." He clapped the guard on the shoulder and left the security station.

Making his way through the quiet compound, Drew swiped his key card to enter the living quarters, greeting the guards at the access points to the private wing.

Drew didn't stop to question what he was doing, although his brain was sounding an alarm that grew louder with every step he took. Once he would have gone to her without hesitation.

Before he had touched her.

Now he had to ignore the alarm bells clanging in his head. When he was around her, which was the bulk of his days, he needed to get away from her, so he could get a grip on his reactions. Hyperaware, to put it mildly. But when he finally got away from her, he couldn't stop obsessing about her. He was screwed either way.

He let himself inside her suites, part of a wing off-limits to all but the NRPG and the kitchen and housekeeping staffs. Dragging a decorative blanket off the back of a sofa, he went to the French doors that opened to the balcony and tapped on the glass. Mirie was so deep in thought that the sound must have startled her, because she spun around sharply, eyes wide. Then stepping away from the door, she allowed him to come outside, as if finding him in her living room in the wee hours was the most natural place for him to be.

"Drei, what are you doing up so late?"

She wasn't wearing a bathrobe, but a filmy dressing gown that molded to her curves in the wind.

She didn't seem remotely concerned to be caught half-dressed.

He supposed they were past that now.

Wrapping the blanket around her shoulders, he covered the sight that was already causing his pulse to start slogging through his veins. God, he was a mess.

"It's freezing out here, Your Royal Highness."

Mirie.

Her name echoed in his head, another ghost of a forbidden memory he had to find some way to forget, as she stared up at him, a frown teasing the corners of her mouth. A mouth that had yielded beneath his so eagerly.

Drew wasn't nearly distanced enough from *that* memory, either. The rest of his life was going to be agony if he couldn't figure out how to manage some distance. Just the thought of kissing her chased off the cold the way no blanket or coat ever could.

"Thank you, Drei."

Her voice wrapped itself on the wind, bit through him with the same force. Maybe not the rest of his life, he reminded himself. Only until Excelsior reactivated him. Of course he'd been in Ninsele for fifteen *years*. No help there.

The smudges beneath her eyes were more noticeable by starlight. Maybe because she wore no makeup. The smattering of freckles across her nose was visible. So appealing.

For a long moment, he stood there like an idiot, not saying anything, the gently formed rebuke about being outside without a coat completely forgotten.

"You couldn't sleep, either?" she asked, reminding him of the question he hadn't answered.

"I was waiting to hear from the general."

"Has he learned anything?"

Drew stepped away from the door, repositioning himself to break the wind and provide her some relief. "The Hungarians reported a low-flying aircraft that made an unauthorized crossing into Ukraine."

"You were right, then. This is good news."

"The general seemed pretty upbeat."

"You don't sound so optimistic."

"Whoever funded those hired thugs probably rented the transport copter, too."

She nodded. "You don't expect a connection?"

Even if there was one, he wasn't confident they'd be able to do anything with it. But he didn't want to piss in her cereal by pointing out that her military was not up to par. "That would be a big oversight for someone who has been pretty thorough."

She considered that, tipping her head to the side, her blue-gray eyes dark in the clear night.

Drew wondered if he was the only one feeling awkward right now. Was she as aware of him as he was of her?

She looked reluctant, as if she wanted to say something, but wasn't sure she should. "I heard you were awake late last night, too."

"Where did you hear that?"

"One of the kitchen staff said you raided the *savarina* that was soaking in rum for today's staff luncheon."

"They knew it was me, hmm?"

"Apparently." The wind lifted her hair and sent tendrils floating around her face, making her look surreal, like an angel in the starlight, as she considered him thoughtfully. "I didn't know you had a sweet tooth."

Something about that seemed to bother her, although only God knew what. That they were even having this conversation bothered him. *Personal.* So now that they'd gotten naked together they were going to become drinking buddies?

"I don't have a sweet tooth," he said.

She eyed him curiously. "No?"

"It was the rum. I like to drink."

That made her smile.

His heart pounded hard, and he had only himself to blame. He was the one who'd barged in on her, so she wouldn't freeze. He was the one who didn't hightail it out of there after delivering his care package of a blanket. So now he was back to staring at her again, knowing he should head back through the door and let her get back to staring out into the starry night.

Drew couldn't seem to make himself move. All

these years he'd guarded her, lusted after her, but never once could he remember feeling so worried that she might think he was a drooling moron staring at her.

He'd made love to this woman, for Christ's sake. Shouldn't that make him feel more comfortable around her?

He finally forced himself to move, but when he reached for the door, Mirie said, "Please don't go, Drei. I have something to say."

He stopped, braced himself.

Her smiled faded, and she sighed softly, the sound of inevitability. "I owe you an apology."

"Really?" Another brilliant reply.

She met his gaze, and he recognized the way she steeled herself, had seen her do it a thousand times. A slight squaring of her shoulders, a lifting of her chin.

"I took advantage of our situation in Alba Luncă," she said simply. "I crossed a line I had no right to cross, and you were gracious enough to let me. I was upset and overwhelmed, but I was wrong to impose on you."

He would never forget her plea to him in the cave, try though he had since their return. Mirie had no clue what it had cost him to answer her request, no idea she asked for the one thing he had been scared to death to give.

He had already been so in love with her, and touching her had only made his situation so much worse.

Drew had never known a time in his life when his response mattered more, but he could think of nothing to say, nothing that wouldn't reveal everything he felt, and that was a burden she should not bear. His stupidity, his lack of discipline, his raging emotions were barely under control anymore.

Every single response that flitted through his head only sounded stock and unworthy, capable only of minimizing the way she felt, the enormity of the way he felt about her and the way they had made love. She couldn't know how he really felt.

Not now. Not ever.

So he stared at her like the idiot he was, the dumb-as-an-ox bodyguard who was all fists and no brains, until the silence grew so alive he could have taken aim and fired a shot through it.

She broke it this time. "I don't want my weakness to affect our relationship."

"That's why you're apologizing?"

Pulling the blanket around her more tightly, she nodded.

"You don't have anything to apologize for." And drooling moron that he was, he went for reassurance, something, *anything* to smooth away the raw edges of her expression, the worry that only added to those she already bore. All he wanted to do was reach out and run his fingers along her lovely face. "I sure as hell didn't do anything I didn't want to, so don't worry about that. What man wouldn't want to spend time with such a beautiful woman?"

And *that* came out all wrong. He'd known it would. The clichés were flying, making a joke of her need and his feelings for her. This was beyond painful.

But his words did—*mercifully*—level the playing field.

Drew knew it the instant her smile reached her eyes. Humor gave her something to latch on to, and she grabbed on with a choke hold, lightening up the mood and the moment.

"I assumed we would go back to the way things were between us." She shrugged, not a little sheepish. "That was naive on my part. Everything feels changed now."

So many things were happening inside him right then. Did everything feel changed because she felt something for him, or because he was blasting his emotions all over her? Or was she apologizing because she was sorry they'd had sex?

There was no way she could have mistaken the way he'd lost his control. They'd have gone for round three if the general hadn't made contact when he did.

Drew had no clue what to say to reassure her, how to clarify what he felt without revealing what he felt. He only knew he wanted her at peace. Not guilty. Not worried. Not awkward. He'd lived with his feelings a long time. He'd deal with them now.

"You have more strength than any woman I've

ever known," he said quietly and watched understanding transform her expression.

"I was mourning Bunică. I was remembering… the past."

Another cliché. Geta had been right to withhold the letter. She'd known how her death would impact this woman who had loved her so much.

"I worry about you sometimes," he admitted, deciding to bridge the distance and lead the way back to comfortable.

That surprised her. "Why?"

Drew willed himself to say what he meant this time, not to botch a few declarative sentences and offend her.

"You're at a time of your life when your future should be unfolding like an adventure. You should have people to laugh with and care about and love. You have your country, and I know you want to give the people security. But you're still a woman, and from where I'm standing, your life appears… isolated."

She gave a short laugh, only there was no humor in the sound this time. She looked thoughtful. "Bunică used to say heaven isn't on earth. I remember that whenever I feel as if all I do is work, and the progress isn't balancing with the effort. There's just always so much to do and so far to go."

"That much is true," he agreed. "And you work nonstop."

Leaning back against the wall, she cast a sidelong glance at him. "That's pretty rich, coming from you."

Now it was his turn to shrug. She had no idea.

"I've been muscling my way through feeling lonely. I thought if I ignored it, I'd get used to it, or at least be able to handle it until I came out on the other end. I thought I was stronger. And I was." Another sigh. "Until Bunică."

Until fear and despair had disarmed her.

"Once the unification and stabilization plan is in place, things will settle down."

Drew nodded. He had never been her confidant, but she needed to talk, so he let her. Maybe, just maybe, if she unloaded what troubled her, shared what she felt, she might not wind up feeling so overwhelmed. He was a good listener. She could trust him with her thoughts. Who was he going to tell? He didn't have a life, either.

But as he listened to her chat about her hope that life would settle down after Ninsele was on its way to accession, he wasn't convinced grief was her biggest problem.

"Would you like an unsolicited opinion?" The question was out of his mouth before he had a chance think better of it.

"Solicited."

"Maybe making some time for yourself will help, and because you work so much, so does your personal staff."

She huffed indignantly. "Are you telling me I'm working everyone to death?"

"I'm telling you man does not live by bread alone. Or a woman by duty. You said it yourself—you need balance."

"As soon as we get the unification and stabilization plan in place, I'll have more time."

"I'm sure you will. But that big goal is still a ways off. You should set little goals. It's easier to find a few hours in your schedule than making time for a two-week vacation."

"A two-week vacation." Her eyes fluttered shut, half-moon lashes resting on her pale cheeks. "Sounds like heaven."

"Heaven's not on earth, remember?"

Then she shook her head, wisps of hair catching on the breeze, twining around her lovely face until she had to brush them away. "I can't rationalize scheduling any leisure time with so much still to be done anyway. I'm not able to go out and join a health club or take a run through the city, which means unless I meet some friends at church because that's the only place I ever go…" She let her statement trail off. "That and the courthouse when the high court is in session."

"Probably not the best place to meet people." An evasion if ever Drew heard one. "All true, of course, but you're an effective mediator. There must be some sort of compromise."

She tilted her head, considering. "I could upload my personal information to one of those friendship websites. 'Seeking companions to share similar indoor interests at my place.' What do you think?"

"I'll be working 24/7 to protect you from weirdos."

"I thought you worked 24/7 already."

"I do."

She pursed her lips, thoughtful. "'All applicants must have a flexible schedule and no problem becoming a target for revolutionaries and assassins.'"

Drew liked that she could find something in there to poke fun of. There hadn't been much to make anyone laugh around this place lately. "Looks like I might get my own vacation. You won't find many takers for that ad."

"My point." The humor vanished as quickly as it had come. A glimmer like the stars on this clear winter night.

Pushing away from the wall, Mirie crossed to the balcony's edge with a few liquid strides and peered out at the grounds. "I'm not good friend material. I couldn't even go to a funeral without jeopardizing people. Maybe even costing them their lives. I wouldn't feel right about asking people to take risks for the sake of my social life. I worry about everyone who lives here. You, Georghe, Helena, the general."

She knew what could happen to the people she cared about even sequestered in this compound. And she did care. He witnessed proof of that caring every day. Even toward him, although he had been part of the woodwork until a few days ago.

But Drew also understood why she'd wound up turning to him for companionship in the cave. He witnessed proof of her loneliness every day, too.

From where he stood, Drew could see the weight settling on her slim shoulders again. Her body suddenly a wisp in the night. All traces of humor gone.

He didn't want it to go. "What about a compromise? Do something to balance your time, so you're not always working. You do that with the unification and stabilization plan. You and the council set goals, work toward them, switch gears, work on something else. There's got to be room for some downtime."

"I should make half a friend? Make it a little easier to dodge bullets?"

"No," he snorted. "You've got friends."

He would be her friend.

She glanced over her shoulder, her profile stark against the dark night as she considered him.

"I said downtime," he explained. "Squeeze something into your schedule that's not work every once in a while. Something that you can look forward to."

"Like what?"

"I don't know." Of course now that he'd made the suggestion, everything he might suggest sounded stupid, so he tossed out the least idiotic of the bunch. "Walking the grounds instead of always exercising inside. Or having a picnic instead of eating in the conference room."

She frowned. "A *picnic,* Drei?"

Okay, maybe not the least idiotic. It was dead winter and Eastern Europe wasn't exactly the tropics.

"Yes, a picnic." The idea didn't sound so ridiculous aloud. She had once loved hiking in the mountains with her friends. Geta had always packed a food basket. "You have to eat, so what's wrong with taking lunch outside once in a while?"

She motioned to everything around them. "Besides the weather, you mean?"

His turn to eye her skeptically. "I hadn't noticed the weather deterring you."

She pulled the blanket more tightly around her.

"Have the kitchen pack a basket. It'll be a lot less work for them. Be like a mini-vacation instead of lugging those catering trays to you three times a day. And Helena has been fighting a cold for weeks. Fresh air and vitamin D will do her good."

His mother had been a big one for saying illness stemmed from lack of fresh air and vitamin D. Of course they hadn't done anything for the Alzheimer's that had robbed her of life long before her death, but until then, she'd been healthy.

"A picnic," Mirie repeated as if the idea might be growing on her, too. "Maybe one day I'll surprise you all."

He hoped she would because she sounded better,

as if getting an apology off her chest and having something to think about had lifted her spirits a bit.

This conversation had lifted Drew's. Everything inside him was still shrieking like warning sirens, but he continued to stand there running his mouth, playing Dear Abby as he sucked in the sight of Mirie half-dressed in the dark. His feelings for her hadn't been balanced *before* they'd made love. He'd hardly slept since.

Yet he stood there practically vibrating inside as he chatted as though he was her friend, promising they wouldn't let what happened in Alba Luncă interfere with their relationship.

A lie. The biggest he'd ever told, and that was saying something.

CHAPTER SEVEN

MIRIE HEARD THE name and came to a stop in the middle of the living room. With the diamond pendant in one hand, she turned to the television as the news anchor delivered a report.

Not good. True, the announcement appeared to be only a mention at the end of the broadcast, but this was a legitimate broadcasting network.

Judging by his frown, the anchorman was equally unconvinced the information he relayed was newsworthy. But he dutifully read from the teleprompter as video appeared over his right shoulder, and delivered his bit impassively.

"Luca Alexander Vadim, the man claiming to be the son of the late King Alexander II, deposed monarch and father to Her Royal Highness Mirela Selskala, signed a declaration of paternity at the Civil Court yesterday...."

Mirie stared at the man in the video, walking down the steps of the courthouse, her heart suddenly pounding. At this man's age, there were few reasons to establish paternity—one would be if this man intended to apply for citizenship.

And make a bid for her throne.

Anger would have been a much better defense against the heaviness that suddenly cast a pall over her mood. This man's lies were only one more thing to deal with.

Tonight of all nights.

Even if she had been inclined to believe that her father had cheated, maybe a mistake to be learned from and forgiven, Mirie saw nothing familiar in the face displayed on the television. Nothing in the man's features. Nothing that brought to mind her beloved Papa or any of her brothers. Nothing of herself.

"The time, Your Royal Highness." Helena swept into the room, aghast to find Mirie still in her dressing gown. "Look at the time. You're not half-ready yet."

Helena herself appeared lovely with her blond hair in a chignon, her deep blue dress both simple and elegant. Her expression collapsed into horror when she followed Mirie's gaze to the television.

"Oh, no, no, no. Since when do you watch the news?" She plucked the remote control from Mirie's hand. With a deliberate motion, she flicked off the television. "No more of that."

"You knew." Not a question.

Helena rolled her eyes. "Of course we knew. Georghe and I were determined not to let this nonsense spoil your evening."

"You didn't think anyone would mention it?"

"This is your ball and your guests. Who would be so rude to ruin the evening with unpleasantness?" She set the remote on the entertainment center. "Let me help you into your gown. Then we can finish your hair. The guests are already arriving."

Tonight's reception and ball was a centuries-old tradition marking Freedom Day, resurrected upon Mirie's return. As a national holiday, schools and businesses closed and people celebrated their heritage and independence with parades and festivals all over the country.

The royal family had traditionally hosted a ball in the palace, inviting officials from all twenty-eight provinces and prominent citizens reflecting all aspects of Ninselan life.

"My gown is out already," Mirie said.

But Helena had already vanished into the sitting room and a dramatic sigh drifted through the doorway. "I knew you would look even more beautiful than last year. Hard to imagine, but you do. You'll look the part of a princess tonight."

"I had a skilled adviser with an eye for fashion." Who was, at the moment, fawning over the blush-colored gown with the fitted lace bodice and layered tulle skirt.

"She served you very well." Helena giggled as she circled the dress form and began unfastening buttons. "Oh, this is breathtaking. Any way you can forgo the sash?"

"Hardly. It's Freedom Day."

"I know. I know. But this dress doesn't need any accessories but a smile."

"I can manage that." She'd had a lot of practice playing to the crowds. But she wasn't thinking about her guests as she stepped into her ball gown. She was thinking about the man who'd be standing beside her, dressed just as sharply for tonight's event. The man she couldn't dance with.

"Then we'll have a wonderful time tonight, Your Royal Highness. We'll dance and drink champagne and talk to people about something other than problems and politics and policies. We should celebrate. This gown was made to be holding a crystal flute. Or Prince Charming."

Mirie smiled then, remembering Drei's charge to make time for small pleasures among all the work. "What should we celebrate? Sadly, it's not Prince Charming for either of us."

"Life."

"Life, then." Setting the pendant on her vanity, she was careful not to tangle the chain. Helena wasn't usually so whimsical, but the Freedom Ball had that effect on people.

Once upon a time, Mirie had been easily caught up in the excitement, too. When she'd been a young girl awestruck by all the beauty in the ballroom on this magical night. Her brothers had run screaming from the thought of dancing, preferring the parades and sporting events that got them away from their tutors for a day.

Not Mirie. For days, she trailed her mother, who oversaw every aspect of the preparations from the ballroom decoration to the testing of recipes for the banquet.

When the day of the ball arrived, she'd helped her mama choose jewelry, decide whether to dust her cheeks with warm or cool powder. And for her effort, Mirie was rewarded with a special place on the stairwell of the grand foyer to peer through the baluster as the guests arrived.

She could still remember how she felt to be so breathless she grew dizzy with excitement.

Her Christmas gift on the year of her eighth birthday had been a designer gown of her own to wear to the ball. Mama had only smiled when Mirie chattered about what she'd wear when she was finally old enough to attend, how she'd style her hair, what jewels she would wear, what boys she would dance with.

But Mama had been listening very closely.

Mirie remembered opening her Christmas gift that year and lifting out the gown from the sparkling tissue, a ball gown that was the embodiment of her imagination. There'd been a tiara and glittery shoes that looked like glass slippers.

But the best gift of all had been realizing she was finally old enough to leave the stairs and dance the night away.

That excited young girl with her big dreams had grown into this woman whose reflection stared back from the floor-length mirror with such a detached gaze. Yes, the gown was quite lovely. Yard upon yard of tulle so she'd appear to be floating on a cloud.

That description popped into her head through the distance of many years. She could remember her papa's description of her lovely ball gown on that Christmas morning so long ago.

That gown had been tulle and lace, too.

Maybe she wasn't as detached as she thought, which was too sobering a thought. So she inhaled deeply and tested her smile. Much better.

"The sash, please, Helena." They added the final touch, adorning Mirie in the colors of the Ninselan flag—blue, silver and white—and then they were ready to go.

Drei waited outside her suite. He had traded his usual nondescript sportswear for a stylish tux that made it impossible not to notice the way the lines hugged his broad shoulders or how the white dress shirt shocked his complexion, made his green eyes sparkle like jewels.

Her gaze devoured him in a sweeping glance, and in that instant, time stopped. The distant chime of the quarter hour faded to silence; the hallway with its vaulted ceiling and crown molding dissolved into nothing.

She had that sense of him as a stranger again, a

man she knew so intimately, but didn't really know at all. The breath caught in her throat when approval flashed in his gaze. One glance became a moment they shared alone, too intimate for Helena, who stood but a step behind, so close she might feel Mirie shiver.

She saw a flicker of surprise in his bright green eyes, as if he, too, couldn't drag his gaze away, remembered all that had passed between them and hadn't meant to show his emotion. His glance became a physical force that invoked a reply deep inside her, an awareness that brought the moment to life in a way only he had.

Then just as quickly, his expression settled into the stoic mask again, and Mirie wondered if she'd only imagined that look.

"Your Royal Highness" was all he said, but his voice caressed her the way it had in the fire-soaked darkness in a cave, the starlight cold of a clear night.

And she might still have stood there, making no reply, only staring at Drei so caught up in her awareness of the moment, had Georghe not arrived.

"Come, come," he said in a rush. "Your guests are awaiting their princess."

Drei dropped back to her left, his expression unreadable, while Helena and Georghe rushed along beside her, escorting her to the grand foyer, where she would make her formal entrance. Then all thoughts of handsome bodyguards and lying imposters were gratefully forgotten as she was announced.

"Her Royal Highness Princess Mirela."

The chatter of the crowd silenced. For one long moment, Mirie could almost feel the breathless excitement from her childhood as though years hadn't passed and nothing had changed. The grand foyer had been draped in banners of blue, silver and white, while the Ninselan flag hung from the high baluster.

Forcing her expression to relax into a welcoming half smile, she slowly descended the stairs to the orchestral strains of the national anthem filtering through the open archways that led to the palace ballroom.

Then she plunged into the dazzling crowd.

There was conversation and laughter. The guests nabbed Mirie's attention away from anything other than their demands for her time, for chances to familiarize her with their causes.

She discussed palace art and the upcoming dedication of the new state-of-the-art medical center—the first new facility to be constructed in Briere in fifteen years. At some point Helena pressed a champagne flute into Mirie's hand and continued to supply names of guests she didn't know well.

The philanthropist who wanted her to make a humanitarian appearance at a new resource center for children with autism.

The abbess from a religious order who invited

Mirie to sponsor its foundation for children orphaned and uprooted during the civil war.

Mirie listened with interest, requested some to contact her office at a later date and praised all charitable efforts on behalf of the citizens whom she served. All the while she was aware of Drei just behind her, so close her full skirt brushed his legs every time she moved.

Then came time for her speech. Georghe reappeared to escort her into the ballroom, which had been set up for the banquet.

"All set?" He plucked the nearly full champagne flute from her hand and passed it to Helena, who handed over the note cards. "Helena, water for Her Royal Highness."

"You're not tipsy, are you?" Georghe asked.

"It's a ball, Georghe, remember? We're here to have fun." At his scowl, she added, "But no worries. I've only taken a few sips. Promise."

He was still eyeing her skeptically when Helena returned with a tumbler from which Mirie took a few obligatory swallows to clear her throat.

She patted Georghe's cheek, lifted her skirts and left him to follow her to the dais. Drei took up his place in the wings, where he always was, but Mirie was so aware of him now, ready to intervene on her behalf, a James Bond–style rogue who moved so easily through the crowd, vanishing when he wanted to be invisible, seeing everything with eyes that missed nothing.

How had she ever *not* noticed what a dashing figure he cut in his formal wear?

Mirie delivered her speech, which was well-received, then formally began the meal, of which every detail was perfect. She couldn't have been more pleased afterward as she led her guests to smaller salons to freshen up or partake in an after-meal brandy and cigar, while the staff broke down the banquet setting.

During that short break, the ballroom transformed into magnificence. The highly polished floor of inlaid wood gleamed beneath the light of the chandeliers with dangling crystals. Gold-leaf designs formed archways around the mirrored walls, and outside the windows the grounds sparkled with thousands of blue, silver and white twinkle lights.

His Serene Highness Prince Ulrick was the first to escort Mirie to the dance floor. He was blond like Drei, and possibly a bit taller, yet Mirie felt nothing when he held her in his arms. His hands were too soft and his smile too boyish, although he was two years her senior. He was pleasant enough, but he talked too much and possessed none of the lean grace of the man whose gaze Mirie felt on her right now.

Did Drei always watch her so closely?

A ridiculous question. *Of course* he watched her

closely. How could he protect her if he didn't watch her closely?

She was the one who'd never noticed the way his gaze followed her through a crowd before. He melted into the periphery, but his gaze never left her. She was the one who wondered what he thought about her dancing with another man.

Was he more aware of her now than before?

Ulrick said something, and Mirie scrambled to laugh—at least she hoped laughter was the right response. She had no clue what the man had said because her attention ricocheted back and forth between questions about Drei.

Did he think she looked lovely in her princess gown?

Was he as painfully aware of her as she was of him?

She didn't think so. He'd seemed at peace the other night when they'd spoken on the balcony. He appeared quite able to put Alba Luncă behind them and deal with the aftermath, the change to their relationship. He'd implied that he was her friend.

Is that what two people were after they'd made love when there was no intention of continuing a relationship?

They'd certainly spoken more casually than ever before, more personally. Did that make them friends?

Mirie only knew that the man she'd never noticed before seemed to be the only man she could see tonight.

Poor Ulrick. She smiled again and forced herself to pay closer attention to his chatter until she finally broke free of his embrace.

She caught a glimpse of Drei as her next partner claimed her. His expression was as unreadable as the marble bas-reliefs of cherubs and dead ancestors that presided from the crown molding. They had much in common with him, she realized. Hovering over the festivities, never joining in the fun.

Only they probably didn't mind. Did Drei?

The night wore on. She tried her best to charm her dance partners, but there was only one man she wanted to dance with tonight, and he wasn't going to ask her. Dance after dance. Toast after toast. After the archbishop, who'd been her father's closest friend since their school years, had asked her twice how she was holding up since losing Bunică, Mirie decided she'd had enough. A moment alone was in order so she could collect herself.

Escaping her guests took twenty minutes and throwing poor Helena to the wolves, but Mirie finally worked her way out of the ballroom and toward a suite set aside for her use.

She stepped inside, and the door shut softly behind her, blocking the music that filtered from the ballroom. Mirie inhaled deeply, willing the sudden quiet to wash over her.

Maybe she'd sipped too much champagne. She only sipped, never drank, so attentive serving staff constantly replaced her flute to keep her fresh. Her only true gauge of how much she'd consumed was the way she felt.

Right now she felt only restless and distracted.

Checking her appearance, she touched up her makeup and absorbed the tranquillity. She knew how to be "on" as her papa had called it long ago, her smiles continuous, her conversation personal and her laughter ready. But tonight had become a struggle, and her heightened awareness and mildly vibrating insides could be calmed only by being alone.

Not alone.

Drei stood outside in the hallway. That was the real problem. Mirie didn't even have to close her eyes to imagine him, such a dashing sight with his usual black attire broken by the cut of his jacket, the white at his chest, standing on the outside of the events looking in.

She was already pulling the door open before she could think better of it.

There he was, exactly as she'd imagined him, his expression just as stoic, just as conscientious.

Maybe she should ask his secret for keeping focused on the job. She'd never had trouble before, but now…

"I don't imagine you're having much fun tonight."

His eyebrow arched ever so slightly. "I'm working, Your Royal Highness."

"Me, too. But weren't you the one who advised me to make more time to have fun? It's a ball, Drei."

"Crowds are a challenge on a good day. They require my undivided attention. Especially tonight."

"Because of the trouble in Alba Luncă?"

There it was—the memory square between them. Mirie hadn't intended to bring up *that* subject, but it was just there when she opened her mouth.

"Until we know who was responsible, we have no choice but to ramp up our efforts. Especially on a night like tonight."

"A ball?"

"A logistical nightmare."

She could have left Drei's reply there, should have, but the words were out of her mouth with a lack of impulse control that was so rare for her, and unexpected.

"But wouldn't you rather be dancing?"

His gaze narrowed. He knew exactly what she was up to, striking up this conversation. Asking personal questions where there had been no interest before.

"I would rather see to your safety," he said diplomatically in an answer that was no answer at all.

And she wanted an answer. Suddenly, the most important thing in the world to her was knowing whether he noticed her the way she'd noticed him. Was it really so easy for him to dismiss what they'd shared? "We're in the palace with the NRPG and video surveillance everywhere. You can't relax a tiny bit and enjoy yourself?"

He shook his head. "Aren't you enjoying yourself?"

Such a simple question, but one that meant he didn't mind being engaged. Was he being a friend?

"I suppose," she said honestly. "The night is work. I'm trying to find balance."

"Any luck?"

None. She wasn't about to share the reason why balance wasn't happening, so she offered, "My partners are lacking."

"Really? You've danced with a prince, two counts, a bishop, an international banker and the son of a billionaire."

His job was to notice everyone who came near her, but that didn't seem to matter right now. Everything about her mood suddenly awoke, as if his admission had sparked a chemical reaction inside her. Reason argued that she was making his attentiveness way more personal than it was.

But reason didn't seem to have a lot to do with this feeling. Mirie liked the idea that he might care what man put his hands on her. And even if that wasn't entirely true, the feeling made the night not feel like such a waste.

Suddenly, she felt alive again, as alive as she'd felt in the cave. The music filtered in from the ballroom, making the hallway feel like part of the ball even though only she and Drei were here. But they were dressed in their formal wear, and the sconces bathed the hall with a golden glow that was both festive and warm.

"Dance with me, Drei."

"Your Royal Highness." Her title became an admonishment. Indeed, everything about him disapproved her boldness. His hard expression. His narrowed gaze. His tone.

But all the champagne of the evening had dulled some of her nerves, and Mirie didn't care. She felt bold.

"I thought we were going to be friends now. It's okay for friends to dance together."

She wasn't being honest at all. She wanted a reaction from him, some hint he felt *something* after what they'd shared. So she moved toward him, left him to bear the burden of accepting or denying her request.

His features sharpened, and his nostrils flared. Some expression she couldn't identify. But in one fluid move he had her, hand in hand, arm a vise around her waist, and caught her against him so hard she gasped aloud. The shock of his hard body against hers felt as if she'd finally come home.

Mirie melted against him with laughter tumbling from her lips as he whisked her around in a tightly controlled motion in perfect tempo with the music. Their first dance.

Drei could dance.

She wasn't surprised. Why would she be? He was an agile, athletic man who moved invisibly from a cottage in Alba Luncă to a palace in Briere, from a snowy mountain to a boardroom, from her bodyguard to her lover to her friend.

His movement was fluid, his command complete as he tucked her neatly against him, a little too close. Had Ulrick taken such liberty, she'd have trod on his foot and forced him to keep a respectable distance.

But with Drei... Their bodies molded together, remembering. She rested her cheek against his shoulder, reminded of the warmth of his skin, the steady rush of his pulse. Inhaling deeply, she smelled *him* beneath the hint of cologne, some masculine scent that suited the night's formal festivities yet was somehow unique to him. She trembled when he rested his cheek on the top of her head. They'd lain together in the firelight this way, their bodies aligned, their legs entwined, their hearts beating as one. Now they moved in another rhythmic motion that felt as natural as making love had.

The moment became charged with awareness, so perfect that all the disappointment and agitation that had marked the rest of the night was forgotten.

"The wrong partner can suck all the fun out of dancing," she whispered. The way the right partner made dancing magic.

"Maybe it's not your partners," he suggested

mildly, his voice a rough rumble in the quiet. "Maybe it's because you've been dancing at this ball your whole life."

She lifted her gaze, considering. "I suppose that could be, except I never danced at this ball. Not until we returned to Briere, anyway."

And there was her reaction, finally. He gazed down at her with his brow furrowed. "Not before the war? I misunderstood. I thought this ball was a tradition dating back centuries."

"It is. My parents hosted the ball before the war." She glanced past him in the direction of the grand foyer where the Ninselan flag hung from the baluster. "I used to sit on the stairs and watch everyone arrive."

"Ah, you weren't old enough to attend."

She smiled wistfully, remembering a ball gown so similar to the one she wore tonight. "Almost, but not quite. The year I was old enough to attend was the first year in three centuries there was no royal family to host the ball."

CHAPTER EIGHT

DREW STARED AT the letter, the wobbly scrawl on the page barely legible. He recognized Geta's hand, didn't doubt the authenticity. But the contents rooted him to the spot, and he stared blindly at the pages.

Trust Drei, no matter what. There is more to him than you can know.

In a letter filled with sentiments and counsel from someone who had loved Mirie, all the expected appreciation and gratitude and approval, this old woman had gone on to say that she would commit no more to writing.

Trust Drei.

Had this letter just blown his cover?

Disbelief had Drew scanning the pages again. Everything in him argued against that conclusion. He'd been in place for *fifteen years*. He had no overt ties to the agency, no control to oversee his movements. That he knew of, anyway.

How could Geta Bobescue have possibly known?

She couldn't have, which is why the idea didn't make sense. She had contacted Oskar after her escape, because she'd trusted the retired close-protection guard with the secret of Mirie's survival. But how could Oskar have had any interaction with a covert United States security agency? No one but the operatives, the president and an oversight committee even knew Excelsior existed.

Shaking his head, Drew willed the quiet in his suite to calm his racing thoughts. He tried to think past his surprise, to make some sense of the impossible. Refolding the letter, he slid the pages back into the envelope and placed it inside his room safe, locked out of sight.

The one thing he did know was that he couldn't give this letter to Mirie yet.

Drew closed his eyes, and the sight of her filled his head, the stunning woman who'd entertained her guests with grace and confidence, always welcoming, always *on*. Her words of the previous night haunted him.

There was no royal family to host the ball.

She hid her loneliness so well.

How many of those closest to her even suspected? Helena? Georghe? Had he even understood the depths of her isolation before she'd reached out to him in the cave?

No. Drew had only known he hadn't seen the lighthearted young woman from long ago, the young woman who'd grown up to be the solemn and dedicated woman he'd fallen in love with.

God, he ached to hold her right now. The girl known as Mirie had been slipping away, minute by minute, day by day, and he was the only one left who knew who that girl had been. And he wasn't about to let her go without a fight. He wanted to make her feel better. He'd spent what remained of the night after the ball searching for ways to do that.

He'd thought this might be the right time for the letter, to be touched by someone she'd loved so much.

But even his good intentions, to share comforting words from beyond the grave, had blown up in his face.

Geta had sealed the envelope, not to keep him from reading the contents as he'd first thought, but to keep Vlas, or anyone else, from reading them. She'd clearly understood the risk of putting such obvious implications in writing.

Had she suspected he wasn't who he claimed to be?

How was that even possible?

Raking his fingers through his hair, Drew tried to wrap his brain around what Geta and Oskar might have known about him.

Oskar's knowing about Excelsior was ridiculous, but the opposite was easily believable.

Excelsior had its finger on the pulse of global politics. The agency would have monitored the effects of the coup when the royal family was murdered. It would have known the key players who had been in place around the king, and the dictator.

Given the United States's interest in the area, Drew wouldn't be surprised if Excelsior had had an operative in place at the time. For all he knew there could be operatives in place now. Active, mission-ready operatives.

Or other sleepers like him.

Both types of operatives served legitimate, albeit vastly different functions—short-and long-term insurance policies, so to speak. One high-risk. The other quality, long-term protection to count on when one least expected to need it.

Moving to the window, Drew stared out at the grounds, tried to corral his thoughts. From this side of the palace, he could see over the compound walls and view the city that unfolded down the mountain, tight sloping streets crowded with buildings in crazy pastel colors like eggs in an Easter basket. That was exactly what he thought the first time he'd visited Briere in the spring. A European version of San Francisco.

The city was quiet today, the colors muted beneath the sullen gray sky. Everyone would be recovering from the festivities of Freedom Day, which had fallen midweek this year. But the national colors still covered the wintry scene, banners strung between street lamps, crisscrossing the streets. No doubt the slushy cobbles would be filled with trash from the fireworks that had exploded until dawn.

This city was the reason Excelsior had targeted Drew.

He'd been Marines Special Forces with an affinity for this part of the world. The agency director had later told Drew he'd unknowingly worked on several high-risk missions with other Excelsior operatives, all of whom had reported that he was just the caliber of officer Excelsior recruited.

The agency ran black bag operations at its finest, and the director was known within the ranks as hardcore, a leader who inspired the kind of loyalty that made people willing to die for United States national security. Drew undertook training and his mission objective with that same belief.

He'd given the past fifteen years of his life to serving the cause. Working in Ninsele, getting as close to the inner workings of the government as he could, staying informed about the politics and military, keeping Mirie alive, waiting for the time he was reactivated and called to utilize the cover he'd spent so long establishing. Just the thought that he might have undertaken this mission without knowing all the information outraged him.

How was he supposed to do his job if he wasn't privy to the mission parameters, to *all* the players. What possible reason would Excelsior have for letting people like Oskar or Geta know it was sending an operative into an unstable country?

Ninsele was *still* unstable. The dictator may have been deposed and the civil war officially ended, but this country was still a hotly contested gateway between the East and West for traffickers who would move their information, their arms, their radioactive materials and their *people* illegally. And the eventual destination of everything on the global black market was the United States.

Drew stared out at the city still showing the scars of war—freshly painted buildings beside those disfigured from bombing.

Excelsior would serve its mission objective. No question about that. But it wasn't talking about some short-term mission here. He had established a life undercover, becoming part of the fabric of another society. The deepest sort of cover.

And this job came inherent with its own set of unique demands. Demands that had been difficult for him in particular.

Was that what bugged him?

The director had known how Drew's upbringing had sent him on a collision course with mortality. Drew had been an extreme risk-taker, didn't feel alive unless he was tempting fate. After all this time he suspected he'd simply been trying to outrun the hand life had dealt him.

The farm. The family business. Alzheimer's.

But he'd only come to realize that with age and maturity. And by being forced to stop running. Without this mission, it would have been only a matter of time before he'd wind up dead. Excelsior had recognized that before Drew had. His first conversation with the director had put that square on the table.

"You've got the ambition and the abilities we value

in our organization, Drew," the director had told him so long ago. *"But judging by your track record, you're likely to get yourself killed and probably sooner than you'll expect. So the question is—do you want to put your skills to use on behalf of our nation's security or do you want to keep chasing thrills until your luck runs out?"*

Would the director have sent Drew to play a role when the people closest to him had already known who he was?

Not all of them. Not Mirie. She obviously didn't know. And couldn't. So what was he going to do with this letter now?

When he gave it to her, he'd need solid answers for the questions she might ask.

There is more to him than you can know.

What the hell did Geta mean? If she'd known he wasn't a Romanian close-protection guard, then did she expect him to fess up to Mirie about who he really was?

And what would Mirie think to find out the man she'd trusted for over half her life wasn't who he claimed to be?

The man she'd made love to, danced with, smiled for.

Jesus Christ. What a mess. He needed to reason through this with a clear head, not the sleep-deprived mess that was his brain right now. If he ever slept again. Every time he'd closed his eyes he only saw Mirie. In his arms. Underneath him. In her ball gown. Naked.

Turning from the window, he caught sight of the digital clock on his bedside table. "Damn it."

If he didn't relieve Jozsef right now, he'd miss catching Mirie alone before the meeting, and there wouldn't be another chance all day. The council was gathering to update security plans for next week's EC talks.

Drew took off out of his suite, slipping the audio transmitter into his ear as he hurried through the halls toward Mirie's wing. Under normal circumstances the council would have taken the day after the Freedom Ball off, but they couldn't afford to lose that much time. They were scheduled to submit their updated security arrangements to the personal heads of security of the high representatives tomorrow, and in light of the attacks, their current plan needed to be revisited.

Mirie couldn't catch a break, because nothing could be simple around here. Drew had no clue why, but that much was true. The European Commission comprised representatives from each of the member countries, so the NRPG wasn't looking at safe passage for one arriving flight, but arrivals from all over Europe and Britain.

Ninsele's resources could get a group from the airport to the royal compound with heightened security. But they were stretched to secure the arrival of many flights, which meant transporting the representatives to the compound individually or securing them at the airport until all the flights landed. Either way was a logistical juggling act for a military with finite limitations.

If the council didn't come up with an impressive plan to reassure the individual security heads of their representatives' safety, if only a few decided the risk of travel was too high in light of the recent attack, postponement of the talks was a reasonable option. And all Mirie's work, all the council's work, to reach this historic goal would be wasted. Only the passage of time would prove that Ninsele had stabilized enough for safe travel.

That same time would give Ninsele's opposing factions the chance to garner more supporters.

And he wondered why Mirie was struggling, willing to risk her life to get the hell out of this compound.

No, he didn't.

If the Ninselan people knew what was best for them, they'd be tripping over themselves to help her get the EC here. Ten years beneath a dictator's rule had all but annihilated the country, and without help there would be no stable health-care system, economy, education, employment.

No future.

This wasn't rocket science, yet people were divided

on what they wanted. Center-left. Center-right. Socialists and nationalists on either extreme.

Until these factions learned to compromise and unify, no progress would be made. And thugs would continue to exploit Ninsele for its prime real estate.

He arrived at Mirie's suite just as the door opened and she appeared, looking fresh for someone who couldn't have slept for long. Or at all, which was an epidemic around here.

His gaze took in everything at once, and the sight of her soothed the raw places inside him.

After dismissing Jozsef, Drew forced aside all thoughts of the letter he didn't know what to do with and took his place beside Mirie for the walk to the conference room.

"Good morning, Drei," she said with a smile, the memory of last night still between them. "Did you sleep well?"

"Didn't try to," he admitted.

"So we'll bully our way through the day together. Good thing there'll be fresh coffee."

"And good news."

She came to a stop beside him, curious. "Really?"

"The priest from Alba Luncă was brought out of his coma last night. He's still in intensive care, but his condition has been upgraded to stable."

Her gaze widened. "You've been checking on him?"

"I knew you were concerned. And from what I

could find out, the rest of the injuries were minor. Cuts and bumps and bruises. Everyone in Alba Luncă seems to be on the mend."

Except for him, of course. He was still carrying the scars inside. Robbing him of sanity and sleep.

Mirie's expression melted into pleasure, her beautiful face suddenly lit up as she flashed a high-beam smile. Reaching up on tiptoes, she kissed his cheek. "Thank you, Drei. For caring, and for such wonderful news. I'm grateful and relieved."

Drew stood there with his cheek tingling and his heart pounding. Everything that had been missing last night was suddenly there in her expression. One heartfelt smile. A glimmer of the girl she'd once been.

But that smile also drove home how selfish he was. Sure, he'd wanted to make her feel better, but he also liked being her rock star. And suddenly all he could think of was how she would feel to discover who he really was.

He was *not* the person she should be looking to for companionship. No matter how much he wanted her to.

It took everything Drew had in him to say, "It was my pleasure, Your Royal Highness."

Some of the light went out of her smile, pleasure fading by slow degrees. He didn't give her a chance to reply, but motioned in the direction of the conference room. "Shall we?"

Her gaze searched his, all the light draining away, and then she nodded, understanding that the exchange was over even if she didn't understand why.

He'd offered what he could. He wished that was an identity on the attacker, but… That was that.

Mirie may have melted in his arms, but he had no right to encourage her. He had nothing to offer. She could never know how he felt. There was no possibility of anything between them. He was her protector. She was his responsibility. Nothing more. Even though they'd shared a night and a dance.

It had to be that simple.

TODAY WAS THE PERFECT day for a celebration. Mirie unbuttoned the collar of her coat and inhaled the crisp air. The simple act of breathing helped to clear away the fugue of a long morning. Moving helped, too, getting blood to flow.

They had a lot to celebrate. There were only a few days left until Ninsele's guests would arrive and the talks would begin. Thankfully, everything was going according to plan.

After the general had informed her the NRPG had exhausted their leads in discovering who had funded the attackers, Mirie decided to reach out to Carol Holderlin, the president of the European Commission, before presenting their protection plan to the high representatives' private security.

Neither Georghe nor the general had wanted Ninsele to look more unstable than it was, but Mirie couldn't live with herself if she didn't come clean with Carol. They'd been working closely to make these talks happen, and it wasn't as if security concerns were going to come as a shock to anyone.

The decision had turned out to be a good one.

Carol had offered to arrange helicopters from a Romanian air base to transport the representatives between the private airfield and the royal compound, which they deemed the safest way to travel. That had solved a big problem, which freed up the NRPG to focus resources on securing the airport. The representatives' private security had been reassured by Carol's involvement and agreed to proceed with the talks on schedule.

"It's a lovely day." Mirie held open the door to the portico of the west wing.

"A picnic, Your Royal Highness?" Helena stepped through, looking exhilarated as the wind blew her hair, as if she, too, welcomed some fresh air. "This is unexpected."

"And long overdue," Mirie agreed. "It's warm for February, and we've been cooped up for too long. I have it on very good authority that a picnic is the perfect way to interject some balance into our busy schedule."

She couldn't resist looking at Drei, who still stood inside, and found him watching her. He remembered every word of that conversation. Mirie could feel it as a connection between them, one that soothed her frayed nerves.

Not Drei, though, she thought. He stood distant and detached, his professional mask firmly in place. She reasoned that this was probably a good thing. She was too much a woman when she looked at him.

Not a friend. Not a princess. Just a woman who remembered the taste of his mouth on hers.

But reason didn't ease her disappointment when he didn't acknowledge her efforts to follow his advice in any way.

"Drei, give me a hand with those chairs," Georghe said, retrieving the hamper.

Something in Drei's expression flickered, as if he'd had to drag his gaze away, and that one tiny look annihilated her disappointment and sharpened her senses, so the bright winter sun seemed to glisten on the snow-covered grounds and the wind seemed to cut with a fine edge. She had to drag her own gaze away when Drei headed to Georghe with long-legged strides.

The moment was over, but she was still so aware of him, broad-shouldered in his woolen coat. His hair was neatly cut. The man must have had a thousand haircuts during the years, yet she'd never noticed until now how perfect his hairline was at his nape or the way a few sprigs sprang onto his forehead when freshly cut, as if only time and some growth would make them lie back down again.

She chided herself for having such a soft observation about such a hard man, but her fingers tingled at the memory of that silky hair beneath her touch.

"Where should we set up the table?" Helena asked.

Mirie scanned the grounds. "Anywhere there isn't ice. Over by the fountain, maybe."

A picnic in the snow.

Regardless of who suggested the idea, it was a good one. The incongruity felt like a tiny rebellion in her dutiful world. She had no idea what the kitchen would pack for an impromptu meal on short notice, but folding chairs had been provided, the kind people took on outings with carry straps.

Drei slung two chairs over each shoulder. He said nothing as he followed her, but Mirie was reminded of long summer days in Alba Luncă. Football games at the field behind the school and lazy afternoons spent at the lake in summer. The sun had shone in crystal skies, and the mountains cut off that idyllic realm from the real world. He'd carried her chair then, too.

But her relationship with Drei during that time had been another one entirely. She'd been young, which was the only real excuse she had for the love-hate relationship with her bodyguard. He'd been a constant reminder that she wasn't like everyone else, that she didn't fit in and never would.

He'd been an impediment when she wanted to be alone with her friends, or her boyfriend, a mute conscience whenever the chance arose to do something experimental or…*fun*. No sneaking a smoke or a sip from someone's flask without Drei's presence to remind her he'd only go back and tell Bunică.

That had been his job, of course, but she hadn't empathized at the time. The more she'd yearned to fit in with her friends, the more distant her true identity had become. That was when resentment of her shadow could flare up on a whim because when Drei hadn't been impeding her fun, she hadn't thought about him at all. In fact, he'd been a handy pack mule on those trips to the lake and a savior whenever someone accidentally locked his keys in his car or blew a tire on the rough mountain terrain.

Poor Drei. She bit back a smile while watching him set up the chairs. Perhaps she should apologize for her behavior.

"Not one word about picnics to anyone," Georghe said. "This has to be our secret."

"A secret?" Helena asked. "From whom?"

"My grandkids. They begged me to take them outside after church, but I told them to wait until spring. I pitched a tent in the family room instead, and they weren't happy with me." He spread his hands in entreaty. "If they hear I've been on a picnic, I'll be spending Saturday nights sleeping outside in sub-zero temperatures. You'll be looking for a new chancellor."

Georghe had moved into the palace only after his

wife, a lovely woman who had long battled cancer, had died. She'd been the love of his life, and the move had helped him grieve easier. Now the only time he got away from work was on Saturday nights when he stayed with his daughter and her family.

"Un bunic dulce." Mirie laughed, enjoying the idea of him as a sweet grandpapa. "Now this is something I didn't know about you. You're a slave driver here."

"He's the slave driver?" Helena emphasized the *he* and stared pointedly at Mirie.

"Not even Her Royal Highness and the state are as demanding as those young beasts." He heaved a dramatic sigh and hoisted the picnic hamper onto the ledge of the fountain. "I could say I had no choice in the matter. It was royal decree."

"Blame me, why don't you." Mirie feigned unhappiness. "You really think your grandkids will find royal decree a reasonable excuse? They're high-energy little boys. Just explain that you're old and you can't keep up. They'll have mercy on you. They're very kind children."

Georghe looked horrified. "Old?"

True, the man was barely sixty-five, but she nodded anyway. "You can either keep up or you can't, Georghe."

He scowled but didn't reply as he set up the table with Drei's help, who still hadn't said one word about her picnic. Mirie wondered what he was thinking, if he approved.

She told herself to let his silence go. She had no right to dictate the shape of their friendship. Especially when he'd already been both gracious and obliging.

Georghe set the hamper on the table.

"What I want to know is if I need to start worrying about you," he said. "Are you so tired of work that you need a break? Is that why we're outside eating our meal?"

Mirie chuckled. "No worries. I just wanted to enjoy the peace of our grounds. The view has been distracting me for weeks, and I know how much work is waiting for us."

"A picnic is a wonderful idea," Helena said enthusiastically.

"I'm glad you like it," Mirie said. "But to give credit where credit is due, the idea wasn't mine but Drei's."

Mirie knew the instant the words were out of her mouth that she was only trying to involve Drei.

Mirie's declaration brought immediate responses from Georghe and Helena, who both looked surprised.

"That's even more unexpected than this picnic," Georghe said. "Feeling cooped up, Drei?"

"Thought the cold air might wake you up," Drei shot back. "You do know you suggested housing the president separately on the third floor of the east wing three times."

Georghe grumbled, Helena laughed and Mirie found herself smiling as she unpacked the hamper, glad he was finally getting into the spirit of things. She withdrew plates and bowls and flatware. "I worried that the kitchen wouldn't be able to come up with something on such short notice, but they prepared a feast."

Wine and cheeses. A chicken and shrimp platter. Crusty, fresh bread and tea cookies.

"What is that?" Georghe eyed the wine narrowly. "Did you tell them the general's coming, and we have a long afternoon? We should get another thermos of coffee. *Hot* coffee."

"We've been drinking coffee all day," Mirie pointed out.

"That's so we get some work done."

"This weather is glorious." Helena's nose was already pink and her cheeks flushed from the wind. "Exactly what we need to get us thinking clearly for the afternoon session."

"This weather is frigid." Georghe reached for the wine bottle. "If we drink this, we'll all need a nap."

"I think it was sweet of the kitchen to send it," Mirie said. "I told them we were celebrating."

"What?" Georghe asked.

Mirie unpacked the corkscrew. "We're celebrating

the talks, of course, old man. All the work we've been doing. The fact that everything is still on schedule."

Georghe only scowled. "I'm serious. We can't afford to lose the afternoon."

"Trust the kitchen staff." Drei plucked the corkscrew from Mirie's hand. "They sent a Viognier. It's pretty light-bodied for a white. Not something that'll put everyone to sleep if they don't drink the whole bottle. Who's planning to hog the bottle?"

"One glass is my limit," Helena assured him.

"Is wine a hobby of yours, Drei, or do you just like to drink?" Mirie asked with a grin, remembering his excuse for late-night kitchen raids.

That got a laugh from Georghe, but Drei only positioned the corkscrew to open the bottle. "Just stating the facts, ma'am."

She watched as he withdrew the cork and passed the bottle beneath his nose, an absent gesture that revealed so much more than he had. Drei liked wine. Another simple thing about this man she hadn't known after all their years together.

"Okay, Georghe. May we negotiate a compromise if we agree to drink only one glass? Is that agreeable to everyone?"

"Agreed." Good humor creased Georghe's features, his mood successfully turned around despite the cold.

"Fine by me," Helena said.

"And me." Mirie placed a set of flatware beside each plate. "What about you, Drei?"

She wanted to include him in the fun, but he set the bottle on the table and said, "I'm on duty, and unlike your work, mine doesn't allow me even one glass."

He plucked the chicken breast from his plate, grabbed a napkin and left Mirie frowning after him as he crossed the lawn to stand at his usual post beside the door.

Always an outsider looking in.

CHAPTER NINE

SLEEP WASN'T IN the cards. Not anymore. Maybe never again. Who knew? Drew sure as hell didn't. The only thing he knew was that whenever he closed his eyes, he saw Mirie. Ethereal, as she had stood on her balcony with her hair and filmy lingerie twisting on the wind. Floating through the ballroom, as she had on the arms of a puppy-faced prince.

Happy, as she'd appeared during her impromptu picnic in the snow. Until he'd left her standing there, anyway.

Breathless, as she'd looked naked in his arms.

That image was imprinted on the backs of his eyelids, the memory on his brain. He was a lost cause.

He stared up at the ceiling of the security station—the only place in the compound with systems capable of allowing him to run untraceable searches.

For all the good it had done. He was missing something important, something he didn't have the resources to find.

The night-duty guards didn't pay any attention to Drew as they monitored the live feed. The general had been in and out all night long. Another person with better things to do than sleep. They should start a club. He would probably find Mirie back on the balcony.

He resisted the urge to roll his chair over to the monitors and check. She was a distraction he couldn't afford. He was still obsessing over the way she'd looked when he'd left her picnic.

Had it been only hours ago?

But he couldn't encourage her interest in him, and he possessed zero ability to focus around her.

His job took precedence over making her smile.

Drew wasn't buying into the whole vanished-without-a-trace theory. They had corpses and egress over borders, which meant they had one glaring variable in their security efforts for the representatives, who'd be arriving in a matter of days.

The NRPG could prepare all it wanted, but it would never cover every eventuality. It couldn't prepare against an unknown enemy, which meant there would be weaknesses. Drew's money was on the airport. No matter how they transported everyone once they got them on the ground, they had to keep them alive until all the flights arrived.

There would be media coverage complicating their job, but there was no way around the press. Much of Mirie's success in reclaiming her throne and ending the civil war had been a direct result of skillfully using the media to cast a spotlight on what was happening in Ninsele under the dictator's rule.

She was a modern young woman with an understanding of what motivated people and how to subtly lead them to the point. Her media efforts had shone a light on the conditions in Ninsele until NATO had become involved. The ensuing transparency had undermined the dictator, and then Mirie and her supporters had been able to oust him.

But using the media was double-edged. When she'd provided headlines that sold newspapers, she'd been their darling.

Mirie of Alba Luncă.

But as the larger-than-life headlines had yielded to real news about purging corruption and baby steps toward becoming a candidate country with the European Commission's support, many media outlets manufactured controversy to peddle their papers.

Now even the few outlets that had remained newsworthy were buckling under the fact that too many people wanted theatrics. Paparazzi were still trying to get close to the compound even with the posted unit. Every other day some headline ran speculation on some imagined drama.

Prince Ulrick Visits Royal Palace.

Photos of the prince's car were printed along with speculation about whether or not the princess had taken a lover.

Drew would make sure that overstuffed prince found himself on his head in the street if he came sniffing around Mirie. The only thing that had saved him on the night of the ball was that Mirie clearly wasn't interested.

She'd been interested in *him*.

Slumping in the chair, Drew rubbed his temples. Working for a covert national security agency also had double edges.

He should have been able to contact Command and peel away the layers around Luca Vadim, who'd done exactly what he'd said and filed for citizenship based on his mother's birth.

But Drew couldn't do a thing except work with what Ninsele had to offer, so Vadim was just ticking along with his plans, working the media's interest. The Ministry of Justice could withhold its response to his request for citizenship for up to thirty days, but beyond that would appear to be a stall tactic and provide more bad press than Mirie could afford right now.

Just yesterday, Vadim had plunked down five hundred thousand lei on an old building in downtown Briere with the intention of turning it into a law office. Pumping big money into the economy was another way to get on the fast track for citizenship.

The man didn't seem deterred that he was still facing some very public DNA testing.

And that bothered Drew.

With his agency's help, he might have been able to find out who was funding Vadim. But he hadn't even been able to track whoever had hired the copter and the assassins. Instead, he had to accept that he'd run into a dead end. And Mirie's life was at risk because he lacked the means to get answers.

The general showed up and said, "Walk with me."

Drew shut down the system. They left the security station, which was housed in the public sector of the palace, the hub as the general called it.

"Anything?" the general finally asked. He didn't sound too hopeful.

"Vadim is either exactly who he says or whoever created his cover has far better resources than we do."

The general sighed. "I've never been one to believe in coincidence."

"Me, either."

They walked along in silence until the end of the hall, where the general swiped his key card through the scanner to access the administrative wing. Drew knew what he was doing—keeping them passing through the radar, and under it. Nothing out of the ordinary, but they were in the muted zone. No one would overhear their conversation.

Not without the general knowing, anyway.

"How's she holding up?" he asked.

"She's dealt with threats before."

"True, true. But she's lost someone she cared a great deal about and faced an attempt on her life.... She's anxious about the talks, and I haven't provided her much reassurance."

Drew didn't want to get sucked into a psychoanalytical discussion about Mirie's mental health, so he said, "She seems to be finding constructive ways to channel her stress."

The general smiled beneath the bushy mustache, reminding Drew of Yosemite Sam minus the hat. "So I heard. I was sorry I couldn't make it for lunch."

"Good times."

Regardless of how Mirie had felt about him leaving, being outside had been good for her. Maybe she'd sleep tonight. Now he was sorry he hadn't checked on her before he'd left.

"We've got to cover Forensic Medicine," Drew said.

"You're worried about Vadim's declaration of paternity."

Drew nodded. They all knew Mirie's feelings on the subject. She believed the man who had been a loving husband and father would never have acted without integrity. Drew thought he understood why she believed that. But Drew also knew Mirie had an eight-year-old's memories of her father. She'd never known the sort of man he'd been. An indiscretion might have been nothing more than a temporary lapse in judgment for a hundred different reasons.

"It's our job to make sure we get to the truth," he said.

"The task force is in place at Forensic Medicine," the general said. "Three of our most trusted men, all with a history with the royal family. They'll over-see all the testing and deter any attempts at bribery."

"That's a start."

But a start didn't resolve the problem of limited resources. Or an exquisite young woman who was slowly suffocating from their attempts to protect her.

"Come, Drei," the general chided. "I see your worry. We've stopped them before. We'll stop them again. Have faith."

Drew was out of faith tonight. The general was looking to *him* for reassurance, so they could con-gratulate each other on doing all they could when they weren't doing nearly enough.

MIRIE TOLD HERSELF she suffered from nerves. The countdown to the representatives' arrival was on; they were down to the final two days, and there weren't enough hours to oversee details. Every morn-ing she awoke to a list of things to accomplish, and every night she retired with just as many items on her list. For every one task she completed, she added two more.

Was it any wonder she lay awake, staring at the ceiling? Was it any surprise she was dreading the day ahead because she knew how exhausting it would be?

When she wasn't worrying about the representa-tives or their safety, she was obsessing about Drei. Nerves didn't explain why she'd never before noticed that he had his hair cut every three weeks. Or that he liked wine and sweets.

The entire kitchen staff knew Drei raided the refrigerator in the wee hours. Helena passed off her desserts after meals in the conference room. How had Mirie never noticed that Drei ate a few cookies during afternoon coffee breaks, and then wrapped a few in a napkin to stuff in his pocket for later?

Nerves didn't explain why she yearned to go to him now and feel his arms around her, taste his mouth on hers.

Mirie rolled over with a desperate sigh. Even as a child, anxiety could get the better of her, so her mother had affixed glow-in-the-dark stars on the ceiling above her bed.

If you should awaken with worrying thoughts, Mama had said, *you should count the stars and imagine the angels hiding behind them until your mind quiets and you fall back to sleep.*

Perhaps she should ask Helena to order some of those stars…because the only things to count right now were all the new things she'd discovered about Drei.

Thrusting off her blankets, Mirie finally got up. She would employ this time rather than yearning for a relationship that wasn't fair to Drei or possible for her.

Pulling on her robe, she stepped into her slippers

and left the bedroom, not bothering to flip on lights as she went.

A large part of her wanted to simply curl up on the sofa with a cup of calming tea and escape into a movie.

But avoidance was a luxury she couldn't afford tonight. Action-adventure films would only wind up her nerves more. A cute romantic comedy would only fuel her thoughts of Drei and happily ever afters. She didn't watch dramas, didn't find the bittersweet tug of emotions entertaining.

She would brew tea and work in her office until the desire for sleep came. *If* it came. If not, she would shower and get on with her day.

Feeling better having made a plan, she headed toward the kitchen to make her tea and caught sight of the night guard through the glass panel by her suite door. For some reason the sight brought her to a stop, and for an unexpected moment, she stood there, staring at the shadow of the wrong man.

Drei varied his schedule. He didn't care to establish a predictable routine of all nights or days, and he couldn't watch her around the clock. As a child she'd believed he possessed the qualities of a ghost, but not anymore….

Carrying her mug of steaming tea to the door, she greeted Jozsef, the guard whom Drei favored and had personally trained for this task. A man whom Drei trusted, which should bring Mirie peace. But she felt only irritation as Jozsef left his post to follow her at a discreet distance.

She was so lost in her mood that she didn't notice her route to the administrative wing. It was the quickest route to the security doors, although she generally didn't come this way unless engaged with Georghe and Helena. But now in the quiet of late night, the hallway lit only with sconces high on the walls, she suddenly awoke to her surroundings.

Tat-tat-tat-tat-tat.

The sound echoed in her head as she passed the doorway to the private living room where her family had gathered often to share life, and so ironically gathered together to meet death.

Would there ever again be Christmases with twinkling lights and gifts in sparkling paper in this home where she'd been born? Or birthday celebrations with sweet cakes and hugs and laughter?

Silence was her only answer.

The way she felt inside. Quiet. Dead, even though she was the only one who still walked these halls, haunted by memories she no longer allowed herself to recall.

Except in moments of her greatest weakness.

The last time this palace had felt like a home was on January 17, 1996. Now she just fixed her eyes on the goal, put her head down and worked, worked, worked.

Until a freezing afternoon in a cave, when she

learned there was still a heart beating inside her, yearning.

Hurrying past the doorway to so many memories, Mirie found her irritation mounting with each step. She didn't want to go to her office. Only her head wanted to work now.

She wanted to go find Drei.

But with a guard on her heels and video surveillance equipment overhead, she lacked the freedom to do that. He was forbidden to her on so many levels. He'd never pursued her. She'd imposed herself on him. On the surface he was all wrong—a commoner, older than her by a decade, a staff member.

She wasn't a woman who could simply involve herself with a man because of attraction or shared interests. She had boundaries and considerations that impacted the state. Her choices were subject to critique by her people. A casual romance with one of her staff would spawn a headline like:

Princess Hires a Lover.

Or *The Princess and the Protector.*

So why did Drei *feel* so right?

Mirie waited impatiently as Jozsef circled around her to swipe his security card and gain access to the administrative wing. She felt stifled by restrictions, edgy from sleeplessness and decidedly ungrateful for all the many blessings in her life.

The most important of which was life itself.

Flipping on the lights, she wished she could banish

her thoughts as easily as the shadows and settled herself at her desk. The tea was cooling now.

No sooner had she taken the first sip with the hopes of clearing her thoughts than Helena showed up.

"Your Royal Highness." She swept past Jozsef, who stood at his post outside the office door, pulled the door shut behind her and approached the desk, positively scowling. "You should be asleep."

"I could say the same for you."

Helena held up her hands in surrender, conceding the point. There was nothing sleepy about her, even though she was dressed in sweatpants and a bathrobe with her hair piled high on her head.

"I don't guess anyone's sleeping," she said. "There's still so much to do, and we're down to forty-eight hours."

"Who else is awake?"

Helena inclined her head toward the common office that occupied the space beside Mirie's, where the equipment was kept for the convenience of all the staff. "You didn't know Drei is working in there?"

"No idea." Mirie's heart started a slow throbbing at the mention of *his* name.

Foolish, foolish woman.

She eyed Helena, though. "Why did you think I knew?"

Helena only shrugged, looking mildly abashed as if she'd been caught speaking out of turn.

Something was clearly troubling her, so Mirie asked, "What's on your mind, Helena?" Then she waited; the only encouragement she had to offer was patience. She really wasn't up to more concerns at the moment.

Helena half sat on the edge of the desk and folded her arms over her chest, thoughtful. "I'm worried about Drei."

Mirie's heart stepped up its beat, fluttering almost painfully. Her anxiety, a problem all night, spiked. "Why?"

Their gazes met. "Drei isn't sleeping, either. He hasn't since your return from the funeral."

"Like the rest of us, he's preparing for our guests. You can't be sleeping all that well, either, if you're up noticing who else isn't sleeping," Mirie pointed out with a casualness she didn't feel.

Helena hesitated, but only an instant. "I'm worried about how worried Drei is about you."

"He's paid to worry about me."

Helena shook her head. "He's a man who spends most of his time with his eyes upon a very beautiful woman."

Mirie hadn't expected such candor and forced a neutral expression. Sinking back in her chair, she stared up at Helena, who was watching her closely. Mirie knew this woman, valued her opinion, had always relied on her to speak plainly if she had concerns, even personal ones.

"I'm not sure I understand," Mirie said.

But that wasn't entirely true. Everything inside her wanted to believe she did understand, that Helena was seeing something in Drei that Mirie had missed.

"I can only imagine that sharing such a frightening situation together changes everything, because something's different about you, too. But I wasn't sure you recognized how deeply he feels his responsibility for you. He hasn't found the men responsible for trying to harm you yet, and I think that's put him in a very vulnerable place right now."

So many things struck Mirie in that moment. How could Helena see so much about Drei, who wore his professionalism like a shroud? Or was she simply ascribing Mirie's emotions to him? The truth was that she'd been the one making the demands, trying to figure out where they stood in their changed relationship.

Changed because of *her* needs.

What did Drei feel for her? Mirie couldn't say. He'd been careful to keep distance between them since the picnic. Why? Because she was making him uncomfortable by asking him to dance, because she'd wanted to know more about his likes and dislikes, because she'd tried to include him in a picnic? That Helena worried that Mirie was carelessly overlooking his feelings meant her actions were plainly obvious.

Suddenly this conversation felt too personal, as if Helena had seen something that was Mirie's alone, something she didn't want to share, but that righteousness was only a defense, because Helena was right.

Mirie's reactions to Drei had been all over the place since their return. Was it any wonder that the people she spent so much time with would notice?

Was that why Drei kept his distance?

"I appreciate your sharing your concerns, Helena." Mirie didn't know what else to say. What she felt was hers alone. So personal, and so powerful, that she couldn't share it as she might have discussed her confusion about a state business matter. "I'll give some thought to what you've said."

"Good night, Your Royal Highness." Helena pushed herself away from the desk. "I'm going to try to get a few hours of sleep, so I'm of some use to you tomorrow."

Under normal circumstances, she would have reassured Helena that her work was always valued, but Mirie wasn't sure how she felt right now, so she just said, "Good luck."

Helena just smiled and slipped from the room. Mirie stared after her, trying to make sense of her reeling emotions, trying not to read her own desires into what Drei might think or feel. She'd only *seen* his kindnesses.

And the distance he'd been putting between them. No small feat for a man always on her heels.

But she needed to sort through her own feelings.

She'd resolved not to impose on Drei, but her moods changed every time they were together, so she'd been impulsive instead. So unlike herself. But Helena was right about one thing—Mirie didn't want to be insensitive, not to Drei, who'd only been caring and kind.

Because he felt his responsibility so deeply?

Or was there more to the way he felt?

Had he been unable to forget making love to her the way she'd been unable to forget him?

That idea throbbed to life, a forbidden hope that gained speed all too quickly, fueling her imagination. If she assigned even the smallest part of the turmoil she'd been feeling to Drei… Was it possible he was thinking about her?

Would it matter if he had?

It would, but only to that place deep inside her that was all woman. A place that wanted to be wanted by this handsome, courageous man who'd never expressed any interest in her before making love to her so exquisitely.

Mirie told herself she was an adult, responsible for her choices, her actions and their consequences. Indeed, these past few weeks had been an exercise in dealing with the aftermath of *one* choice and the impact on everyone around her. Mirie suddenly wanted to go to the office, wanted to see Drei.

She shouldn't go. She shouldn't fan this tiny flame of hope inside her, or selfishly involve Drei in her fantasies, but she couldn't stop herself from getting up out of the chair. She knew she shouldn't, but she did anyway.

He was so close, and she just needed to see him right now. Just one look to help soothe the churning feelings inside.

The knob turned silently beneath her hand, and the door opened with but a whisper. Still, he had turned to face her before she'd even stepped inside.

And she ached at the sight of him.

He stood in front of the fax machine, dressed casually in faded jeans that rode low on his hips and a shirt unbuttoned at the collar that left his throat bare. She could see the shadow of hair on his chest, remembered the feel of it beneath her cheek.

But it was the expression on his handsome face that made her breath catch. The slightest softening of his hard features as he watched her, the way his eyes lingered on her as gently as a caress, as if in the drowsy hours of late night, he couldn't shield everything behind the mask, maybe didn't want to.

He faced her without saying a word, but he didn't look surprised to see her. He waited, the chill quiet of the night reminding them both that they were alone.

Mirie wasn't sure what she'd needed beyond seeing him, but she'd been right about one thing. Just being near him soothed the chaotic places inside her, calmed all her uncertainty.

She refused to spoil the moment with conversation when there was no need for words, only feelings.

She refused to distract herself from the sudden clarity she felt inside. She came to life beneath his gaze. It was that simple. There was no more denying the way she felt, no more confusion.

Mirie wanted him to want her.

It didn't matter that fanning the flames of her desire was foolish in the extreme. It didn't matter that any normal relationship was forbidden them. She wanted him to feel what she felt more than anything, wished with all her heart that he might care for more than her safety.

She let her gaze linger on him a moment longer before slipping out the way she'd come.

CHAPTER TEN

"How ARE YOU looking on the inside, Major?" the general asked over the audio transmitter.

Things were looking good, but that was only because Drew stared at Mirie, dressed crisply and professionally in her business suit. She was media-ready for the press conference with her hair swept back in a sleek twist that left her fresh-faced and glowing with a calm excitement that was hers alone. Six years worth of her time and effort finally came together as she sat in conversation with the president of the European Commission and several of the representatives.

Scanning the perimeter of the VIP lounge for the hundredth time since the last arrival, Drew said, "All clear, General."

And it was all clear. For the moment. Drew couldn't help but feel as if this was the calm before the storm although everything seemed in order, and the feeling had him on edge.

"Excellent," came the reply. There was a so far, so good in there. "The last flight will be on the ground in ten minutes."

Once the high representative for foreign affairs

and security policy and the remaining two representatives arrived, they would begin the press conference and the next phase of security. For Drew, anyway. The NRPG was already well under way with clearing the select group of reporters chosen to cover this historic event. He had been on the committee that had handpicked each one given security clearance.

"Want me to inform Her Royal Highness?" Drew asked.

"I already alerted Georghe," the general said. "He's keeping everyone entertained, I'm sure."

"You know it."

But while Georghe ran around attending to everyone's needs, Mirie played hostess. The royalty she wore like a comfortable bathrobe was so evident in her sparkling laughter, the way she rallied the representatives, drawing each into the conversation with an effortless awareness of how to include people that was so natural to her.

She was a mediator, a negotiator and a skilled politician. Drew also knew she genuinely liked the European Commission's president, Carol Holderlin, a woman from the United Kingdom whose five-year term would carry Ninsele through a fair portion of this foundational process to become an acceding country.

Mirie hoped these talks would raise pride in her countrymen and bring hope of a promising future.

As always, some people would agree this move was promising and others wouldn't. But Mirie, as always, would attempt to bridge the distance between them. After all her work, she deserved to see some discernible measure of success.

Drew sure as hell would do everything in his power to help her accomplish her goal. But his Spidey senses were tingling big-time, as his brother, Jay, had once been fond of saying.

Drew could practically see his younger brother's grin, a slow smile that hid a sharp wit and a people-savvy nature that made him a favorite everywhere he went.

The thought almost made Drew smile. Jay was the genial brother, the social brother, the brother who had never left home, while Drew was the one who had run screaming after high school graduation without a backward glance.

And in that instant, the longing he felt for what was left of his family came down on him like an avalanche. The sudden emptiness stunned him, made him think about what Mirie had felt in the cave, a sense of disconnection so powerful the distance might never be bridged.

God, what was wrong with him?

He shouldn't be fighting this hard for focus. Not during this most crucial outing. Mirie setting foot outside the compound again.

He scanned the perimeter of the VIP lounge again.

Three exits. Windows that sat two stories above the ground. Egress by two stairways and one elevator. The NRPG surrounding the private airfield. The personal security details of the representatives on both ends of the exits. Security was tight. The choppers were in place to transport the representatives back to the compound.

There was no room for distraction, and no reason for Drew's gut to be going wild. He hoped it was only the buildup of all the anticipation, all the work and the sleepless nights pulling the security plan together. But deep down, he suspected that he was too emotionally invested in the outcome. Not because of Ninsele, but because of Mirie's investment in the future and the life she had given up in the process.

"The dogs have arrived," the general said.

"What happened with them?" Drew asked. "They were supposed to be here before we arrived."

"A problem with the truck on the transnational. The mountains played games with the cell service so it took time for another truck to arrive."

Back to the trouble with sharing resources. The dogs had come from Romania. A generous country. Probably because it understood the grief Ninsele endured now since its history didn't look too different.

"The handlers checked out?" he asked.

"Every one," the general replied.

"How's this going to impact our time frame?"

"Hopefully not much. I've got the handlers moving already. I'm shooting for covering all areas before the flight lands. Probably won't make it, but we shouldn't be off by long."

Drew should feel better, shouldn't he? Maybe the dogs were what bugged him. The NRPG had its security plan in place. Any deviation from the carefully planned details was cause for concern. The dogs were one more layer of protection around the representatives, and around Mirie.

As if on cue, Georghe sidled up to her and whispered in her ear. She inclined her head slightly in acknowledgment. He was probably giving her the news about the late flight or the dogs, Drew guessed. Whatever the interaction, Mirie glanced at Drew.

Their gazes collided across the distance, such a small glance that managed to suck all the air from the room, managed to command his attention completely. Her eyes looked steely from this distance, some indeterminate color that was neither blue nor gray, yet somehow both. He saw the emotion in her face, so carefully concealed, yet entirely obvious.

To him, anyway.

She sought reassurance that all was well, as if she, too, felt edgy. And in that moment, he also knew he wasn't the only one fighting to rein in his emotions. It would go a long way if Mirie would stop looking at him as if she had suddenly noticed he was there after all these years. As if he was someone other than the man who had been guarding her for a good part of her life, and she wasn't sure what to make of him now.

She didn't want him. She didn't *know* him. She wanted only what he offered. Protection. Once that had been physical protection, and security. Now he had extended his reach into the realm of emotional protection, as well. Calming her when she was frightened. Comforting her when she needed reassurance.

Making love to her when she wanted.

Jesus. Drew was a mess. Dragging his gaze away, he scanned the perimeter of the room again, marked the exits, the movements of the NRPG guards, the representatives. He wasn't sure how he was going to rein in his reactions, but he knew he had better find some way to get a grip on himself. Today was not the day for even deliberating the problem.

"Plane's starting its descent."

Drew exhaled. He was more than ready to get everyone safely back to the compound. For more reasons than one. "Affirmative."

Taking stock of the representatives he would soon escort under guard into the room that had been converted into a secure press area, he was just glad the delegation was not any larger than it was. Of the twenty-seven members of the Holderlin Commission, only the president and high representatives of various relevant departments would hammer out the preliminary plan. International Cooperation. Humanitarian Aid and Crisis Response. Justice. Fundamental

Rights and Citizenship. Regional Policy. Financial Programming and Budget.

Including Mirie, the total number of their group was a manageable ten. They were trying to keep things secure but relaxed, to not give the impression to the representatives, or the public via the media, that this historic gathering was a militarized event, which was precisely what it was.

"Flight's arrived," the general said. "We'll proceed as planned. By the time we get the representatives cleared and to the VIP lounge, they should have just enough time to freshen up and greet Her Royal Highness before we're through with the dogs and move everyone for the press conference."

"Affirmative."

Three moves. Off the flights and into the VIP lounge. From the VIP lounge to the press area. From the press area on to the choppers. Each step of the way secured. Each step of the way with a plan for egress. Neat and clean.

Georghe went over to Mirie, and she announced, "The flight has landed. The rest of our group will be joining us shortly."

There was more conversation, and Drew walked the perimeter, touching base with each pair of guards posted at the exits.

"How are your complements?" He referred to the teams posted on the opposite sides of the exits.

Three teams. Three affirmatives.

So far, so good.

The general put the move into play, and Drew glanced at Mirie before making his way to the staff entrance of the lounge, the route where the remaining representatives would be brought through. The most easily secured route between the tarmac and the lounge comprised only guarded hallways and one stairwell. The service elevator had been shut down.

She chatted animatedly with the president, her smile engaging, her silk suit clinging to her long curves in a way he shouldn't notice. She didn't glance his way this time, and he was pleased to see that her spirits were high, was relieved they were about to get this show on the road.

The remaining representatives arrived. The exit was barred again. There were greetings and welcomes. Georghe buzzed around offering hospitality. Drew made contact again with the teams, ensured the exits were secured, especially the stairwell that would be used to move the representatives to the press area. Now it was only a matter of waiting until the general cleared the area with the dogs before they would move into the next phase.

"Impose electronic silence. Over," General Bogdanovich growled over the transmitter.

Electronic silence.

Standard procedure in the face of a heightened threat.

The dogs had found a suspicious package.

They weren't going to catch a break, were they?

Drew schooled his expression and moved in Mirie's direction, positioning himself between her and the nearest exit, trying not to draw her notice. This was the last thing she needed to worry about right now.

Georghe didn't miss a beat.

He appeared quickly and eyed Drew questioningly. They'd worked together so long, a part of the intimate group around Mirie, one glance was all it took to convey that something was up. Drew hoped the general could identify the problem and contain the threat quickly because no one would be getting a sit-rep until he did. They'd be waiting in the dark.

Drew shouldn't be surprised by how fast a situation could go to hell, but he always was. One second everything checked out, ticked along just fine, then the next, *wham!* Straight to hell that fast.

Thanks to dogs trained to detect bomb vapors.

Every cell in Drew's body shifted into high alert. He wanted to know what the dogs had found. This airport had been locked down, all flights canceled for the past seventy-two hours, a ghost town but for the NRPG that scoured and secured every square foot of the facility and the Ninselan militaries surrounding the perimeter of grounds.

How was it even possible to get *anything* in here?

Mirie was greeting her guests with no clue there was any problem downstairs. And with everything Drew had in him, he willed that problem to resolve quickly, so she wouldn't have to be briefed about the problem until after the talks concluded and the representatives were in airspace well over Ninsele on the way to their respective homes.

He hoped a bomb didn't detonate and blow the damned roof off the facility along with everyone in it.

Then the minute *tap-tap-tap* of the knock code at the stairwell door sounded. Drew knew he wasn't going to get his wish. Mirie heard it, too, and glanced up in time to catch Drew making his way to the opening door. He took one look at Jozsef's face and the look on the younger man's face stopped him cold, sent a blind chill of premonition through him.

"Major." Jozsef motioned Drew away from the guards.

"What's happening?" he asked in a low whisper, bracing himself for the news.

But there was no possible way Drew could have ever prepared for the pistol Jozsef thrust into Drew's side. For one stunned second, Drew thought this man he'd personally trained for close-protection detail was a thug who had betrayed the NRPG.

But that was only until Jozsef said, "Stuntman miraculously awoke from a coma."

Then Drew could only stare. The man wasn't a thug at all, and the only thing miraculous was hearing that name again after fifteen long years.

Stuntman.

His code name for Excelsior.

MIRIE KNEW SOMETHING was wrong when she heard the knocking. The NRPG communicated via transmitter and radio. Their posts had been secured. No one should be entering the VIP lounge.

"What do you think, Your Royal Highness?" Carol asked.

Mirie turned to Carol, a woman in her early fifties, who had risen to prominence as president of the commission through her longtime work in domestic protection, a woman whose petite build and bright yellow suit hid a passion for her work that won over people.

"Forgive me. I was distracted from your question." Mirie forced herself to converse normally, did not want to raise suspicions, although her own concerns were making her vibrate.

She didn't see Drei. He must have slipped out the door to deal with whatever situation had brought Jozsef to the VIP lounge. She had no clue where Drei had gone, but knew he would never have left her under any circumstances.

He hadn't left Jozsef behind, or assigned any of her other personal detail from what she could tell, which was alarmingly unusual. He never entrusted her protection to anyone but those he'd trained himself, but she saw no additional security, no one but the guard teams posted at their doors.

Carol smiled kindly. She understood better than anyone the mountain of logistics that had paved the way for this gathering. "I asked if you were aware of the recent findings on education. I thought they might be of interest since we'll be including educational progress as one of our objectives in Ninsele's plan. We just published the report this week."

"Thanks." Mirie willed her racing thoughts to focus. What had Helena said about this report? Helena who monitored relevant developments and briefed Mirie. Bless her.

"I was aware," Mirie said, and the memory was there when she needed it. "The findings are interesting. I read through the report and thought the correlation between higher education of the teachers and the quality of learning was timely. We want to maximize our youth's potential, and if we need to look at the certification criteria of the teachers, there couldn't be a better time. We're getting ready to set our goals."

"That's just what I thought." Carol was clearly pleased. "Our commissioner of Education, Culture, Multilingualism and Youth isn't scheduled for this talk. But she'll visit soon. I think you'll like her. She's goal-focused and works really hard finding the resources to prepare people to enter the job market. She has done a tremendous amount of work on the Moving Skills Forward project."

The International Cooperation commissioner commented on a recent conference where they'd reviewed education, not with the idea of standardization, but with what he believed was a better approach to accurately assessing the needs of the educational systems of individual countries.

"The EU is, after all, a cooperative of many different cultures," he said. "Some vastly different in fundamental design, yet all with unique needs and diverse resources."

Mirie nodded, distracted again by more knocking. This time Georghe headed to the door and was there to greet the general, who strode through, imposing in his dress military uniform and grim as he addressed the team at the door with a few curt words.

Then he exchanged a somber glance with Georghe, and her heartbeat throbbed as the general caught her gaze and both men moved toward her.

Had something happened to Drei?

"It's time for the press conference," the general said simply, glancing around again with a frown.

She exchanged a glance with Georghe, who looked worried and confused. No, she wasn't overreacting. Something was wrong.

General Bogdanovich looked grim and unreadable beneath the bushy brows and mustache. "Come, Your Royal Highness." He wrapped his fingers around her arm and guided her toward the door.

The general was frightening her. Or maybe it was Drei's absence that had her unsettled. As long as he was with her, she was safe. He would never allow anything to happen, was always watching anyone who got close, always kept her informed.

Where was he now?

She wanted to ask Georghe, but was forced to re-assure Carol and several of the representatives, who seemed to sense that something was going on. Mirie smiled dutifully, allowing the general to escort her through the door and down the stairs, but when she heard the NRPG directing the representatives behind her, advising them to move quickly and quietly, Mirie knew they weren't heading to the press conference.

They were being evacuated.

REACTIVATED? NOW? AFTER fifteen years? If Drew had one second to wrap his brain around what was happening, he would reevaluate his priorities. Re-activated? As in Excelsior needed him to carry out a mission?

Or they thought his time in Ninsele was up?

As it was he could only bounce back and forth between the reality that duty called in the form of Jozsef—code name: Pagan—who needed Drew's help to stop an international incident. Drew's im-pulse was to evacuate Mirie, but Pagan resisted that plan with a loaded weapon.

Drew's impulse was to cause an incident in the VIP lounge by showing Pagan what he thought of a pistol shoved in his ribs.

But Pagan's next words stopped Drew cold. "The dogs located an RDD at a security checkpoint. The general wants the princess and the representatives out of here, but the minute he starts evacuations, he'll alert whoever planted the device. We've got to find the perp before he knows we're on to him."

A couple of things hit Drew at once.

First and foremost was that the general needed to rethink his plan. They couldn't risk an electronic transmission without the possibility of detonating the bomb, and he didn't need a primer about the effects of a radiological dispersion device or the political fallout of blowing up the Ninselan princess along with nine visiting dignitaries from various countries.

But knowing this didn't solve Drew's problem because he wanted Mirie out of this facility *now*. The greatest danger of an RDD didn't come from the radioactive material that contaminated everything within reach, but from the blast site.

But Mirie wasn't going anywhere without an explanation or the representatives, so unless he hoisted her over his shoulder, and carried her out the door…

Jesus Christ. He hadn't heard his code name in fifteen years, and within fifteen seconds, he was effectively between a rock and a hard place. Pagan would get another fifteen seconds before Drew pulled *his* pistol.

"Let's go." He opened the door and didn't look back.

But with every step he took away from Mirie, the

need to protect her was a physical, violent force that opposed every step. He hadn't assigned anyone to her detail, and she'd be wondering what had happened to him.

Pagan was on Drew's heels, briefing him as they descended the stairs. "The device was placed in a food service area close to where the media are being held for the press conference."

Damned terrorists. Fame whores, every last one of them.

"I can't figure out why the perp hasn't detonated already," Pagan said. "The dogs went nuts. The general got the handlers out of the terminal, but the media are right there, if the perp wants an audience."

"Then the perp didn't come in with the media."

Pagan's expression narrowed. "No one else here, man."

"Wrong. There are a lot of people around here," Drew said when they came to the armed guards at the exit.

"Has anyone unauthorized left?" Drew asked.

"No."

They passed into the terminal and found the media still cordoned off, a tight group of professionals with video equipment and microphones.

"Did the media get the memo about electronic transmissions?" Drew asked, worried a reporter would make a call and accidentally detonate the bomb.

Pagan nodded, then glanced at another team of guards posted at the cordoned area. "Do you recognize them?"

Drew scanned the faces. He recognized every one. Invitation only, so unless one of them was an undercover terrorist with a death wish… "They've all been cleared and their equipment wanded and X-rayed. We're looking for someone in NRPG regs."

"Son of a bitch," Pagan spat out. "You know the posts—"

But Drew was already on the move, mentally eliminating positions as he headed across the small terminal.

VIP lounge—clear. Concourse—clear. The only places left were the tarmac, mechanical hangar and administrative offices, which were all areas not visible from the concourse. There was already a device in food service. He hoped it was the only one.

Dirty bombs were aptly named, and he and Pagan were already operating on borrowed time. The tarmac guards and NRPG captains all communicated via radio. They would have received the order for electronic transmission silence. Their perp hadn't gotten the memo, or there was a good chance he would have known he'd been made and blown the place sky-high.

Drew reviewed the security positions.

Their perp had to be stationed on an eyeball team, one of the pairs of guards posted at intervals within eyeshot of each other. They stood like beacons down every hallway leading off the terminal, a layer of invisible protection so no one unexpected could access through the wings. And the representatives wouldn't see how tight security really was.

That left the mechanical hangar and administrative offices. Drew went for mechanical, which afforded the most visibility.

He scanned faces as he passed the guards, mentally placed faces with names. No one stood out.

Pagan was in lockstep behind him, both of them trying not to break into a run and raise an alarm. Drew identified the NRPG guards as he passed.

Ene.

Ciobotaru.

Neacsu.

Sollomovici.

Rom.

Bochinsky.

The general would get Mirie and the representatives out down the employee stairs. Once they arrived in the terminal, they might buy a few more seconds because it would appear that the representatives were heading to the press area.

But they would pass by the cordoned section and head out the nearest exit, which would take them onto the tarmac. That was the general's quickest route. He would instruct the media to fall in behind the representatives, and once that happened, their perp would know he'd been made.

Then it was only a matter of a simple radio signal to detonate the bomb. Drew's money was on a cell phone.

"Who's that?" Pagan asked.

Drew followed the direction of the gaze. "Yonescu."

"Then our perp isn't down here."

Which was not entirely true. They were looking for someone unfamiliar, but the perp could easily be an NRPG guard with a radical connection and a mission. A spy like Pagan. Maybe even a sleeper like Drew. And if that was the case, then they would have to mark him when he made his move.

Which would probably be too late to stop him from detonating the bomb.

They didn't say a word, but headed back toward the terminal. The only place left was the administrative wing. Drew willed them to find an unrecognizable face. Just one, so they could take action.

But catching a break wasn't happening.

Drew knew it the instant he got within eyeshot of the terminal again, saw the team of guards at the staff stairs moving in formation away from the door.

They were out of time.

He didn't stop. He kept moving across the terminal with Pagan on his heels, closing in on the administrative wing, which brought them closer to the press area and the action.

Closer to Mirie.

The door opened, and Drew watched the representatives file through, the guards from the lounge flanking them at intervals. Several glanced around nervously, as if sensing that the situation was not playing out as anticipated.

There was Mirie.

At the very end of the line, lovely in her blue business suit that made her eyes more blue than gray. He could tell by her strained expression that she knew the situation had gone balls-up. She was flanked by the general and Georghe. Both had her discreetly by an arm, able to redirect her easily.

Doing Drew's job.

If she noticed him, she gave no indication, and he forced himself to look away, a sheer act of will that became physical when everything inside him ached to be with her. *He* was the only one he trusted with her safety. *He* was the one she looked to, the one she counted on to protect her. The one she looked to for comfort. Drew did not care what she wanted from him or why she wanted it as long as he could give it. So, so simple.

There were only seconds until the first of the representatives passed the cordoned area, before it became obvious that the situation was not playing out as expected.

Drew scanned the perimeter of the terminal for any movement, shifted his gaze between the administrative wing and the mechanical hangar, his gut on fire as confused whispers erupted from the press area and the media realized the representatives were not stopping.

Time was up.

Mirie was still in the terminal. Why had the general and Georghe not evacuated her first? But Drew knew they would have wasted more time arguing with her to get her to leave before the representatives. She was the honorable captain seeing to all hands before the ship sank.

The guards pulled open the exit door, directing the first of the representatives through. The people seemed to be moving in slow motion.

He watched the first few representatives clear the door, then scanned the administrative wing again. No one moved. Nothing happening out of the ordinary.

Excelsior training hadn't changed in the fifteen years since he had been trained, he realized, when Pagan positioned himself at Drew's back. They both began to rotate, scanning everyone and everything for any sign of movement.

No one seemed to notice. The media focused on

the departing delegation. Several reporters broke formation and appealed to the guards for information.

"Go, go, go," looped inside Drew's brain, willing Mirie through the door as every second ticked by backward.

Until he caught movement in his periphery.

A guard named Nistor, in full NRPG dress with insignias on his chest. The man watched the delegation, eyes widening in surprised horror, then he raised a hand toward his face.

He was clutching a cell phone.

"Pagan," Drew growled, and leveled his pistol.

The shot rang out through the terminal, a lingering echo that preceded an eruption of reactions.

The sound of running feet.

Breathless whispers.

A scream.

Nistor went down, and the cell phone skittered across the linoleum floor like a shot.

Pagan was already in motion, heading after that cell phone, but it was the guard who had made up the other half of Nistor's team that Drew noticed— the look of rage on the man's face and the sidearm he pulled from his waistband.

Drew did instinctively what he had been trained to do.

Lunging at Mirie, he covered the distance in one flying leap. He collided into her, Georghe and the general like a bowling ball into pins as he squeezed off the shot.

Almost instantly a bubbling red circle bloomed on the gunman's forehead, but not before he discharged his weapon.

CHAPTER ELEVEN

MIRIE OPENED HER eyes to an unfamiliar bedroom. She had no memory of arriving here. Wherever *here* was. A room that might have decorated the pages of a home decor magazine. From the wooden furnishings, mismatched with eclectic perfection, to the deep shades of eggplant and gold on the walls and bedding.

There were beaded lamps and windows that cornered the room. Mirie could tell from the sun that it was still early. She wasn't in a hospital, which might have provided a reason she felt as if she had been run over by a tank.

Her chest felt tight, and every breath she took hurt. A lot. Her head throbbed, and her mouth was dry and swollen.

A woman entered, and Mirie vaguely remembered she'd seen this woman before. The hair. Pale blond and shiny like glass. Hazy images of that hair swinging silkily as the woman leaned over the bed.

Mirie must have made some sound because the blonde turned and smiled warmly. She had the bluest eyes. So blue they looked purple like meadow flowers.

"How are you feeling, Your Royal Highness?" she asked.

"Dry." The word scratched through her throat like gravel. What was wrong with her?

She didn't have the energy to ask.

The woman only inclined her head and stepped out of sight. She couldn't have left the room because she reappeared only moments later with a foam cup. She was careful not to touch the bed as she leaned over Mirie.

"Try this." She touched Mirie's mouth with a small sponge and rubbed moisture on her lips until she could open her mouth.

"Better?" the woman asked.

Mirie nodded but wasn't sure if her head actually moved. "More."

The woman wet the sponge enough so Mirie could suck the water until it dribbled into her mouth. The act of swallowing was an effort, but the moisture eased her terrible thirst.

Mirie didn't think this woman was a nurse and wanted to know what had happened, why she was here with a stranger and feeling horrible, but even the effort of swallowing wearied her. Her eyes fluttered shut again, and she wondered where Drei was. And Helena and Georghe. It was so unlike everyone to be gone at the same time.

When next Mirie awoke again, she felt much clearer. She must have been given some sort of medicine to make her sleep. Now the fog was lifting, and she raised her head to look around.

Definitely not a hospital, yet there was medical equipment scattered around the designer furnishings. Items she recognized. An IV bag with tubing that hung from a metal pole. A tray of bandages and scissors. A plastic water container and a supply of Styrofoam cups with lids. A blood pressure cuff.

Now with some clarity of thought, Mirie recognized the tightness in her chest. She'd been bandaged, and her every breath felt sore. She tried to remember what happened, but could only recall the feeling of panic. The feeling overwhelmed her, was so potent she drew a deep breath, and her chest ached so intensely she thought she might be sick.

Carol. The talks. Mirie had met the representatives at the airport. The general had hurried them past the press.

Drei had vanished.

Fear.

She had felt his fear as if they'd been physically connected. The mask had vanished, and that had frightened her more than anything else.

The door opened. The blonde came in on light steps, in an obvious effort to be quiet, not realizing Mirie had awakened.

"Where am I?" she pushed the words out in a weak voice that sounded like a stranger's.

The blonde glanced at the bed, her smile kind. She was a woman who only knew how to smile kindly, Mirie thought.

"You're awake, Your Royal Highness," she said brightly. "How are you feeling today?"

"Clearer." That much was true.

"That's a good thing. You're in a safe house."

"Where?"

"We thought it best to get you out of Ninsele for the time being. But we're not far, still in Europe."

The woman spoke Ninselan, but with a slight accent. That accent and half answer managed to clear away the very last of the lethargy.

"Where is Major Timko?"

"He'll be along soon."

Not an answer. Mirie refused the water. Her anxiety was making her head spin.

The woman frowned as if realizing her answer had not been well received, and then set aside the cup.

"You were shot, Your Royal Highness," she explained. "The bullet would have gone through your heart if your bodyguard hadn't gotten you out of the way. You have a lot of stitches and probably a fair amount of pain since the bullet grazed a rib."

Mirie considered that. She did recall Drei plowing into her, a solid wall of muscle. Her knees had buckled. She remembered nothing after that.

"Was he hurt?"

Something about the question made the woman smile. "Only his pride, I think. For not getting you to safety."

Drei would hate that she had been harmed, which in no way explained why he wasn't here with her. He was always with her.

Until the general had evacuated the VIP lounge. Now she remembered. Drei had been there one moment, gone the next. She had been surprised by his disappearance. He never left her side without telling her who would replace him.

Mirie didn't like any of this. She didn't like having to be told details she should remember. She most especially didn't like how this woman was intentionally stingy with details.

Mirie's head throbbed in time with her heartbeat the harder she tried to think and pull together the pieces of what had happened, what questions to ask.

One question came easily. "Was I hit in the head?"

"You have a concussion from the fall. The doctor has reduced your pain medication, but if you're uncomfortable, just say so."

The last thing Mirie needed was medication. She couldn't think as it was. But she knew something wasn't right. She needed to focus, to remember, because pulling information bit by bit out of this woman was irritating her.

"Who are you? Who is the doctor, and where are my people?"

To Mirie's surprise, the woman sat in the chair beside the bed, as if she were a friend settling in for a visit. But they could talk now with Mirie only turning her head on the pillow. The pressure in her head eased.

"I'm Violet, and I've been overseeing your care."

"You're…a nurse?"

"No. There's only the doctor caring for you now. We believed it best to keep your situation tightly contained."

Death threats seemed to plague her lately, so that was no surprise. But… "Who is *we?*"

Violet frowned. "I know you have questions, Your Royal Highness, but I'm not authorized to answer them. I'm sorry."

She seemed genuinely contrite, and Mirie tried to tamp down her annoyance, knew anxiety and pain were making her edgy. She would only get flies with honey anyway. "Tell me if any of my people are here."

"Only Major Timko."

Had Drei and the general opted to bring her here for safekeeping? If so, why wasn't he here explaining the situation? He would never just leave her lying here injured and wondering. This was so unlike Drei.

"When will I be able to see him?"

"He shouldn't be much longer." She reached for the pitcher. "How about that water now?"

But Mirie only stared, her decision made. She wasn't doing anything until she spoke with Drei.

"I'VE ANSWERED ALL of your questions. I've been answering them for the past seventy-two hours. Now you answer a few of mine," Drew said, then added as an afterthought, "Sir."

The only thing Drew could say was that Excelsior's director, Simon Brandauer, looked as wiped as Drew felt. They had been locked in this interrogation room for three days around the clock, stopping only to hit the bathroom, which technically didn't count as leaving since it was attached to the room.

Food came and went. He had only an approximation of what time of day it was since he'd been stripped of all his electronics and there wasn't a window in the room. Except for the observation panel that ran the length of one wall. He wondered who might be watching, but didn't have a clue.

Debriefing fifteen years took time.

But Drew had reached his limit. He had acted in good faith, but he was done cooperating. He worked for this organization. He was not a political hostage.

Simon stared at him from across the table. His expression was unreadable. He was a big man, and Drew recognized how big because he was big himself. He didn't look too many men straight in the eye, but he did this one.

Simon wore the past fifteen years fairly well, all

things considered. More gray in his hair. Less humor, definitely.

But he was in good company because Drew had no humor at all. His brain ached from speaking English for so long, and he was beyond tired, the past seventy-two hours nothing compared with the preceding weeks. Drew was done playing nice.

Simon might not know or care. Drew had met the director only a handful of times, during interviews, after each phase of training. Simon oversaw every aspect of Excelsior, so not even sleeper recruits got past him.

Maybe Drew should feel honored the director had traveled all this way to personally debrief him.

He didn't. The only thing he cared about right now was getting answers to his questions.

Simon stood and went to the sideboard to pour water. "What is it you want to know, Drew?"

"Her Royal Highness. Let's begin there."

Mirie was the *only* thing he was interested in.

She had been taken by NATO medics, and he had not been given one update on her condition since. He wasn't sure whether this was a terror tactic on Simon's part, a reminder that Excelsior was in control, but it was no oversight. That much Drew knew. Mirie's blood had dried to an ugly brown on his clothes.

Simon didn't reply immediately, and Drew braced himself. He had administered triage until the NATO troops had contained the air terminal: compression to stop the bleeding, wound assessment and a vain attempt to delay shock. He knew where the bullet had penetrated, guessed by the exit the wound was clean.

That much had been a relief, at least. The traitors Nistor and Kraveks had been armed with Ninselan regulation weapons—FN Five-seveN pistols, non-expanding bullets.

Thank God.

Except that Mirie never should have been in the line of fire. Drew should have gotten her clear completely.

And would have had he not abandoned her.

When he thought of the sequence of events, the split-second decisions… His hands tightened around the sides of the chair, fingers clenched against the seat when he realized how one missed opportunity, one unnoticed glance, one too many steps, might have resulted in game-changing consequences.

Detonation of the bomb.

A bullet through the heart.

Mirie.

"Her Royal Highness is recovering well." Simon met Drew's gaze, openly gauging the reaction of his news. "In this house, under heavy guard. She'll be safe until she can be moved."

The sudden image of Mirie as she had looked the first time Drew held her appeared in his head. Not in the cave when she had been naked, but in the chapel altar, bundled heavily in wool and fur, the scent of her clean and fresh like fallen snow.

He wasn't sure why that memory struck him now, but he could see her face as she had pulled him into the hideaway, her expression all worried and urgent. And relieved.

He had not been the only one protecting that day.

Drew forced himself to think past his own relief right now, forced himself to manage the impact of Simon's reassurance, to move past the fear that had dogged him every long hour of these past three days, and the simmering resentment that he had been forced to wait for news about her condition.

Maybe even that he had been kept from her.

"What is the extent of her injuries?"

"Twenty-two stitches. The bullet grazed her rib. For all intents and purposes, it's a glorified flesh wound."

The words filtered through Drew, a palpable something that eased the tightness of tired muscles and strained nerves. Finally put to rest the niggling fear that he had not been told her condition because something had gone wrong. He would not put it past Excelsior to keep news of her death from him if the agency thought it would interfere with its debriefing.

That sort of hard-core dedication to mission was what had originally appealed to Drew about this agency.

He was older and more mature now. And Mirie

was alive and safe for the moment. That was all that mattered. The rest of his curiosity was nothing more than filling in the blanks.

"Those NATO troops were practically on top of us," Drew said. "The EC never said a thing about NATO. We coordinated with the representatives' personal security. They expected trouble?"

Simon returned and half sat on the edge of the table, perhaps feeling the effects of the endless hours on a wooden chair. Folding his arms over his chest, he stared down at Drew with a gaze that revealed nothing. "They didn't. I did. I received intel that there was a tie between an organization I have under surveillance and some members of the NRPG."

A leak in the NRPG.

Drew was growing more agitated by the second. If Excelsior had been sure of a connection to the NRPG, sure enough to keep NATO troops in the wings—an impressive feat in its own right— shouldn't its agents have known about its suspicions?

And Drew wasn't talking about the active field agent, either, but the sleeper trying to keep the princess alive.

Obviously Pagan had not known Nistor and Kraveks were the ones who had planted the bomb. But both those men had been assigned to details on the journey to Alba Luncă, too. Had they provided her coordinates to the enemy?

"A leak might have been helpful to know about,"

Drew said. "Since I'm the one responsible for the princess's safety."

Simon did not concede the point and considered Drew stoically. "You did what you were supposed to do. You reactivated when you were needed and avoided an international incident, not to mention thwarted an assassination attempt on Her Royal Highness. Your performance has been exemplary. The princess was never your mission objective, only a means to infiltrate Ninsele."

Everything about that statement came at Drew wrong. How could Mirie only be a means to an end when he had spent every waking moment of the past *fifteen years* protecting her?

"You'll have chaos if anything happens to her." Drew forced the statement out with a calm professionalism he didn't feel. Not even remotely. But he wouldn't give Simon the satisfaction of seeing how closely his words had hit home. "She's the only thing standing between power grabs by an awful lot of factions that aren't interested in anything but controlling borders to capitalize on Ninsele's geography."

Simon conceded that point with a nod. "Precisely why I put an active operative in place."

Drew knew that Jozsef had been with the NRPG for a number of years now. Long enough for Drew to tap him as one of Mirie's palace protection guards. "What about the other two guards? The leaks. What do you know about them?"

"Not enough, I'm afraid. They appear to be two fanatics willing to jihad to free Ninsele from the monarchy's oppression. They were recruited by the people behind the organization I'm after. This organization is making quite a name for itself peddling abandoned nuclear batteries it's picking up all over the former Soviet Union. It's supplying terrorist cells that want to jihad all over the U.S."

Drew didn't need to be told that portable thermoelectric generators contained sizable amounts of highly radioactive materials. Nuclear weapons materials on the black market were a cause for concern—for everyone, not just the United States. But not enough countries had the resources to police the flow of nuclear matter around the globe. The United States was one of the few that could, and did.

"What's the connection to Her Royal Highness? Ninsele's leak is only a lead to whoever you're after." Not a question, and Drew didn't like where this conversation was heading.

"I had a team seize 3.7 kilograms of plutonium-239 in an undercover sting operation a month ago. From Ukraine straight through Ninsele and on its way south. Her Royal Highness has accomplished a great deal here, no question, and I'm committed to supporting her efforts. But Ninsele is a bleeding artery. Traffickers are using this country like it's a duty-free."

There was no denial. Not of Simon's claim or the

way Drew's pulse upped its pace at the thought that Excelsior needed to maintain a presence in Ninsele. "Sounds like you need your people in place here, then."

Simon arched a brow. "I have some thoughts about that. You want them now or do you want to shower first?"

"Hit me." Drew had been stinking up this interrogation room for three days. His next stop was Mirie's room.

Simon glanced absently at the observation panel as if he, too, wondered who might be watching.

"NATO could have kept the troops in Ninsele to keep the peace, but we have an active monarchy. Princess Mirela wanted to handle the situation internally. That's her right because it's her country. But the rest of us deal with the fallout until she gets the situation under control."

"She's doing that."

Simon nodded. "Agreed, but not quickly enough. Even if Her Royal Highness and the EC hammered out a stabilization plan during these talks, which is ambitious for a first meeting, the plan has to be implemented. Internal transparency will take time. I'm not telling you anything you don't already know. The political situation around here has to be stabilized. The government has to be restructured. We are talking years before Ninsele repositions itself and builds up the resources and transparency to protect her own borders. And that's if Her Royal Highness lives to keep up the work. She's a target."

"That's what I'm here for."

There was a beat of silence, and Simon leveled his gaze. "There's my concern."

"What?"

"The princess was never your mission."

"I am well aware."

"Are you? From where I'm sitting it seems as if your mission objective may have gotten a bit fuzzy."

Drew frowned. "Is this a test? I won't defend myself. I've been guarding Her Royal Highness for fifteen years. Of course I'm concerned about her well-being. And you just told me my performance has been exemplary, so exactly what are you worried about, sir?"

"That it's going to be hard for you to leave your post."

Leaving his post meant leaving Ninsele.

And Mirie.

That came at Drew sideways.

He was an Excelsior operative. Never once had he questioned his loyalty. Not once through all these years. That was the problem. He hadn't thought about it.

"Active operatives are assigned controls, Drew. They change mission objectives and maintain enough contact with Command to keep them grounded. You don't have those anchors. For all intents and purposes, you were dropped off in Ninsele and left to live your cover, so you were in place when we needed you.

"That's a special mission objective that takes a special type of person. There's never been any doubt in my mind that you were up to the task. You've done stellar work all these years. You've gotten close to the pulse and stayed there. You've kept Her Royal Highness alive, which has also been your goal, if not your actual mission objective. Excelsior couldn't have asked for a better performance. That's why we briefed Pagan on your status. We couldn't get anyone else in, not without blowing our cover. The best we could do was pull in NATO troops to mop up the mess if there was trouble."

And there had been.

Excelsior wasn't a large agency, and it was exclusive as hell. Complete autonomy with a budget it didn't have to answer for. The most efficiently trained operatives comprised one of the most elite Special Forces organizations in the world.

"If Ninsele is such a problem, then why are you pulling me in?"

"Because what I need you to do is going to blow your cover," Simon said simply.

Nothing about Drew's reaction was simple. Not the hollow in his gut or the tightness in his throat. "What's that, sir?"

"Princess Mirela trusts you, Drew. I need you to

convince her to cooperate with the United States to lure out the person trying to assassinate her."

Drew sank back in his chair, and shook his head as if to clear it. "You want to use her as bait? Am I hearing you right?"

"It's in Her Royal Highness's best interest, too."

"How's that?"

"I've got a solid connection between Luca Vadim and the organization I'm after. The one that recruited Ninsele's guards for this terror attack. It provided the radioactive material used in the dirty bomb. If it had gone off, we wouldn't be having this conversation. There would be a crater where the airfield had been and NATO would be trying to mop up Briere from radioactive contamination. Vadim is preparing to take his claim to the throne to court."

"He'll have to take a DNA test."

"And he will. It will positively identify him as the late king's illegitimate son."

Drew stared. "He's legit?"

Simon shook his head. "He brokered a deal with a big shot in the Forensic Medicine Institute. Someone whose word will be difficult to refute. That person will manipulate the data."

Jesus. No wonder Vadim was so confident. He'd paid off someone in charge. Mirie didn't need more trouble. She needed to be recovering from a gunshot wound that might have killed her.

"It'll be beneficial for her to work with us, Drew. You must see that."

"You'll expose Vadim as an imposter?"

"I'm not worried about Vadim's identity," Simon said. "I need him to lead me to the organization funding this bid for the throne. That's what this is all about. If this organization puts its man on the throne, it'll put a stop to any bid to join the European Union. Ninsele's borders will stay a conduit between East and West the way it was during the authoritarian regime. Her Royal Highness is the only obstacle in the way."

Drew knew this wasn't going to work for Mirie. Not when Simon spoke of her throne as collateral damage and hadn't mentioned one word about the people. There may be warring factions. But the one thing all Ninselans had in common—they had all suffered under the dictator's rule.

Whether they hadn't been able to seek justice from a fair legal system. Or lacked adequate health care. Or necessary police protection. Or a basic education.

They had all suffered.

But Simon didn't mention that.

He didn't mention how Mirie had lived most of her life preparing to take the throne or confined to the royal compound for her safety, so she could accomplish what she had for Ninsele, which still wasn't enough.

He didn't say one word about the years she'd given to her duty.

Or about how Drew had spent the past fifteen years of his life earning Mirie's trust only to betray it at Simon's request.

But what brought Drew up out of the chair, though he was nearly too exhausted to stand, was the way Simon seemed to be a mind reader when he said, "This is not your life, Drew, even though it may feel like it."

Simon had gotten that part right, at least.

This did feel like Drew's life.

CHAPTER TWELVE

MIRIE WAITED UNTIL Violet left the room before pushing herself up. Her entire chest rebelled against the effort, but after a few moments, the sensation subsided.

Shoving away the covers, she maneuvered her legs around until she could dangle her feet over the side of the bed.

The pain was not too bad. Her side felt hot and tight, sore on the inside, but as long as she breathed gingerly, she could move just fine. She was made of far more than a little pain, and very determined not to appear weak.

Not when her world had narrowed to an invisible doctor and Violet of the no answers.

Where was Drei? Was he in trouble?

Were *they* in trouble?

Mirie was not obligated to accept anyone's help, and she would not accept help. Nor would she take anything by mouth. Not drink or food, and certainly not medicine. She would take nothing from people who could not be troubled to answer her questions.

And she had many. About what had happened to

Carol and the representatives. Had they been transported from Ninsele? And if so, by whom—choppers that should have transported them to the royal compound? Those questions led to questions about whether or not they had postponed the talks indefinitely, what they had told the media and whether or not they would be willing to return to Ninsele.

Then came questions about why the general had evacuated everyone from the VIP lounge in the first place. Where had Drei gone? Who had shot her?

"Pah." She waved her hand in growing irritation. As soon as she could safely stand, she would head straight out the door and demand some answers. If she didn't get them, she would continue walking out the next door, and the next, and the one after that. Until she was home. Or someone shot her, whichever came first.

But Mirie had not even placed her feet on the floor before hearing hurried footsteps. "She's in here."

Mirie had hardly grasped that Violet spoke her direction in English before the door opened, and Drei appeared, filling the doorway with his broad shoulders and welcome presence.

Mirie could do no more than stare, every thought and ache forgotten, her eyes so greedy for the sight of him. His expression collapsed; all the stern lines that chiseled his face into stone melted away at the sight of her. His green eyes softened as if the meadow in spring gleamed with morning's dew, a look of such profound relief. Every tiny worry that had barely compressed inside her, that had simmered for so long threatening to erupt into panic, calmed.

He was here now, alive, and whatever had happened they would face and make right. Drei would protect her. Not only with his life, but his strength. Knowing he was with her gave her strength. Mirie had not realized it until that very moment.

But as she basked in that feeling of *right,* she shifted her gaze from his face to drink in more of the sight, and suddenly struggled to make sense of his appearance.

He was disheveled. The black shirt and pants with the knife-point creases were wrinkled. His sleeve was torn. There were stains as if moisture had dried to ugly stiffness. Blood?

Her blood?

He still wore the same clothes after all this time?

She met his gaze again, questioning, but her unease grew at the change in his face. She had never seen this expression before, but she sensed his reluctance, and somewhere deep inside her shrank, did not want to face more trouble.

She braced herself. "Drei?"

He crossed the distance in two long strides. Suddenly, he was kneeling before her, so she had to look down into his face. She had to resist the urge to reach out and take his hands.

"Your Royal Highness," he said. "You're okay?"

Violet pulled the door shut quietly behind him, leaving them alone.

"Drei, are you all right? Tell me what's happened, and where are we? That woman would tell me nothing."

"Tell me how you are."

She waved off his concern. "I'm fine. Sore. But you? Where have you been? Are you well? I understand it has been days since the representatives arrived or was that a lie?"

"No," he said slowly. "It's been three days."

"Who are these people that they don't see to your needs? Where is the general? Are we in trouble?"

She hadn't realized until that very moment how much she sought his reassurance, hadn't realized until no reassurance came. If anything, his expression grew more bleak, more troubled.

"I'll tell you everything." He didn't pull the chair around but remained kneeling. "There was a bomb. It was discovered next to the area we set for the press conference."

He called the device a "dirty" bomb and went on to explain that the blast was only one problem because the nuclear matter could have contaminated the whole of Briere. Mirie listened with growing horror as he explained why he had left her in the VIP lounge, how close they had come to ruin.

"The general had no choice but to evacuate everyone, but we feared once the men who had planted the device realized they weren't going to get their audience, they would detonate."

"So the representatives are all right? Everyone got to safety?" she asked. "No one was harmed?"

"Only you."

There was such softness in his voice that Mirie could feel his relief overriding her horror. She clung to the feeling as he explained how NATO troops had been close enough to assist with the evacuations when there had been need, how they had diffused the bomb and provided medical attention for her.

The widespread implications rendered her speechless. That so many people might have suffered… For what? Power? Control? Were these things worth killing for?

"How is it possible I owe you even more gratitude, my dear Drei?" She was so overcome she could not stop herself from reaching out to slip her hands over his, needing him to understand, wanting to feel a physical connection between them and not caring about anything else just then.

Only that he knew how she felt, how much she wanted to erase that concern from his face, the heavy burden from his shoulders. He bore so much on her behalf.

Drei only stared down at where her hands covered his, and looked wistful. That stoic, beautiful face that revealed so little emotion suddenly looked as overwhelmed as she felt.

He was weary. She had only added to his burdens since demanding to return to Alba Luncă.

"Have you been speaking with NATO, Drei? Are they such poor hosts that they couldn't see to your needs? And how is it they should be involved? Carol mentioned nothing."

"Carol didn't know."

"Oh." That stopped Mirie. There was more to this tale. She knew as surely as she knew the general would not have been able to make that sort of arrangement without Carol's assistance, nor would he have ever concealed it from the Crown Council.

Drei exhaled heavily and sat back on his haunches. Her hands slid from his, and Mirie forced herself not to react, though she felt hurt that he would pull away from her.

"I've been speaking with a liaison from an American national security agency. This security agency is who arranged for NATO to be nearby in case we needed them."

Mirie frowned. American? That might explain Drei's condition. Luca Vadim had come from America.

"I'm confused," she admitted. "What does America care of our troubles?"

He explained how this American agency had been tracking the trafficking of nuclear materials, how these materials had been traveling over Ninsele's borders and into the hands of terrorists who used them to fashion destructive weapons.

Mirie listened and felt the weariness that had vanished at the sight of Drei weighing down on her again. She knew there were abuses. They all knew. The general had strengthened military presence at the borders, had increased the customs guards drastically.

Still, their efforts were not enough.

The political party that most loudly resisted inviting the European Commission to Ninsele was believed to have ties to criminals who would use her beautiful country as a clearinghouse for all sorts of evils.

She knew they had not solved the trouble, had impeded only those easily deterred, but they simply had no more resources to divert. The military was stretched thin as it was.

"But how did the Americans know our plans, Drei? I certainly haven't authorized any communication with this country. I haven't asked for their help. Or NATO's."

Of course she hadn't. She had been busy putting on a show of stability for the EC's benefit.

"We're on their radar, Your Royal Highness." Drei met her gaze, and there was something so sad in his eyes. "And they have their agents all over the world to monitor these situations so they don't get out of hand."

Maybe she shouldn't have been so surprised that Drei seemed so knowledgeable about what Americans were interested in half a world away, but she was. "Are you saying they have an agent in our country, Drei?"

He only nodded.

Mirie wasn't sure what she'd expected, but such a simple admission only angered her. Not the anger of outrage, but of apprehension, and fear. The truth was coming, she recognized it in the growing distance in Drei's gaze, and that truth would change everything. She could feel that with every shred of premonition she possessed.

"You knew of this person yet said nothing?"

He met her gaze and said, "I'm the agent."

For a long moment, a moment that dragged on another lifetime, Mirie could only stare into the face she'd thought she'd known without seeing, blinded by an admission that made no sense yet impacted everything.

Oskar handpicked this man to protect her, trained him personally. To protect her.

"It's true."

His voice seemed to come at her from a distance, across the chaos cluttering her thoughts, making reason a struggle. Such a struggle.

Drei had been her constant companion for fifteen years, since before Oskar's health had failed, before he had died. Drei was with her when she awoke in the morning, when she closed her eyes to sleep at night.

She trusted this man.

She had given him her body.

This man who had not been hers. Never hers.

And it was that realization more than any other that finally penetrated her shock, felt real. Mirie shrank from him, and the movement made her wince from the sudden motion, the pain causing her to clench her teeth.

Drei reached out to steady her, but she blocked his arm with her fist. "Do not touch me, liar."

Her words rang out harsh in the quiet.

Now he looked hurt, but he masked it quickly, said quietly, "Forgive me."

She didn't know whether he sought forgiveness for his touch or his lies. She didn't care. The only thing Mirie cared about was the look on his face, the knowing she saw there. This man had beheld her needs, her most private thoughts, her deepest yearnings, but she hadn't known him at all. She had thought him hers, loyal, trustworthy. And as she stared at him in growing understanding, she only wanted to hide from the truth, from the explosion inside her, a collision of everything she believed and felt. Or thought she had. Now she only saw weakness. Her own.

"You spy on my government and tell your government our secrets, and you think—"

"No, I don't."

His raised voice startled her.

"I have never told your secrets. I have had no one to tell them to. I'm a sleeper agent. I came to Ninsele as your close-protection guard to do exactly what I've been doing for all these years. Protect you. The situation has been unstable. I was here as a precaution, in case I was needed. I was reactivated to help avoid an international incident."

Reactivated. International incident.

Spy terms from a liar.

She had gone to this man in her weakness. She had been needy, and he had been the only man she could trust.

But Mirie remembered all the times she had thought of him throughout her days, the thousand little things. Ball gowns and balconies and picnics.

And lying naked in his arms.

All a lie.

Because the man she had known was a lie. The man she had pursued, had trusted with her weakness. But Mirie knew right then that she was wrong. She had dismissed her need as weakness, but her feelings were really so much more.

If she had reached out to Drei for closeness, the only man within reach, she would not feel the way she did right now. So very foolish.

And so, so hurt.

DREW GLANCED AT Mirie from across the cabin of Simon's jet. She sat in a seat beside a window, staring out at the Atlantic Ocean. She wore a bright orange jumpsuit that made it easier to move with the bandages around her torso. She looked like a political prisoner.

She probably felt like one, too.

Her profile might have been sculpted of marble. With her hair swept away from her face, she tormented him with the sight of her grim expression, the delicate curve of her cheek, the freckles sprinkled across her nose, the compressed mouth that hinted at very unpleasant thoughts. She had not spoken to him since Simon had shown up in her bedroom at the safe house and introduced himself by his official cover.

Special liaison to the United States Security Council.

The *special liaison* had proceeded to detail Ninsele's situation. Simon had complimented Mirie on her achievements, of which there had been many. He had outlined most of them to prove he'd been paying close attention to everything happening in Ninsele. Then he explained the ways he'd been supporting her regime from behind the scenes.

There had been quite a few of those revelations as well, Drew admitted. Actions that went far beyond putting active and inactive operatives in place and wielding influence with NATO.

Then Simon had explained his areas of concern.

From Ninsele's bleeding borders to Vadim's connection to an organization supplying nuclear material and arms to terrorists. Simon explained how Mirie had become a key figure of interest not only to the United States, but also to the countries being targeted by these terrorist organizations.

The United Kingdom, Israel, Algeria, Iraq, Turkey.

He had explained things about the bomb that Drew was hearing for the first time. While the NRPG traitors had been extremists, they had been recruited by an organization with another goal entirely. The bomb had been a message. The enemy was prepared to use whatever means necessary to terrorize Ninsele's people, so they would resist any government pursuing EU candidacy. In effect, cutting into the enemy's profit margin.

Had the bomb detonated, the message would have been clear: *We can get at your princess. We can get at the representatives of any country that tries to help you. We can get at* you *because the effects of the bomb will poison every person in Briere with radiation exposure. We can bring down your economy because decontaminating the city will cripple Ninsele's treasury.*

A message of terror and intimidation.

Simon had not minced words, and had manipulated Mirie into the middle of a volatile global situation, where she was being held accountable for what crossed her country's borders.

It was the only reason she was on the jet right now. But she did not entirely agree with Simon's assessment, and she had no use at all for the high-handed way he had coerced her.

Mirie did not appreciate the nature of covert operations. Her priorities were the same as Simon's—only reversed in many ways because her responsibility was not to herself or other countries, but to her people. Her greatest concern seemed to be Luca Vadim. If he proved his claim through fraudulent means and she was not in Ninsele to obstruct him, then she was in effect allowing an imposter to step into her rule.

Simon thought that letting the public believe Vadim had a claim to the throne was a small price to pay. They could expose him as an imposter after they caught their enemy. Turning the tables and keeping Mirie out of Briere would do that.

Mirie believed she should be able to discredit Vadim and draw out the enemy without deceiving her people in the process.

Both agreed this enemy trafficker needed to be stopped. Neither minded making Mirie a target.

Simon considered her throne and public perception collateral damage.

Mirie found Simon's lack of regard for her people offensive and shortsighted.

They had reached a stalemate for the moment, while Drew found the entire situation disturbing for the very problem neither Mirie nor Simon seemed concerned with.

Making Mirie more of a target than she already was.

He did not want her safety at risk for the benefit of the United States and other countries. And he felt responsible for putting her in this situation, for exposing her to Excelsior's director, who had unapologetically coerced her cooperation.

Drew knew that Simon had the best of intentions and the resources to accomplish the mission objective with Mirie's help. Maybe he had gone soft these past fifteen years, but watching Simon bully Mirie— or try to—did not sit well with him. But without her cooperation…the simple truth was that she would not be safe until they hunted down the trafficker.

They had been living with that reality for a long time.

Still, she was entirely justified in her unwillingness to use her people as unwilling pawns.

She had every right to feel betrayed by him.

He could not sit still any longer and got to his feet. He stood in front of the window directly across from Mirie, feeling the distance between them as wide as the ocean below.

The interior of the jet, while comfortable, was designed as an in-flight command center. Simon sat at a workstation behind the cockpit, catching up on everything he had missed during his days debriefing Drew. Violet bounced around the cabin, chatting with Simon, checking on Drew, even trying to engage Mirie.

Mirie was not speaking to Violet, either. Not in Ninselan, English or any other language.

Violet seemed unfazed. Taking a seat at another workstation, she slipped on a headset. As the linguistics expert for Excelsior, she would have plenty of work to keep her busy during the flight. Drew had worked with her during his training long ago. She had helped him nail various dialects that had made him valuable in Eastern Europe. She spoke fluent Ninselan, which was probably why Simon had brought her along to care for Mirie.

Or maybe this was a working vacation for Simon.

Back in the old days, Violet had been Team One—Simon's personal team of operatives. The elite of elite. But Violet had told Drew she retired from fieldwork a few years back and married their boss, which sounded like a conflict of interest.

Or maybe Drew was just feeling ornery because Simon had called him out on his feelings for Mirie.

This isn't your life, even though it might feel like it.

Drew had been struggling with his feelings for Mirie for a long time, but the cave had only made the situation a million times worse. Controlling his emotions was one thing, but when Mirie began looking at him differently, began reacting to the awareness between them, she had annihilated his restraints.

Drew had started to hope.

For what, he didn't know. There was no place for them to go. She had wanted companionship with someone she trusted. Period. And even if she had wanted *him,* she could never pursue him. He could never be more than her guilty secret.

That was the reality of their situation. Drew knew it. He had always known it, but he didn't feel it. Somewhere along the way since making love to Mirie, he really had just let himself get caught up in the moment. Their chance encounters. Her newfound concern for him. Their quiet conversations.

He had allowed the pleasure of this change to distract him from reality.

"The captain has alerted me to our altitude," Simon said, circling his chair around, and distracting Drew from his thoughts. "We've reached 39,000 feet."

Mirie turned away from the window for the first time since takeoff. She studiously avoided looking at him.

"We can make the call now?" she asked Simon in English, a beautiful sound with her lilting voice.

God, Drew was gone, totally lost in feelings he couldn't feel, a life that wasn't his.

Had never been, no matter how it may have felt.

"We can make the call." Simon leaned to the nearby workstation and pulled another chair toward him.

Drew watched as Mirie worked her way to her feet with slow movements, the way she pushed up with her arms to avoid bending at the waist. He had already taken a step toward her to help before remembering he wasn't her close-protection guard anymore.

Her scowl promised that his assistance would not be welcome.

But watching her struggle went against everything Drew had in him. He had been caring for this woman since before she had been a woman. Of course he cared about her. Even if they had never slept together, he cared for her safety, and *her*. He would have been inhuman *not* to care.

"Your people have been told you're under the protection of NATO until you heal from your injuries and the threat has been contained," Simon explained as he handed her the headset. "You'll want to stick to that cover story."

Mirie only inclined her head, but Drew didn't miss the mutinous tightening of her jaw. Nor did Violet, who watched him with an expression that seemed to understand all his turmoil, to see how much he cared. She had been a field operative once. She knew how some situations didn't play out smoothly. Not like her husband, who micromanaged from his ivory tower.

Her phone conversation began smoothly, and lasted until they were well along their track over the Atlantic. She spoke in turn with Georghe, Helena and Carol, whom NATO had escorted to the royal compound at Carol's request. Drew wanted to know what was going on in Briere, suspected Simon was recording the conversation. But for the moment Mirie was making the best of her limited privacy, and Drew heard her half of the exchange.

"Call a meeting of the Crown Council to address this terror event. Maybe you can make progress at spurring some national reaction, get people thinking as Ninselans. This was an attack against Ninsele, and the terrorists used Ninselans and their interests as weapons."

She continued, "Then schedule a press conference, Georghe. I want you to publicly address Vadim's claims, and release how we're going to proceed in my absence. Ask Carol to arrange for a third-party company to oversee every step of the process. I'll tell her my concerns myself. She'll find someone suitable. But I want oversight. Especially when they're collecting the samples. We'll insist they run sibling DNA, too. We'll appear to be cooperative, but thorough. That should buy us some time." She slanted a pointed glance at Simon, who only met her gaze impassively. "I'm not sure when I'll be back. Soon, though."

Despite the troubled situation, despite her urgency to help put out as many fires as she could during this phone conversation, the effect of taking action and touching base with her people was visible. Color flooded back into her cheeks as she fired off questions about daily business, made quick decisions and reassured everyone she was recovering well.

She helped Georghe formulate a slant for the press coverage the way she always had around the conference table, and the sight of her taking charge again relieved some place deep inside Drew that had needed reassurance.

It's not your life, even though it might feel like it.

Three days of debriefing had not come close to transitioning him from fifteen years as Mirie's protector.

CHAPTER THIRTEEN

MIRIE WAS NOT impressed by her first glimpse of the
United States. Had the circumstances been different, had she been there to reestablish the honorary
consulate or as the guest of the president, she still
didn't think she would have found anything pleas-
ing. From the air, the flat land stretched in every
direction. Manicured trees outlined pulsing highways as a child might use broad strokes on a crayon
drawing.

On the ground, she found the architecture mas-
sive and plain. Monuments turned the city into a
museum announcing the country's accomplishments
rather than holding them close and safely guarded.
She tried to remember what Papa had told her of
his visits to this place, could only remember what
he hadn't said—that he'd been involved in an affair
with another woman and left behind a bit of himself in a son.

Which she refused to believe. Not without proof.

The safe house they eventually arrived at was as
American as their city. She supposed she should've
been impressed with its sweeping view of the sky-

line from across the river, but Mirie felt only fatigued and angry.

She tried to expunge thoughts of Drei—no, *Drew*—from her mind, yet they always drifted back. And were always met with horror over what had transpired between them in the cave.

She had felt guilty for turning to him in her need, for demanding what he had not offered. Now her moment of weakness taunted her, for she had sought comfort from a man who was a lie.

Had she mistaken Drew's actions for caring?

She'd never considered that thought, not until she was sitting in a plane taking her away from her home and trying her hardest to avoid him.

But he was a part of her, of her days, of her very soul, for every time she glanced over her shoulder, she expected to see him there.

The invisible man who was not invisible at all.

Had she really thought he cared about her? Was that why she had reached out to him?

That would explain why she felt the way she did now, so angry and betrayed. Drei had been her employee. A man paid to do exactly what he had always done. But in her heart he had become more. Drei Timko didn't exist.

The man named Drew was a stranger.

"What do you think, Your Royal Highness?" Violet asked in Ninselan, probably trying to make Mirie feel welcome in this strange, foreign place. "Will you be comfortable here for a few days? Just until you've rested up a bit from the flight?"

Turning away from the long window with the panoramic view, she faced Violet. This woman had been kind to her. Mirie abhorred these circumstances, but she did appreciate the kindness and care she had been shown. She owed a debt of gratitude to these people for averting a tragedy and protecting the representatives when the whole of the NRPG and her military had not managed the task.

Maybe she simply did not like the reminder that Ninsele was still so fragile.

"I will be comfortable, thank you," she said.

Violet smiled. "Would you like a tour of the place or would you prefer to settle in yourself?"

"I'm sure I will be able to find my way around."

Violet inclined her head with a knowing gaze in her flower-bright eyes and retreated, glancing at the director as she went to stand beside Drew, who stood by the door with his hands clasped behind him, in a stance so familiar to her. The director half sat on the back of a sofa. "I intend to do everything in my power to ensure your safety while you're in my watch, Your Royal Highness. Drew has been assigned as your close-protection guard and is still the individual best suited to see to your safety. If you're willing, I'd like him to continue in that assignment for the duration of your stay here."

Everything inside Mirie wished to refuse that request. She needed to think, to regain her strength, to breathe freely again, and she knew that would be easier to do without him there, claiming her thoughts and distracting her with so many feelings she should not be feeling.

But she forced herself to think like a princess, not a woman. The director was right. The man she had once known as Drei had always protected her. Even though he didn't care for her personally, he would protect her for his country.

"Your man is adequate." There was still a weak part of her that did not want to be alone in this country without a familiar face.

Would she ever feel strong again?

The director inclined his head, clearly pleased.

"So, when will we negotiate our plan?" she asked, forcing herself to deal with the real issue.

"Let me propose something, Your Royal Highness, and then we can get together tomorrow to hash through the details. I want you to have a chance for rest."

She was tired. Not physically, but tired of this situation. Of the Americans' interference. Of those who would steal her throne. Of the man she thought she had known. The sooner they made a plan, the sooner they could implement it and she could return home.

"I want to start moving you around the country as soon as you can travel," the director said. "If I keep you moving, I can keep you safe and minimize the risk to others."

Mirie considered what the director said. The talks were supposed to reassure her people and give them faith in their government again. In their hearts, most Ninselans wanted security and a future, no matter what their political beliefs. "You think this trafficker's organization can move around your country more easily than mine? How is that even possible?"

"My country is bigger. More places to hide." The director flashed an uncommon smile that transformed his expression.

For the first time, Mirie felt a connection to the man. She understood the heavy weight of responsibility, too.

"I can operate most effectively within our borders," Simon continued. "We already have a connection to the United States in Luca Vadim. The man has no prior connection to Ninsele except his claim of his mother's citizenship, which checks out. But Vadim didn't even have a passport until a month before he traveled to Ninsele. He was targeted in Whitefish, Montana, which tells me his trafficker will have no problem chasing you down here."

Mirie folded her arms over her chest and resisted the urge to sit down. She could feel everyone watching her. Especially *Drew*.

Did he believe she should cooperate?

Did she even care what he thought?

No.

"If you're sure of the link to Vadim, then it makes the most sense to investigate Vadim and follow that link to the guy in charge of this organization. We can discredit Vadim in the process and spare my people from believing his lies."

The director frowned. "I understand why that sounds like a good plan. But if we expose the one link we have, which is Luca Vadim, then the guy in charge is going to know we're on to him. He'll go underground and wait us out. He'll stop conducting business, probably even relocate. We'll be forced to try to track him down all over again." He stared at her. "But if we don't let him know we're on to him, we can lure him into the open by dangling a big target in front of him. He won't miss his chance to eliminate his only obstacle to putting Vadim on Ninsele's throne. Once he makes his move, we'll get him."

Moving to a chair that placed distance between her and Drew, she sat on the edge and contemplated the director's words.

"Everything you say makes sense, yet you're not addressing my concern. I won't sit back and allow Vadim to deceive my people, the European Commission and the rest of the world with his fraudulent tests and his lies. He must be discredited, or detained, or…" She shook her head and squelched the thought of assassination, although *that* course of action would surely solve the problem.

For the moment, anyway.

"He's my only lead to the trafficker," Simon said.

"My people have endured much in their fight for stability. You must negotiate with me."

Their gazes met. The director's was icy and unyielding. Mirie was tired of this argument. They'd reached an impasse.

"I'll sleep on it," she said simply.

She had to come up with a better plan. One that met both their needs, because she was unwilling to yield this point.

Vadim needed to be stopped. Every minute he spent pursuing the throne created doubt in the Ninselan people and fostered dissension. It undermined their belief that Ninsele could recover from the war and once again provide opportunities and good lives for them.

The director watched her a moment longer, then stood. He glanced at Violet, who went to the door and retrieved a briefcase. She set it on the table that bridged the open rooms and retrieved envelopes that she brought to the director.

"I have something to give you before I leave," he said.

Mirie noticed the sudden scowl on Drew's face before accepting the envelope the director offered her.

"Drew, I have one for you as well," he added.

Drew's scowl appeared to get even bigger, but he crossed the room and accepted the envelope.

That was the last thing Mirie noticed before she glanced down at her official title scrawled in a spidery hand.

And gasped when she recognized the handwriting.

DREW RECOGNIZED THE letter as soon as Violet took it from the briefcase. He didn't bother asking how Simon had gotten it. Obviously he had sent someone to hack into Drew's personal safe.

Pagan? Or another operative?

Drew had not been briefed. He had no clue how many operatives Excelsior had planted in the royal compound. He didn't think he'd get an answer if he asked.

He wasn't surprised Simon had produced the letter. He'd admitted he thought Drew would have trouble leaving his post. Maybe Simon wanted to gauge how much trouble, and what better place to observe a rat in a cage than an Excelsior safe house?

Poking a stick into the cage to see how the rat reacted sounded just like something Simon would do. Maybe not the Simon of memory, but the man standing before him now.

Maybe Simon wanted to get a lock on the relationship he and Mirie had forged over the years, so he knew how to separate them with the least risk to Excelsior. Had he not needed Mirie's cooperation, he might have reassigned Drew after reactivation.

But when Drew was also handed an envelope, all

his thoughts fled as he noticed the obvious age of the paper. The name on the front was handwritten in a withered scrawl, the name of a man who had never existed.

Drei Timko.

As Drew stared at the name that felt more familiar than his own, he thought of the life this imaginary man had led. A life not so imaginary. He felt wrenched from the inside out, until the handwriting jarred his memory.

He must be mistaken.... He slipped the page from the envelope, which, like Mirie's, had been previously opened.

His Majesty, the late king, like his father before him, maintained a cordial and steady relationship with the Americans, impressed as he was by their resilience during the Great Wars. So, in these dark and difficult times, when Ninsele is under attack and its future resides in the willing but weak hands of an old man who gratefully gave a lifetime of service to the Crown, I have appealed to only those whom I dare trust for aid. They have sent me you.

Violet came up behind Drew and rested her hand on his shoulder, a reassuring touch that did nothing to reassure him. He glanced over to find her watching him with a thoughtful expression, and she patted his shoulder, asking without words if he was hanging in there, and assuring him that he would.

The best Drew could do was nod because he was trying to make sense of the fact that Oskar had known who he was all along, but Excelsior had never told him. He had suspected as much after reading Geta's letter, but suspicions were not fact. The only thing Drew was sure of right now was that had he given Mirie the letter sooner, he might have eased her into discovering who he was. She would at least have had a clue something was up....

Glancing over to where she sat on a chair, gripping the pages of her letter, silent tears falling down her cheeks, he wondered what she thought of this correspondence from beyond the grave. If she was comforted or if it caused her to mourn her loss all the more, given that she was half a world away from home.

Drew ached for her, a feeling he had no right to feel, so consuming and real that he vibrated with the intensity of it. He ached to shield her from harm and hurt. To see her smile. To hear her voice again.

To hold her against him.

This isn't your life, even though it might feel like it.

How could he have lived beside this woman for so long and not care about her tears? She had endured more loss than anyone should, and he knew all about loss from his long-ago life. Yet Mirie had not run as he had. She stood tall in the face of adversity and duty. Except for rare moments of vulnerability… And then only Drew knew. Only Drew had seen.

And he had given her over to Excelsior.

He had no defense. He had withheld Geta's letter the way Simon had withheld Oskar's. The way Simon had withheld the knowledge that Oskar had known about Drew all along. Why? Because the information had been considered need-to-know? Because, for some reason, Simon thought Drew would do a better job not knowing that Oskar had sought Excelsior's help?

Drew had no way of knowing unless he asked. But he had believed he was the one who should be making the decisions for Mirie. And by doing so he had done to her what Simon had done to him.

Maybe he wouldn't feel as if he had betrayed her if he couldn't see her tears…. But there was nothing to hide her face. With her hair swept back, there was no masking her wet cheeks, her eyes the color of a rain-swollen sky. Dragging away his gaze, Drew tried to find refuge in the old man's words from long ago.

I would appeal to you with a promise you made between swallows of *ţuică* around the village fire, as I gauged your trustworthiness and tried to ascertain whether or not the Americans had sent me the right man for the job. You did not know I had asked for you and were so eager to prove yourself worthy of this task.

I believed in you. Not at first, but you eventually proved yourself to be strong and steady and smart. I learned to have faith in you, for that was the only way I could die in peace, knowing you would care for our most precious royal treasure. Knowing you would protect her with your life, so she can grow into the princess she was born to be.

The only princess Ninsele has left.

This is a special calling we share, you and me. We know the great responsibility and the great privilege of being needed to keep the royals safe from harm. They are vulnerable in a way most people can't even imagine. We make it possible for them to live their lives without always keeping an eye over their shoulder.

I have no way of knowing how long you will be called to this task. I have no way of knowing what life has in store for Her Royal Highness, or for you as her protector, but I know the young man I share my bottle with will heed his promise to care for her until she gives him her blessing to go, or he lays down his life in his efforts to protect her.

Godspeed, Drei Timko. I hope your life is a long and happy one. Know that you have been the answer to two old servants' prayers.

Simon had kept this letter for so long after Oskar had died; so much had happened in the years since then. Had it been Simon's intent to wait for the "right" time to share an old man's faith in him and reveal that Drew's identity had been known all along? Had Simon kept the letter from him just as Drew had withheld Mirie's letter, believing he knew what was in her best interest?

He remembered the man Oskar had written of—a young man, although Drew had not thought of himself as that young at the time.

Drew glanced at Mirie and found her head bowed low. He could see the loneliness that surrounded her, the isolation that had become her life.

The woman she had once loved as much as a grandmother could touch her only from beyond the grave. Her most trusted friends and advisers were across an ocean, unaware of her situation, trying to hold down the fort in her absence.

And the man she had trusted with her life, and her needs, had turned over the responsibility for her care to an agency that would place her in the crosshairs to try to lure out the enemy.

Drew had believed wholeheartedly in Excelsior's mission—national security. He had found his life's work in the good old U.S. of A. and knew from his years in Special Forces that defending his country made all sorts of unexpected demands of him.

Oskar had been right. Drew had been eager to

prove himself. Protecting the sole remaining member of the royal family during a dictator's regime and a civil war had been his calling. He had learned to value life during his years in Ninsele—not only Mirie's but his own.

And, now, looking at her wrapped in her silent thoughts, Drew wondered who would protect her now. Did Excelsior believe the job was over, that the American government's promise to an old man would end once they tracked down the enemy?

Or would they send someone else to protect her even though she wasn't the mission objective?

Drew had committed himself to her care so long ago. And while they may eliminate one threat against her, there would be others. There would always be others.

Drew wanted to know more about this original agreement. He found it hard to believe that Oskar could have known about Excelsior, so how had the agency gotten involved? And how long had it agreed to watch over Mirie? Who would do the job if Simon decided it had done its part?

The NRPG with its limited resources?

Drew wanted answers, but when he looked around the room, he realized Simon and Violet had slipped out, leaving him alone with Mirie.

Or as alone as one could be in an Excelsior safe house with a perimeter team standing guard outside.

"How did your government get this letter?" Her

voice was rough in the quiet, her eyes swollen from her tears.

Drew faced her, and it was the look of inevitability on her beautiful face that stole his breath. She moved right past her tears to understanding the situation, to putting the pieces in place and assessing the effects. No time for sorrow.

"Vlas gave me that letter at Geta's funeral. She asked him to give it to me and to only pass it on when you were ready to be reminded of the past."

Mirie drew herself upright in the chair, an effort with her injuries, judging by the strain on her face. "She thought you were best able to make that decision for me, hmm? Yet you were not the one to give this to me. What were you waiting for?"

"Until the talks concluded."

She didn't like his reply. He could tell before she even opened her mouth.

"You follow orders well, then."

Drew absorbed the slap of her words, took it on the chin as his grandfather used to say. Mirie wanted to hurt him.

The way he had hurt her.

But knowing that she was hurt eased the sting of her words. Because her hurt meant she cared. Her anger meant she cared.

"Were you ready to be reminded?" He needed to know.

She studied him for a long moment, as if she

wanted to see inside him to the man she thought she had known. And what shocked Drew was how much he wanted to be that man. Not a man who gave her care over to another, but the man with a calling, the man Oskar had seen in him.

The man Mirie had seen in the cave.

"I don't know that any time is better than another," she said. "There is no reminding me. It's always with me."

The resignation in that simple admission made him ache. She didn't ask for pity, didn't give herself any, but Drew could feel the vulnerability that Oskar had named.

And as he had all those years ago, Drew felt an urgency to prove himself again.

She was *his* calling.

Oskar had been right about that, too. Only when she wasn't watching over her shoulder to avoid the next threat could she live the fragile balance that was her life and duty.

"I hope you found comfort in Geta's words." He hoped because he cared so much more than he had ever known.

"I did, and I do. She knew what I needed to hear. She told me I must be true to myself. I have been trusted with duty and obligation, and I must fulfill my purpose while still living a full life. Because that is my true purpose—to live. No one else in my family got that chance. She didn't want me to squander that gift."

Drew had read the letter, knew the words Geta had written, but only Mirie had understood the message.

"She's right."

Mirie glanced at the letter he held. "What did Bunică tell you?"

He seized this chance to bridge the distance between them. A momentary truce; Drew knew that was all this was. Mirie was much more than a beautiful princess; she was a skilled negotiator. "This is not from Geta, but Oskar, written a very long time ago."

"And you've only just received it now?"

Drew nodded.

She met his gaze then, a glance they had exchanged a thousand times. He knew she wanted to know what kind of agency he worked for, the kind that would withhold letters and use monarchs from weaker countries to achieve its goals.

But she did not ask. Their momentary truce was just that. She was practical enough to know she was among people she could not trust. And she no longer had him watching her back.

His loyalties were divided now.

Crossing the distance between them in a few strides, he handed her the letter without a word.

He watched her as she read it, wanting to be the man to provide the security she needed to find mo-

ments of laughter with friends during an icy picnic,
to seek physical pleasure in a cave.

Maybe Simon was right, and Drew had bought
his cover, had believed this life he had lived was his
own. Or maybe Simon was wrong, and Drew was
living life exactly as he was supposed to. Excelsior
had only been the means to get him from Charlotte,
North Carolina to Ninsele in Eastern Europe.

He didn't think it mattered either way.

Not when he had committed himself to this
woman. Not when he felt about her the way he did.

When she glanced up at him, resignation had
chased away all remnants of tears. "Oskar sought
your government's aid. Bunică hinted that there was
much I didn't know."

He nodded. He had read her letter the way Simon
had read his. Everyone had an agenda.

"You know our situation better than your director does. If nothing else, you know it from an inside
perspective." That simple truth cut deep. "Do you
agree with what your director would have me do?
Do you think I should allow an imposter to make
gains in my absence?"

There was so much more to her question than what
she was asking. Like Geta's letter, the words only
hinted at the true message.

Even if he'd had a solid answer, Drew knew better
than to speak freely in this house. "I think we would

do well to sleep on Brandauer's suggestion. We can look at it with fresh eyes in the morning."

Their gazes collided, an impact he felt right to his gut. And understanding shadowed her blue-gray eyes.

"So, what do I call you since Major Drei Timko no longer exists—Special Agent Candy?"

Her mispronunciation of his name and assigning him an FBI title missed the mark in so many ways Drew might have laughed. Except nothing felt funny right now. Not the question he saw on the beautiful face that had once trusted him. Not the way he felt inside.

"Drew."

"Sounds a lot like Drei, only different." Then she got to her feet and headed down the hall without glancing back, finally taking her tour of the house.

But she had talked to him.

It was a start.

CHAPTER FOURTEEN

"In news from around the world, the Royal Palace of Ninsele, a country in Eastern Europe, has released a statement that EU talks were aborted last week after an attempt on Her Royal Highness Princess Mirela's life...."

Mirie stared at the news report, struggling to keep up with the accented English. It didn't help that the television screen was the size of a dinner plate and the car's engine and the roar of passing vehicles made the task more difficult.

"Did he say the stabilization and unification talks would be rescheduled for as soon as I've recovered from my injuries?"

Drew stared at the television and nodded. "And that the president of the European Commission has released the same statement through her office."

"Good for Georghe and Carol," Mirie said. Finally, some good news. Such a positive statement should redirect people from the disturbing reports about Luca Vadim's scheduled DNA test at the Forensic Medicine Institute.

Georghe had released an official statement that

an unbiased private company had been retained to oversee the process for security reasons.

When would this nightmare end?

Mirie found the fact that her entire life had been boiled down to a ten-second blip on the evening news sobering. But here in America, Ninsele was only a tiny country half a world away.

"Please, no more." She sank back into the plush seat of the car with its darkly tinted windows while Drew used the remote control to shut off the television.

Then it was just the two of them, alone but for the driver in the front seat behind a partition of glass. Bulletproof, of course.

At least she was alive, as Bunică had reminded in her letter. Alive, just to be frustrated and shot at and ignored.

She and the director had stalled on their negotiations, and time was running out. They had been deliberating nonstop for forty-eight hours on the nuances of their priorities while the very situation she did not want to happen was unfolding beyond her control.

Vadim was gaining a public foothold, undoing six years of hard work and cooperation among different factions. The director had finally insisted on moving her after they failed to reach common ground. He was responsible for a visiting princess who had not entered the country through diplomatic channels.

He would not risk her safety any more than necessary. So he packed her up into a car and they were on their way. He promised to continue their negotiations as soon as she was safely settled, but Mirie knew he had simply used her safety as an excuse to outmaneuver her.

No doubt he was in his command center, laying a trail for the trafficker he hoped to lure. In the battle they fought, he would win with patience because time was Mirie's enemy.

Drew had been equally frustrating. She was not sure what she had expected of a man who would lie convincingly for so many years—she supposed his actions could be interpreted as commitment to his cause. Knowing that Oskar had appealed to the Americans for help had tempered her anger with Drew only a small bit. She told herself that she couldn't take his actions personally, but there was nothing about the man that felt anything *but* personal.

He had not once defended her to his director, or stuck up for their cause. *Her* cause. Major Drei Timko was an American named Drew, who had no real ties to her part of the world, no matter how fluently he spoke her language.

Men.

"ETA, ten minutes," came the voice of the driver through a speaker system.

Mirie turned from the window to find Drew watching her. To her surprise, he left his seat in an athletic burst of motion she hadn't expected and was suddenly beside her, so close he seemed to swallow up all the space.

He handed her a water bottle. "How do you feel? You've been sitting a long time."

"I'll be stiff when we get wherever we're going," she said simply, trying not to respond to the look in his green eyes, a look that was so familiar.

A look that was a lie.

But her heart raced anyway. Not even her own heartbeat was under her control anymore. If it were, she would have torn her heart from her chest and branded it a traitor to the Crown.

But all thoughts of rebellious hearts and traitors vanished when Drew leaned in. He reached into her collar for her throat.

"You chain is caught, Your Royal Highness," he said. "Let me untangle it or you might break it when you move."

She didn't know what he was about because her chain with the religious medal she had worn on the day of the representatives' arrival was around her neck exactly where it should be, lying against her chest above her throbbing heart.

But his rough fingers caressed her skin, making her pulse leap beneath his touch. She could feel the warmth of his breath against her ear when he whispered, "You have a choice to make. We can continue to the safe house and play by the director's rules, or we can run for it and handle the situation our way."

Run for it?

For one stunned instant, Mirie's heart didn't beat at all, simply stalled in her chest as she tried to make sense of what Drew had proposed. Handle the situation their way?

"The clasp is stuck in your hair." He fumbled idly with her collar. "I'm not hurting you, am I?"

"No, no," she replied automatically.

To leave the protection of the American director would mean trusting Drew.

A man she no longer knew, and had never truly known.

Mirie let her eyes flutter shut as she struggled for breath. She was a secret visitor to this country. Her people thought NATO had seen to her care. And they had. She had no idea what the director had told NATO when he had spirited her away.

Trust Drei, no matter what. There is more to him than you can know.

What if Bunică and old Oskar had been deceived?

Mirie had only the feeling in her pounding heart, the feeling that with Drew she had always been safe.

"I'll go with you," she whispered beneath her breath.

There was a flash of something in his expression, but Mirie didn't have time to ruminate on what it might be.

"Do what I tell you quickly. No looking back, and no worrying." He patted her collar. "There you go. Is that better?"

"Yes," she said, sounding quite normal although she felt as if her heart would leap out through her throat.

She watched him settle back into his seat as if nothing important had transpired between them.

But everything had changed.

FOR THE FIRST TIME since leaving Ninsele, Drew had purpose. Watching the unfolding scenery through the windows, he had tracked their route since leaving the safe house. He hadn't been told where their next location would be—a standard precaution—but judging by the terrain they passed, he guessed Simon intended to keep Mirie blanketed within the anonymity of the masses in a highly urban area. A solid plan.

But Drew had been considering other possibilities. Mirie would not yield her position, and Simon would simply proceed around her under the guise of security.

Neither really had a choice.

Their loyalties placed them at loggerheads. Mirie's primary concern remained the effect on her people, while Simon's goal was putting an end to the threat as fast as possible, regardless of the cost.

Drew checked his watch for the time.

ETA, four minutes.

Stealing a glance at Mirie, he found her watching him, eyes wide, expression unsure. He had surprised her. And she had surprised him. He hadn't been convinced she would jump on the chance he offered. Not when it meant taking off with him.

A week ago she had believed in him without question. Now, not only was the truth between them, but he hadn't earned any points these past two days by allowing Simon to attempt to coerce her compliance.

But the sight of her now soothed away all his rough edges. She looked unsure, but resolute. She had agreed to trust him for the moment. He would provide the opportunity she wanted to publically disprove Vadim's claim while staying a step ahead of Simon, who wouldn't miss the chance to keep laying his trail to draw out the trafficker.

And Drew would keep her alive. That was his area of expertise, the one area where Simon's resources would not give him the advantage.

ETA, three minutes.

Mirie eyed him curiously, her lovely face pale above the dark wool of her coat. There were smudges beneath her eyes, but she was healing well, according to the physician. Still, Drew could tell she was fragile from her injuries. He noticed the effects: the low energy level, the discomfort that made it difficult to move, difficult to sit.

He had factored her health into his plan.

Her injuries were a ticking time bomb. She would need care for the stitches, and he couldn't take her to any kind of medical facility. Anyone looking at her would recognize the gunshot wounds and be required by law to file a report.

ETA, two minutes.

Their gazes met across the distance, and she searched his face for something—some hint of the man she had thought she knew, maybe. Or some reassurance that together they could accomplish what she wanted. Maybe both.

Drew couldn't say. He got lost in the connection between them, her beautiful face, the knowledge that they were on borrowed time. He had taken the past fifteen years for granted. Always having her in sight. Never thinking about the day when he finally looked around and she wasn't there.

He damned sure wasn't going to waste one more second of the time they had left together.

ETA, one minute and counting...

She was worried. He could see it in the tight lines around her mouth. A week ago she would have trusted the details to him without thought, trusting that he would brief her about whatever she needed to know. He no longer had her faith.

That was what he intended to correct.

Mirie had to know that whether he was a Romanian close-protection guard or an American operative, he cared for her.

The car came to a stop.

"Just wait here," he said and smiled, hoping to reassure her, even a little.

He could feel her gaze on him as he signaled to the driver to unlock the door. Then he exited the car and assessed the situation.

The car had brought them inside a parking garage. Drew marked the perimeter team, posted inside and outside the doors to the building, behind the car at the garage entrance. He wasn't surprised the place had steel performance doors that would drop fast for maximum security.

No problem. He'd anticipated containment. Excelsior wouldn't risk satellites catching sight of Mirie as they moved her. But so far, so good. This wasn't a private garage, but a basement facility, which told Drew the safe house was the building above, rather than a residential house.

That was a stroke of good luck.

Marking the surveillance cameras, he circled the car as the driver opened the door to get out, leaving the engine idling.

Everything was standard procedure.

Drew grabbed the door and held it. "Everything checks?"

"Affirmative," the driver replied. "The director said to tell you he wouldn't arrive until this afternoon."

Drew nodded. That was actually sooner than anticipated.

"I'll get her," Drew said, waiting until the driver

cleared the door before stepping around the door himself as if about to let Mirie out.

He slid into the driver's seat instead.

Drew had the door shut and locked and the car in gear before the driver pulled his sidearm.

He gunned the engine. "Get down," he yelled to Mirie.

The driver and perimeter team would target him, trying to stop him before he got away. But Drew didn't want to risk Mirie's life. Bulletproof vehicles and standard procedures weren't guarantees that accidents wouldn't happen.

Mirie knew the drill. They were a team. He sensed rather than saw her comply, didn't glance in the rearview mirror. He was too busy gauging the best spot to steer the car through the descending steel door. Drew needed to catch it exactly where he could maximize the damage, and not get shot in the process.

He was counting on the commotion he caused with sending a commercial steel door into a busy street to create a diversion. The perimeter team would have to contain the situation. With any luck, some well-meaning bystander would call 911.

Drew always had egress. That was his job.

And he had been trained by the best.

The front end of the armored vehicle nailed the bottom of the garage door just as it was headlight high, and the crash reverberated through the empty parking garage, the screech of heavy metal as the door was torn from a pinning on one side.

Then Drew wheeled into the street. His timing had been perfect. He didn't think a shot had even been fired.

Accelerating as he headed toward the nearest cross street, he caught the light and wheeled onto a side street. He assessed the scene ahead of him, the cars lining both sides of the street, the pedestrian traffic. As he slowed to a coast to take another turn, he flipped on his phone's GPS, then shoved open the glass panel. "Are you all right?"

"Fine," Mirie shot back, and the resolve in her voice made him smile. "May I get up now?"

"Why don't you get comfortable down there? Settle in and hang on. You won't be there long, I promise."

He wasn't worried about flying bullets, but he didn't want her getting thrown around by the way he was driving. She couldn't afford to tear any stitches, lose any blood.

The car maneuvered easily, but it had tracking, which meant he had to ditch it fast. Simon would use their coordinates to track them, and it wouldn't take him long. Drew glanced at his GPS.

They were in downtown Philadelphia.

A damned shame, too, since they were surrounded by some of the nation's top airports. They could have gotten anywhere from here or Jersey or New York.

If they could have chanced getting on a plane. They couldn't. Not yet. Not until they got a few steps ahead of Simon.

Drew decided on his route and merged onto the highway, keeping his speed within five miles of the limit, doing everything in his power not to draw unnecessary attention.

He had about two or three more minutes in this car before he would find himself surrounded by flashing lights. He needed to make those minutes count.

"Nearest hospital," he said into his phone.

In seconds, his GPS flashed the nearest location. Two exits. Zero-point-three miles east.

Drew maneuvered through the traffic, kept his pace steady, prayed Simon wasn't standing in Command watching the blip that was this car on a monitor, anticipating Drew's next move.

Since he was operating in a tight situation—in a country he hadn't lived in for a while—Drew's options were limited, but he intended not to be predictable.

Steering off the exit, he assessed the surroundings when forced to kill time waiting for a light at a busy intersection. The traffic was horrific.

He saw the blue hospital sign in the distance, scanned the information for visitor parking by the emergency room. He would ditch the car here.

Hospital. His first unspoken message to Simon.

I'll take care of her.

Drew didn't feel bad. Let Simon chase him for a while. Simon would get what he needed to draw out the trafficker while he found out just how active his operative could be.

And if he didn't like it, which he wouldn't, then he could pursue a court martial, which he would.

After he had captured the trafficker, of course.

Drew was counting on it. And in that time, Mirie could do exactly what Simon wouldn't risk—obtain the information she needed to publicly expose Vadim for what he was: an imposter.

That was the plan, at least.

Drew drove up and down the aisles of parked cars, steering clear of the poles that housed security cameras, until he found what he was looking for.

"Perfect." He wheeled the car into an empty space and tossed the keys under the seat. Going rogue didn't mean he had to be inconsiderate.

Mirie was already on the seat and ready to slide out when he opened the door.

"Let's go," he said. "Do you have everything?"

She met his gaze, and those eyes that could look like a stormy sky sparkled. "Got everything."

She accepted his hand, and her fingers were warm and soft against his. In that instant, he memorized the way her hand fit perfectly within his. A casual touch that he had experienced untold times that suddenly had a finite end.

Helping her from the car, Drew didn't rush her

when she eased to her feet and stretched gingerly. Then he led her to a Jeep Wrangler.

She narrowed her gaze as she watched him make quick work of the door skin. "We're stealing a car?"

"We're stealing a Jeep." Which meant he didn't even have to pull the slim jim from his backpack. He pulled out the drill instead. "Get in."

A couple of well-placed holes and he used a screwdriver as the key. He had the engine running in under a minute.

"That was almost too easy," he said as he threw the gearshift into Reverse and wheeled out of the space.

The Jeep's soft top wouldn't protect them from flying bullets, but this vehicle would get them on the road fast, which was exactly what he wanted right now.

Simon could track a stolen vehicle, of course, but it would take him time. The vehicles in this lot belonged to visitors. The surveillance cameras were closer to the building. With luck, whoever owned this Jeep would be inside for a while. Emergency rooms weren't known for their quick turnaround times.

Exiting the hospital the opposite way he'd come, Drew drove down side streets to avoid the busy intersection. His GPS routed him to the next exit on the highway, still safer than sitting in traffic. Especially when he heard sirens in the distance. He was going to have to ditch his phone soon, too. But not yet. Not until he could dispose of it properly.

Simon would expect Drew to head north to New York City or south to Baltimore. He would also consider that Drew might try backtracking toward D.C., which would be the most obvious and unexpected route—like agent reverse psychology. But Simon wouldn't be sure because he didn't know yet what Drew's intentions were.

Simon would know that Drew was operating on limited resources—no passports or identification—which would restrict his and Mirie's movements in a way that Simon could anticipate.

"We can't stop until I get us ahead of my agency. Then we'll be able to rest for a while." He glanced at her so close beside him. "How are you holding up?"

"Fine." She tucked the drill neatly into the backpack and set it by her feet. "You always carry a drill?"

"I brought along a few things I thought we might need." Not enough, though. Not nearly enough.

"So, what is our plan?"

"I'm afraid it's not much of one," he admitted honestly. "Since I've been residing in your country for so long, I don't have access to all the usual resources. And for that I apologize, since you've been a very gracious host."

He shifted his gaze away from the road to gauge the effects of his words so far.

He wasn't the only one gauging. She met his gaze and said nothing, so he continued.

"The plan is to track down whatever you need to

disprove Vadim's paternity while staying one step ahead of my agency, so they can draw out the person who is funding this campaign against you. Since we don't have a lot of resources beyond a drill and a screwdriver and a few throwaway phones, we're going to make our way doing what we Americans call *roughing it*."

She surprised him by flashing a grin. "We'll be like Thelma and Louise."

Not hardly. He gave a snort. "Bonnie and Clyde, thank you."

"Who?"

He laughed, so grateful for a moment that felt almost normal between them. "You'll have to add that movie to your collection when you get home."

Or maybe he would send her a copy from prison. Surely Amazon could deliver to Briere.

She frowned. "Drew, I don't know what we need to disprove Vadim's paternity. I thought a DNA test would suffice."

Drew.

His name from her lips, for the very first time.

"Don't worry. The general and I have been working on it ever since Vadim showed up. I've got a few ideas."

She liked that, he could tell. Her expression softened around the edges as she stared at the road unfolding before them. She reached up to grab the oh-shit handle, and the tension seemed to flow out of her before his very eyes.

He'd known his idea would appeal to her. He knew this woman so well. He just hadn't known if she would trust him enough to come along for the ride. But here she was beside *him*.

A beautiful princess in a stolen Jeep on an American adventure.

He wished that was all this trip was.

"We're going to have to keep on the move, so you're going to have to promise me you'll tell me how you're feeling," Drew said. "No toughing it out if you feel ill or faint."

He knew this woman so well.

"It's really important, Your Royal Highness. We have to be transparent with each other." He tossed that word out, knowing she would like it. "I don't have the NRPG at my back, but I do have my agency after us, and possibly a trafficker after you. If you pass out in the middle of some situation I don't have control over, I can't effectively protect you."

And he could not live with himself if something happened to her, when he had lured her from the safety of Excelsior.

"Will you agree?"

She considered him for a moment, and then stared out at the cars clogging the highway ahead of them.

"If you promise to call me Mirie."

"I can do that," he said with a casualness he wasn't

close to feeling. "Your Royal Highness will draw attention around here."

She didn't reply, and they lapsed into silence. He glanced at his GPS and mentally calculated his route. If their luck held, he might be able to get them on a flight to the West Coast tomorrow.

He veered east at the next exit. They would take a little side trip through the park and pick the highway back up at the next exit. "How's your arm nowadays?"

"My arm?"

"You had a great rise ball." He held up his phone. "Think you can lob this into the river as we drive over the bridge?"

She glanced out the clear plastic skin covering the passenger door frame and grimaced. "Ah, no problem."

"Without tearing open any stitches?"

"Pah." She gave a snort. "That's a big river."

He didn't think Simon could trace his phone, but he wasn't taking any chances, which meant he needed to unload the phone before they got out of Philadelphia. If he did manage to track it, Drew didn't want to leave any clues to what direction they had taken. Let Simon think they were headed into Newark or Manhattan. Or better yet toward the Canadian border.

He pulled into the right lane and checked the mirrors for any sign of law enforcement. There were no boats passing beneath the bridge, so they were good. "Anytime."

She unfastened the plastic enough to give her leverage, and then she tossed the phone. It arced neatly over the railing and vanished from sight.

She settled into her seat and rested her head back with a smile. She looked pleased but tired. He hoped she might sleep, but didn't suggest it.

The silence stretched between them.

Once they had been able to pass time together without speaking, but everything felt different now.

He was the one to break first, his need to hear her voice too much to fight. "May I ask you a question, *Mirie?*"

She tilted her head to the side, eyeing him curiously.

"Why did you agree to come with me?"

She didn't answer right away, and he wondered what she was thinking, if she was concerned about sharing her truths when she had placed her life in his hands. Again.

"In her letter, Bunică told me I should trust you no matter what," she finally said. "That you would always have my safety as your priority."

Drew only inclined his head. There was nothing he could say that would change the fact that he had deceived her with his identity for all these years. No words would reassure her.

She trusted her nanny and Oskar, and maybe even

Drew's actions of the past, enough to take another chance on him.

Drew understood, and vowed that by the time they parted ways, she would have no more questions about his trustworthiness. She would know that every second of every day of every year they were together had been real.

Because Simon had been dead wrong. Drew had not bought his cover. What he felt for this woman was the absolute real deal.

CHAPTER FIFTEEN

MIRIE STOOD IN the shadow of Drew's broad shoulders as they waited for servers to prepare the order. He protected her from jostling by the fast-moving patrons and the line for service that snaked back from the counter past the merchandise displays.

This coffee shop was not the sort of sleepy café in Briere's city square, where people lingered during long mornings with their friends. And yet it was familiar with its rich smells and laughter. A high-energy version, she decided.

She had begun to feel the effects of her injuries after Drew dragged her into a huge compound called a mall. He had brought her into this café called Starbucks, where they would refresh themselves with coffee and sandwiches while he set up his new laptop computer.

"I need the public Wi-Fi to transfer funds," he explained.

Apparently, money was the one problem they did not have.

"I've been drawing two paychecks for fifteen years," he told her in English. "But I haven't really spent much. I haven't really needed to, since you've been covering my expenses."

Mirie considered that, thought it said a lot about his life, which had been as confined as hers. "You can access your account without your agency finding out?"

"I can." He didn't elaborate.

"If you're rich, you can make a donation to the royal treasury. I'll put it to very good use."

That made him smile, and humor sparkled in his eyes. "Let's see what's left over after we get through with this trip."

"I'm not sure how costly our expenses can be." She lowered her voice to a whisper. "We're helping ourselves to things that belong to others more than we're paying for them."

"Only *certain* things. And only when we have absolutely no other choice."

Mirie understood, as much as she disliked that her needs had placed them in a situation where they had no choice but to take advantage of others. Still, her worry was tempered by an undercurrent of anticipation as she accepted her cup and followed Drew to a table. She wasn't sure whether she was feeling the effect of nerves or excitement or a strange mix of the two.

A week ago, as they prepared for the talks, she could never have imagined so much would happen in such a short span of time. Here she was in an

American coffee shop with a man who was a familiar stranger, wearing a scarf around her head as a disguise, and asking for God's forgiveness for stealing from others.

Her life had taken a very unexpected turn, and now that the shock and fear and despair were clearing away, she accepted that the situation had changed only because it was meant to.

She remembered what the archbishop always said when life seemed to present more problems than solutions.

We haven't found the right solution, and God is leading us off in a new direction.

But had she made the right choice coming with Drew?

She considered her options while accepting the tray with sandwiches and following Drew to a table in a corner by a window, where he could sit with his back to the wall and see everyone in the café and the mall beyond with minimum effort. He seemed more interested in opening his laptop than anything else right now.

Removing the sandwich packaging and the little meals in tiny boxes, she disposed of the wrapping, earning a scowl when she left their table to throw the wrappers in the trash.

He opened his mouth to scold her. "Your Roy—"

She scolded him back with a stern glance.

"*Mirie,* eat your meal. You'll feel better." He

smiled, and she couldn't decide what she liked more—the way his smile transformed his expression or the way her name sounded in his throaty voice.

She sipped her coffee and watched him work. He slanted a gaze toward the street entrance every time the door opened. Periodically, he would look away from the screen to scan the tables around them, and Mirie had no doubt if she asked him for details about the other patrons, he would be able to describe exactly who sat around them.

He behaved as he always had, only now she understood the genius of his masquerade. She had never questioned him or his actions because he had been hired to do exactly what he did. Yet through her, he had gained access to everything that was going on in Ninsele. And by invitation. It spoke to the size and resources of the United States. To pay an employee for so many years to honor the request of an old man....

Mirie supposed she understood why the director expected her cooperation in return now.

Had she been wrong not to give it?

That thought troubled her as she watched people come and go. The life she witnessed in the mall, in this coffee shop, was not so very different from life in Ninsele.

Perhaps that explained her nervous excitement. Mirie had not been in public for so long. She had been confined to her home, hadn't interacted with anyone but those cleared to enter her world. And there hadn't been many of those. They only came for state-related events. Meetings. Conferences. Balls.

She got out for church on Sundays, but, of course, she was a target there because of the predictability of the Mass schedule and her attendance. Many people came with the hope of catching a glimpse of her, but she was never able to visit with anyone for long before she'd be whisked out under heavy surveillance.

She considered what Bunică had written. Had Mirie been squandering the gift of her life? The concern felt very real in this place where friends talked and laughed together, in couples and in groups, around tables or gathered on sofas and chairs.

Mirie had already finished her sandwich by the time Drew finally glanced away from the laptop. He reached for his coffee, which was surely cold by now.

"Did you get everything taken care of?" she asked.

He nodded, swallowing appreciatively. "We just have to do a money transfer, then we'll be done with our errands. We can work on finding a place to sleep tonight."

Drew had planned their day well. There was a store with a wire service within walking distance of the mall, and after receiving his funds, he led her through the aisles to purchase another backpack and water bottles and protein bars to fill it.

"We're not taking the car?" she asked when he led her to a bus stop and handed her some bills.

"No. Best to leave it where it is. The police will eventually recover it and return it to the owners."

The thought made her feel a little better. There had been a security vehicle that drove around the enormous parking lot, which would keep the car safe until someone noticed it sitting there. Or until the director of Drew's agency discovered where it was.

Drew hadn't said as much, but Mirie knew the concern prompted his every decision, which was why after the first short bus ride, she found herself on a big bus bound for Charlotte.

He led her to the very back. The seat was shorter than the rest, but he sat on the outside, which afforded him a view of the entire interior. There was an emergency exit beside him.

Their seat created a cocoon for the two of them as the bus roared to life and the lighting dimmed.

"Why would you do this?" she finally asked, unable to contain her curiosity any longer. She had gone over the series of events again and again, yet was still no closer to understanding. And she needed to know, needed to hear him explain. "You will be a traitor to your government for helping me escape. You may be executed."

He rested his head back against the seat, which tilted the hat he wore at an odd angle. "Prosecuted, but probably not executed."

Mirie searched his gaze for the truth. "Why would

you risk so much, so I can protect my people from an imposter?"

Something about her question made him smile. Just the tiniest hint around his mouth. "My agency wants the trafficker caught. Period. It'll take the most direct route to accomplish mission objective, and it won't risk tipping him off by investigating Vadim. It won't risk your life, either, if it can help it. It's willing to use you as bait, but it needs you safe, otherwise it'll risk exposing our agency. Its hands are tied."

Everything he said made perfect sense. As a head of state she operated by a stricter set of rules. But she wasn't worried about her safety. Not with Drew.

"I'm willing to take the risk. But you know the situation. There's so much unrest already. We need to expose Vadim as a liar fast. *Before* he gathers more supporters and leaves people feeling betrayed and even more unsettled. Do you think it's possible?"

"I don't know. I'm not going to lie. But if the trafficker discovers we're trying to blow Vadim's cover then we'll lure him out that much faster. He's not going to sit back and let us expose his only hope of controlling the throne. If he thinks we're acting alone—which he will because he knows the United States would never risk your life by conducting this investigation—then he'll also think he's that much safer to come after you. With some luck, we'll all get what we want."

Mirie tried to read his expression. He seemed so

eager to prove himself. Or was her heart playing tricks? She had nothing to go by but the way she felt.

Trust Drei....

But he wasn't Drei. He was a man named Drew who worked for Americans, who wanted something in return for the help they'd given to Ninsele. And now he risked his future to help her.

Had she been wrong not to cooperate with Drew's boss? This country had helped Oskar when he had asked. Without Drew she would have been dead in an airport in Briere. Or a churchyard in Alba Luncă. Who knew how many other times?

"I don't want you to be in trouble for me," she said.

He exhaled hard. "Why don't we worry about finding out what we need to know about Vadim and keeping you alive before we worry about me, too?"

She considered that, so aware of their closeness. She had only her feelings to guide her. And she sensed that there was much behind Drew's actions. She knew in her heart that allowing Vadim to progress his claim publicly was the wrong thing to do, just as she knew that there was more to Drew's feelings for her, so much more than he spoke aloud. No man would go to such lengths for her unless he really cared.

After she was finally able to see past her hurt about his deception and reason through her doubt, the part of her that knew him intimately knew that he cared for her.

"Okay, Drew. We'll only worry about right now."
One more decision made that she hoped would lead
them in the right direction. "So, why are we going
to Charlotte?"

To her surprise, he reached out and drew her
against him, so her head rested against his shoulder
and her face against his neck. She remembered the
way she had felt the last time she had lain against him
this way. Exhausted from pleasure. Her every breath
was filled with his scent, his strong arms protecting her from death threats and threats inside herself.

He rested his chin on top of her head and said, "So
you can get a good night's sleep."

WHITEFISH, MONTANA, WAS an American version of
Ninsele, Drew decided as he drove down into Flat-
head Valley, a place protected from the world by
the rugged Rocky Mountains. Close to the Canadian border and the lush forest and seven-mile-long
Whitefish Lake, he could understand why a Ninselan transplant might have settled in this small town
to rear her son.

"So what do you think?" Drew asked Mirie. "Look
like you expected?"

"These are mountains," Mirie said with a shrug.
"I was beginning to think America was one big,
ugly city."

"Charlotte wasn't ugly." His hometown may have
seemed like the most confining place on the planet

when he'd lived there, but maturity had done a lot to alter that impression.

He'd felt a sense of familiarity when they'd gotten off the bus, when he'd seen the tree-lined streets of downtown, when he knew a few miles northeast was a cloistered sixty acres the city had left untouched as it had grown, where his younger brother and his family lived. Just passing through Charlotte had felt like seeing an old friend again.

Mirie huffed in exasperation. "There were trees. I will concede that."

Drew tried to imagine seeing this country from her perspective. He couldn't. She was bound to Ninsele in a way he could never understand—a blood tie that went back generations. But he had witnessed the effect on her, believed she felt the responsibility of her people much more because she was the only one left in her family who could.

"The U.S. is not like your country," he said. "We've got all sorts of geography here. Think big. We've got mountains and prairies and oceans, white with foam."

She eyed him curiously. "I think I'd like to see your beaches. I've always enjoyed the water."

As a teen she and her friends had spent long summer days at the lake swimming, boating, fishing.

Drew didn't know if she'd ever visited any beaches with her family before their deaths, but some of the most gorgeous beaches in the world were within easy reach of Ninsele. She had never vacationed while he'd been with her.

"We don't have the Riviera or the coast of Dalmatia. But we've got great beaches. Very different depending on where you are. Tropical around Florida and the Gulf of Mexico. Pacific beaches along the West Coast. Then there's Hawaii. That's a chain of volcanic islands. Completely amazing. My family used to spend long weekends on the Atlantic while I was growing up. Charlotte's within driving distance of the coast."

She tilted her head toward him and eyed him ruefully. "I'm sorry we couldn't take the time to visit your family. It seems like such a shame since we were so close. I would have liked to meet your brother and see your family home."

"Stopping there was a diversion. My agency knows where I'm from, so once they track us there, they'll keep a watch on my brother until they realize we never stopped. Then they'll look for how we left Charlotte."

Once Simon realized they had gone across the country, the playing field would be leveled considerably. Drew would have a hard time staying a step ahead in a town the size of Whitefish when Simon would know exactly why they had come here.

He just needed to find something concrete to send back to Command, something to cue Simon that there might be an advantage for him to sit back and let his operative assume all the risk.

"I still would have liked to meet him," Mirie said.

Drew understood. He wanted to be the one beside her as she discovered whether she preferred the white sands of Florida's Panhandle or the whaling towns in Maine.

They'd had fifteen years, and now, when the clock was ticking on their final moments together, he suddenly wanted more time, a lifetime of more time.

Did Mirie want more, too? Did she want more than to find her proof and return home?

"Yeah, well, I know my brother would like you. It would be a thrill to meet a princess. He doesn't travel much."

"Does he look a lot like you?"

Drew shrugged. "Looks like me, maybe, but we're nothing alike. He's the steady, responsible brother. The one who hung around to take care of all the family old folks."

Drew had never valued family the way he should have. Not until he had spent so many years away from everyone. By then they were all dead. He wondered what Mirie would think. She hadn't gotten much of a chance to be with her family.

"I can't imagine anyone more steady and responsible than you, Drew. Or more committed. You've been watching out for me more than half my life."

He gave a snort of laughter. "Tell you what, I promise I'll bring you by on your next visit to the States."

But there wouldn't be a next visit. Mirie would go back to being a captive in her palace.

And he would go to a federal penitentiary.

Their time was up. Maybe she would make a diplomatic visit to the capital somewhere down the road when she finally accomplished all she wanted to do for her country.

Reality plunged them into sober silence. And in that silence all he could think about was taking her to the beach, watching her kick along in the surf, listening to her tiny gasps as she found some unique shell or another.

"Let's go over our cover," he said in an effort to redirect his thoughts.

"My name is Irina Boroi. I'm Ileana Vadim's niece. You're my husband. I've come to Whitefish to track down my cousin and find out more about my aunt's death. I want to see her grave." She smiled. "I even have photo identification to prove who I am. My newly altered Ninselan ID."

He had been the one to do the altering. "Excellent. I've told you everything the general and I found out. I'm sorry we don't have more to go on. Everything we came up with seems to point to the fact that Luca Vadim is who he says he is."

"Except for his lies about my father."

Drew nodded. "Birth certificate issued in Maryland says father unknown. Let me ask you a hard question."

She nodded, unfazed, used to hard questions.

"Every time someone has tried to make a claim for the throne, you've said the very same thing—no way. Have you considered that people change as they age, and not one of us is perfect?"

Drew was thinking about himself just then, thinking about how the years had changed his perspective, how he had learned to value life as he watched Mirie give up bits and pieces of hers.

"I have. And if that was a mistake my father made, then I will need to come to terms with the fact that he was not perfect. But these opportunists must first prove my blood runs in their veins."

"How would you feel if you had a half sibling?"

As the town came into view, she said, "I know what you're asking, and I don't know how I would feel to learn I had family when I've lived so long alone."

She stared out at the long stretch of buildings that appeared in the valley. "I think, above all, I would be surprised. If my father didn't honor his marriage vows, it would go against everything I know about him."

She turned to Drew, and he took his eyes off the road to meet her gaze.

"He taught us to act with honor, and even more

importantly, to act with love. If he had strayed from his honor, for whatever reason, he would have owned the mistake. He would never have left a child of his to remain hidden from their identity, to not know the love of family, to feel shamed over a birth that was in no part their fault. That was not the father I knew. You could argue that I was only eight years old, a much-loved princess whose views are colored by immaturity and loss. But I listened to my father barter his life for his family's."

Her smile was so bittersweet that Drew had reached out and slipped his hand over hers before he realized what he was doing.

She glanced down wistfully at their clasped hands. "He used to tell me how he wooed my mother. He saw her at a ball, and she looked like an angel. But she was a Belgian princess and her parents favored a prince from the Netherlands, so she would remain close to them. He fought for her and won her heart. He loved her. He loved us. That is my truth, Drew. I will accept what is proven to me, but I will not leave my people vulnerable to a man who must bribe others to prove his truth."

Then she sighed softly. "I always wished I would find someone who loved me as much as my father loved my mother."

Drew wondered how she would feel to know that much love was already hers. From a man who could never be hers for more than a stolen moment, a man who would never be worthy, a man who would never reveal how he loved her, and had for so, so long.

MIRIE WAS EXHAUSTED and discouraged. She and Drew had spent all morning researching Ileana and Luca Vadim's lives at the library. Old newspaper clippings. Public records. Real estate records. Archived sporting events at local schools.

She had fought the director for the right to prove Vadim to be an imposter. She had insisted he investigate Vadim's claim if he wanted her cooperation to lure out the trafficker. And he had agreed, but only on his time frame, which she believed was high-handed and unaccommodating and essentially useless to her because she needed to go public *now*, before more unrest was caused, before the media seized on her absence to foster more doubt and fear.

If the director wanted her help, then he should be willing to offer his help in return—on her time frame to avoid the damaging effects on the hard-won peace of her people.

But what Mirie hadn't realized until this morning was that the director's lack of cooperation probably stemmed from the fact that he'd known how hard it would be to disprove Vadim's claim, since the man was preparing to submit false DNA results. He had understood the challenges in a way Mirie hadn't, and he hadn't been willing to stall their operation and risk not catching the trafficker.

Drew had known, too. Mirie had no doubt at all about that. Every bit of information they currently had on Vadim and his mother had been the result of Drew's work with the general.

She'd been so naive. She'd heard the director's explanation, but hadn't understood what he meant.

In the library this morning, as she and Drew conducted their research, took notes and made photocopies, she came face-to-face with the enormity of the task before them.

"This is impossible," Mirie finally said, a whisper beneath her breath as the library was an open area and they sat only within a corner of the archival section.

He glanced away from the display of the film machine and frowned. "It's a long shot, I'll give you that, but not impossible. It only takes one piece of information to blow open an investigation. It just has to be the right piece."

He didn't say that searching for that one *right* piece among the growing tapestry of what they learned about Vadim's life was going to take time.

Time they didn't have.

Vadim was a grown man. He had lived a full life before arriving in Ninsele with his lies. He had apparently been quite a sportsman, which hardly seemed surprising given the man's fit appearance and the nature of life in Whitefish, Montana.

Skiing, snowmobiling, dogsledding and other

winter sports drew visitors here for the season. During the summer they arrived in droves to partake in hiking, camping, fishing, boating.

Vadim had made a living serving these tourists. He'd served as a youth ambassador for a local ski resort all throughout his high school years, showing visitors the best trails, arranging their visits to the slopes, providing instruction.

He left Whitefish to attend the University of Montana, then returned home with a law degree to take a job at the same resort, only in legal management. Likely, Vadim had returned home to be close to his mother, since he had resigned his position immediately after her death.

So what had turned a seemingly nice, normal young man into a fraud who would attempt to dethrone her?

That was the question they were left considering as they gathered their research together, all their highlighted clippings and stories and tidbits, and left the library.

"You're being impatient," Drew said as they made their way to the car. "We've only just started looking, and we've already turned up several pieces of new information."

"We have nothing I can take to the media, nothing that will counter the fraudulent DNA results Vadim is preparing to release."

"Not *yet*. But we've only just started looking."

But how long would they have to keep looking before his agency tracked them down? She watched how Drew scanned the parking lot as he opened the passenger's side of the car and held it while she slipped in, always watching, always looking for a threat, always protecting her.

She asked so much of this man, always had, only she had never known, never realized.

He handed her the folder, then shut her inside the car. She watched him circle the front, then slide into the seat beside her.

"What new pieces are you talking about?" she asked.

"I'm talking about Mrs. Vadim. The reason why she has been so tough to track down. The general and I looked into Luca Vadim's history, and he appears to be exactly who he says he is. But his mother is a different story. I blamed our resources in Ninsele, but Mrs. Vadim worked pretty hard to cover her tracks, using small tricks like creating a proprietorship to purchase her home and secure credit cards, so public records came up under the company name."

"What does that mean?" Mirie asked.

"Well, for starters, these kinds of tricks would have deterred most people from tracking her down during her son's early life. It's only become easier to find people because of all the public information on the internet."

"I wonder why she would have been in hiding?"

"My question exactly. Or from whom?"

Mirie frowned. "But how is that a helpful piece of information? It's just another question."

"Questions help us determine where to look next. That's how it works. Trust me." He smiled. "We've still got a few hours until school gets out. I say we run by the Vadims' place and see if we can talk with the person renting it. Maybe we'll come up with something good. I'd like to know more about the investigation into Vadim's mother's death."

His expression softened. He was trying to reassure her. "Then we can catch up with that teacher who gave that quote about Ileana's death to the newspaper, once school lets out. He sounds as if he knew the family well. We don't know what we'll turn up. That's the nature of investigating."

He turned to face her, smiling reassuringly. "You need to trust me on this. We came up with a lot this morning. We know who we need to talk with. Hopefully we'll shake loose some more information, so we can figure out our next step."

"What if there is no luck? What if we learn nothing?"

He watched her with a gaze that seemed to see right inside her, deep inside to all her anxious places.

Could he see her conflict about him? About all he risked for her sake? Did he understand how worried she was for him?

"That's called a dead end, Mirie, and it just means

we have to backtrack a few steps and look for a new direction," he explained softly. "It's a normal part of investigating."

"We're on a time limit, Drew. You know this. I've stalled by insisting on the third-party oversight for Vadim's DNA testing."

He nodded, but still his gaze searched her and his expression was soft. "But you did get that extra time. I've gotten us a little bit more by getting us to Whitefish. Let's not get ahead of ourselves or we might miss something important."

She sighed. "You're right."

"Of course I am," he teased. She could hear it in his tone, see it as humor flashed in his gaze. He wanted to lighten the moment. "So, let's agree to not waste any of our time worrying about things we can't control. We'll keep investigating until we shake loose the truth or until we can't investigate anymore. Every piece of information we find puts us closer to the truth. Try to remember that."

Did he understand that she might not be able to use her diplomatic connections to protect him from trouble for his efforts on her behalf?

If the trafficker was caught, she might have some influence with Drew's agency. But she was in America unofficially. She had no diplomatic protection. She could only remind the director she'd come to America in good faith and barter her help for some leniency toward Drew.

But only if the trafficker was caught.

And how likely was that when they hadn't found any connection to prove Vadim was even a fraud?

She was trying to let go of her fear, but her head raced with the problems and potential outcomes of all the things that might go wrong and defeat their efforts. With all that would be undone if Vadim tried to claim the throne. Six years of her hard work, and everyone around her, including Carol…

He must have recognized her struggle because he suddenly grinned, a fast change of expression that made her notice how closely they sat. "You just want this all to be over, so you can get rid of that wig."

He reached out to wrap a blond curl around his finger, still smiling.

While they had arranged their charter flight in Charlotte, Drew had dyed his hair to a rich brown in the bathroom of the private airfield, but he wouldn't let Mirie dye her own hair. Instead he had provided a wig of long blond curls that effectively masked her hair, along with a good portion of her face and upper body.

"You mock me," she said. Although she knew he was teasing, she appreciated his effort.

He shook his head. "I would never. Even if you didn't make such a glorious blonde."

She frowned, but her heart was pounding harder.

"You're one of those women who actually wears blond as well as your natural color," he continued, unfazed by her lack of response. "Not many do. But some wear it like they were born to be blonde. Scarlett Johansson for one. And Kate Hudson."

She knew exactly what he was doing, and tried to let herself be drawn in. "I had no idea you were so well versed in celebrity culture. Are these actresses you admire?"

He arched an eyebrow. "I thought you did."

"Me?"

"You watch their movies all the time."

"We've never watched a movie together."

He pulled a face. "All those nights when you wake up at one in the morning and can't sleep, remember?"

He guarded her at night as well as during the day, often taking the post outside her suite himself, his broad shoulders visible through the glass. But not always. Sometimes Drew assigned Jozsef or another guard to her detail, but neither of them would ever open the door to check on her at night.

Never once had she considered how her choices were his, how he might be watching over her shoulder all those late nights when she watched movies on the DVD player.

How did he feel about watching *Sherlock Holmes* a dozen times because she adored Robert Downey Jr. and Jude Law?

Did he cry with her when Kate Hudson sat in a closet with the kids who had just lost their parents in *Raising Helen*?

As she stared into his face, lost in those beautiful green eyes, she asked herself what kind of man would give up so much of himself for her, little things, big things, things she hadn't realized he had given up? What kind of man would risk everything to help her now?

And the only answer she could come up with was—

A man who cared.

CHAPTER SIXTEEN

THE TENANT RENTING Luca Vadim's family home turned out to be a single guy in his mid-twenties. One who didn't keep to a normal schedule, judging by the fact that they had obviously awakened him from a dead sleep even though it was one o'clock in the afternoon on a weekday.

Drew knew the second he saw the guy that their cover—pretending to be Vadim's family—wasn't going to work.

"Sorry to bother you, sir," he said, hoping the guy would tell them what they wanted just to get rid of them.

"My assistant and I are scouting this area and need some information. Would you mind answering a few questions?"

The tenant, whose name was Jesse Parmetier, stared at them with the creases of his pillow still imprinted on his cheek.

"Um, yeah. Sure." The guy ran a hand through his hair, standing the brown waves on end, and looked as if he would rather be anywhere than standing in the open doorway with the winter wind blowing on him in comfortable-looking, well-worn sweats.

Mirie surreptitiously peered past Jesse to get a glimpse of the interior. Homey, and not what one would expect from a man they already knew was single from the lease papers. And an outdoorsman by the muscular, weathered look of him.

Drew would bet money Jesse had rented the place furnished. So how many goodies had Vadim left behind?

Enough to warrant Drew breaking in?

Drew wouldn't rule out the option. Not yet, at any rate. "Our production company is producing a documentary about a year in the life of a family that gets fed up with the big city and gives up everything to relocate to Whitefish. Sort of a reality TV deal, only with actual reality."

Jesse blinked again and looked as if something had caught his attention enough to pull him from any lingering slumber. Even Mirie slanted a curious glance at Drew, clearly surprised. Drew shrugged. "We've got a lot of criteria to meet, and I've got to tell you that your place tops the list for an ideal location to shoot the series. And you can't beat the compensation. Not only will our network pay to relocate you to other digs for a year, but we've got a budget in place to get this property camera-ready. You take a vacation for a year—maybe to a fancy condo on the slopes or some place you won't have to shovel yourself out of all winter—and you come back to a completely remodeled homestead without ever spending a dime. We'll even pay to store your stuff. That sound like something you might be interested in? Interested enough to let us take a look around?"

Jesse ran a hand through his hair again, shifting his gaze between Drew and Mirie. "I mean, yeah, sounds like a killer deal. Except it's not my stuff. When were you looking to get in? Soon? Because I've got the place through the summer."

Drew feigned surprise. "You're not the owner?"

Jesse shook his head. "I rent, sir, and unless you want to relocate me, too, I won't be breaking my lease. Hard to find properties around here. There are all kinds of restrictions against vacation rentals in residential neighborhoods. I'm here for an internship with the forestry service, so I'm not making a lot of money. Those rentals are way out of my price range."

Maybe because the guy was still half-asleep or maybe because they were in Whitefish, Montana, Jesse provided more information than Drew had asked for, and without requesting the production company's name or identification. Very good luck. Or maybe having a beautiful woman beside him lent Drew credibility.

Jesse had noticed Mirie. With her big eyes and freckles and lean curves, what man could have kept his eyes off her? And every time Jesse's heavy-lidded gaze slid her way, Drew thought about planting his fist right in the guy's face.

Maybe it was the way Jesse had called him sir, as if he was around Mirie's age and Drew was from another generation. Maybe not. All Drew knew was that he wanted to use his fists to cross the ten years between Mirie and this lazy bum.

Resisting the urge to break the kid's pearly whites with his old-man fist, he made an attempt at evasion. "I can see why you wouldn't want to leave. Can't beat this place. We've scouted quite a few locations, and this one's prime."

"I lucked out," Jesse agreed.

The house was modest. Four bedrooms and two bathrooms according to the property assessment, situated on a six-acre lot. It sat up high enough on the bluff to overlook the state park across the road, which was a hub for recreational activities in the area.

Drew had guessed by the year the house had been constructed that Vadim's mother had purchased the lot and had the place built to her specs. Something about the European design with the turret-style bay windows and wooden stairs that wound from the porch. Add the remote location nestled in the mountains, complete with a barn and a fenced-in area where one could keep livestock.

Still, no one had built this place without a chunk of change, and Drew knew that an envoy working for the Ninselan honorary consulate thirty years ago wouldn't have drawn enough of a paycheck to manage the job. So he mentally added that question to his list of necessary answers. And it bugged him that it wasn't the first time he was asking the question.

Someone had coughed up seriously big bucks to make an assassination attempt in Alba Luncă.

Vadim himself had plunked down a nice chunk of change to buy a building in downtown Briere. Maybe the guy had been saving since he had gotten out of law school, but he wasn't all that much older than Mirie, and considering what student loans were nowadays... Drew found it hard to believe Vadim's Ninselan-envoy-turned-schoolteacher mother had funded his education without help or left behind a healthy estate.

Drew had already run Vadim's credit to find out if the guy had taken out a loan to buy the Danmark Building. No loan, and he hadn't won the lottery, either. So someone with money had footed the bills.

The *same* someone?

"Well, I'll see what we can do about relocating a tenant," Drew said to keep Jesse talking. "I can't promise anything until I speak with the network. Won't know until I ask and it all depends on whether or not the owner is willing."

Jesse glanced apologetically at Mirie. "I don't know how to get a hold of the guy. I've got his name on the lease, but I only met him a few times. He was going out of the country."

Drew flexed his fingers. "That's got to be tough if something needs to be done around the property. The place has a good few years on it."

Jesse shrugged. "I go to the neighbor. Plumbing went bust a month ago. Called up the lady, and she had the plumber here that afternoon."

"That does sound fast." Mirie flashed her most charming smile. "Which neighbor?"

"The lady with the kids the next house down." Jesse gestured to the left.

"Sounds like your landlord thought of everything."

Jesse nodded. "No complaints."

"So you like him?" she asked. The beautiful woman inside the princess had marked the scent of a man's interest.

Drew rocked back on his heels and unclenched his fist to feel the sidearm tucked in his waistband. He could always shoot Jesse in his pillow-dented face if he didn't stop leering. But only after Mirie had finished with him.

"Yeah, he seems okay. Only met him a couple of times."

"You said he was going out of the country. For work? I wonder what his wife thought about that."

A little obvious for an investigative technique, but Jesse didn't seem to notice.

"I don't think he was married. He told me this had been his mother's place. She died, and he didn't have the time to go through all of her stuff and put the house on the market. That's why he rented it to me. I didn't need the standard year lease."

Mirie's expression collapsed. "She died? Oh, how sad."

"Yeah. She couldn't have been that old. I think it must have been unexpected, too, because every time I met him there was an older guy with him. His father, I think. He seemed like moral support."

"They must have been divorced if he didn't live here with her," Mirie said, as if the breakup of any marriage was as much of a tragedy as an early death.

Jesse nodded eagerly. "That's what I thought, too. And he wasn't from anywhere even close because he had an accent."

"Really?" She feigned surprise, eyes wide and her mouth opening to form a perfect O.

Jesse noticed. "Yeah, weird one, too. Not like British or Australian or anything I recognized."

"How nice that he had his father with him during such a sad time. I wonder how she died."

"No clue." Jesse shrugged.

"But the whole situation will work to your benefit with the network if we can get the owner to agree to the house swap," Drew said, before this stupid bum realized Mirie was grilling him with an accent most people wouldn't recognize, either. "Tell you what, rather than waste your time touring the place, we'll get with the property owner and see if we can work out a deal."

Jesse eyed Mirie as if he wouldn't have minded giving her the tour. "Yeah, sure."

Drew separated Sleeping Beauty from Mirie and led her down the front steps to the rental car. He could sense her excitement as she walked beside him in silence, even though her face was hidden behind the fall of blond hair.

"And here I thought you didn't appreciate the nuances of covert operations," he said when they arrived at the car.

"Just another day in the palace." She waved a dismissive hand, but she was beaming. "Diplomacy is my specialty. More than anyone, you should know that."

He only gave a snort of laughter. "So that was you being diplomatic? Glad to hear it. I'd be shocked to find out you were actually encouraging Prince Ulrick's attention the way you just did that kid's."

She came to a sharp stop, blocking his access to the door handle. "Please." She gave a disgusted sniff. Drew laughed and reached around her. He shut the door after she slipped inside, and then went to the driver's side, using the time to transition to a conversation about something more relevant. "All it takes is the right piece of information to send us off exactly where we need to go. And thanks to your impressive performance, we've got more than one piece."

"He was helpful," she agreed. "So, who do you

think the older man with the accent was? We know he's not my father."

Drew slipped the car into gear and made a three-point turn, then headed down the long driveway.

"I don't have a clue, but I'm willing to bet the accent was Eastern European. Maybe even Ninselan, but he didn't recognize your accent. Of course, he was distracted by your smile."

That wiped away her smile quickly enough. "Drew, I was trying to distract him."

"Mission accomplished."

She narrowed her gaze. "Why do you think this person may be Eastern European or Ninselan?"

"The money." He ticked off the possibilities one at a time. "Suddenly, it's a big question again. I'm thinking it might be a connecting link. We've got a Ninselan envoy with enough money to bankroll that property. We've got two separate assassination attempts with pricey mercenaries and an RDD that did not come cheap. We've got Vadim with his expensive new office building in downtown Briere and enough power for someone important at the Forensic Medicine Institute to risk a career to manipulate test results. We've got someone who knows his way around Ninsele with the money to pay for what he wants."

Mirie cocked her head to the side. "So you think one person may be responsible for all these things?"

"It's definitely a possibility. I'm trying to figure out who might benefit enough to lay down some huge sums of cash. And how did Vadim's mother even find this place?"

"She was a Ninselan envoy," Mirie said. "This is exactly the sort of information the Ninselan honorary consulate would provide. I'm visiting America, so where should I go? I'd expect my consulate to have an answer."

"You're right, which brings up the next question—what was she hiding, or hiding from?"

"She wasn't hiding her illegitimate son from my father. If Vadim wasn't an imposter, why would he need fraudulent test results? Why would he wait all these years to stake his claim? I understand he might not have wanted to take on a country in the midst of a civil war, but I've been home for six years. And I'm not buying that he was performing a public service." She scoffed. "I wasn't assassinated, and he didn't leave."

"He went to Ninsele after his mother died. I would interpret that to mean she didn't want him to go."

"So we need to find out why."

"We need to find out who the older guy was with Vadim."

And they needed to get the information without Drew punching anyone or pulling his sidearm.

MIRIE REALIZED DREW was jealous. She had been able to sense his agitation while they were talking to the tenant, agitated enough to openly call her out on it now.

Yes, he was trying to cover his annoyance with his talk of his suspicions about their enemy, but she knew he hadn't liked the way she had smiled engagingly at Vadim's tenant, not quite flirting, but close enough to get the man to speak freely.

It surprised her that Drew had shown his agitation, even the tiniest bit. He was usually so contained. So controlled. She remembered what Helena had said about him spending his life watching a beautiful woman, yet Mirie had never before considered that he had to control himself.

Because he cared for her.

As she sat beside him during the short drive to the neighbor's, she tried to keep her thoughts on their investigation while everything inside her was coming to life with so many realizations about Drew. Actions she had never truly looked at before. Tiny cracks in his armor that allowed his feelings to leak out. All overlooked by her.

All of which pointed to a man who cared.

Mirie had been blindsided by the truth about his identity, by Oskar's having involved the Americans to keep her safe until she could reclaim the throne. But now when she sat so close to him, she could practically feel his stubborn resolve to rein in his responses. Perhaps loss of sleep had worn him down. Or perhaps it was she who had worn him down.

Was watching a beautiful woman different from watching a beautiful woman he had made love to?

Mirie felt a thrill at the thought. Such a greedy, hungry feeling that should shame her for torturing a man so.

Yet she felt only hope.

She wanted to be right, wanted to believe Drew cared about her so much that he was mourning the loss of their life together. For once they found their enemy, she would go home, and he would face the consequences of his choices.

He had already risked everything for her. Did she really need to hear him say the words?

Words, she now realized, that might not come easily for him. He was honor bound to protect her. Not only by his vow to Oskar, but by an oath to his country. And he was a man of deep commitment. She was ashamed that so many years had passed, and she had never thanked him for his commitment to her.

Did it really matter whether he had taken the job for money, or for loyalty to an old royal guard, or to honor a vow to his country, when the end result was that he had cared for her with his life for so many years?

No, she didn't need to hear Drew's words. She needed only to look at his actions and trust what she felt inside. Her heart knew he cared. Enough to give her his loyalty now no matter what the consequences to himself. The knowledge humbled her.

"This has to be it," he said, jarring her from her thoughts. "It's the *only* driveway. I've driven half a mile in each direction just to be sure."

Twisting around in her seat until she could fully face him, Mirie eagerly drank in the sight of him, always so focused and capable. How had she ever looked past him?

He was so weary. There was strain around his mouth, the chiseled jaw he clenched tight as he turned their car and drove through the open gate. His gaze shifting to her, then back to the road again, taking in everything in between.

Always wary. Always watching over her.

She loved him for that.

It was there in her heart. And had been for so long. She didn't question it anymore. That was why she had reached out to him for physical comfort in the cave. And maybe was also why she had taken him for granted for so long. Because to acknowledge her feelings would have meant acknowledging the fact that she could lose him, too, as she had lost all the others she had loved.

"Are you okay?" he asked, seeing everything in her face.

Always seeing everything. How could she have ever overlooked so much caring?

"I'm well, thank you."

He arched an eyebrow as though he didn't believe her.

She smiled, a smile that bloomed up from within her. So filled with gratitude was she in the face of such devoted concern that the feeling stole her breath. "I am well. I promise."

And she was. She had never been alone because Drew had always been there, always cared. Somewhere inside, she had always known that.

And the knowledge was bittersweet as life tended to be. He had always cared for her and only now did she possess the clarity to see the truth. Only now, when they spent their last days together, had she come to feel the love that had always surrounded her.

Maybe Mirie was not so well, after all.

"We'll stick with our original cover this time," Drew said. "We'll try to, anyway. I'll know what to say once we see this lady. Just follow my lead."

"Are you not concerned this woman will tell the tenant?" she asked him.

"Sleeping Beauty already went back to bed," he scoffed. "We won't tell her we spoke to Vadim's tenant. Got it?"

Sleeping Beauty. She bit back a smile and nodded.

And then they were knocking on the neighbor's door, and Mirie had no time to dwell on anything but remembering her cover story because it turned out that Elizabeth Van Brocklin had been a very close friend of Ileana Vadim's.

"Her niece?" Elizabeth stood in the doorway, shocked. Then in an instant, her expression trans-

formed into a warm welcome, and they were ush-
ered into the sturdy log house.

The first thing Mirie noticed about Elizabeth Van
Brocklin was that she laughed easily. With her blond
hair and warm eyes, she maneuvered them through
the foyer and hallway of a house filled with family
life. Helmets were sitting on the bench inside the
door. Coats haphazardly hung from a rack, camouflage beside bright pink wool. Ice skates and hockey
sticks were strewn about, and the smell of something
baking filled the air.

"Drop your coats here, and go get warm by the
fire. Let me get you something to drink. Coffee?
Cocoa?"

"No need to trouble yourself," Drew said.

But Elizabeth wouldn't take no for an answer, and
within minutes they were all seated in the living
room in front of the fireplace, sipping hot chocolate
with marshmallows that floated on top, chatting as
if they had known each other all their lives.

"I don't know what we would have done without
Ileana after my husband was killed in Iraq. The kids
were still pretty little. Wyatt was in first grade and
Madison was a baby. I had been staying home with
them, but then I had to go back to work, of course."
She shook her head at the memory, and then gave
a dismissive nod. "But in the end it worked out the
way it always does. Luca had gone off to college, and
Ileana had empty-nest syndrome big-time. She knew

what it was like to raise a family alone. She was like a mother to me, and a grandmother to the kids. She came to everything—Wyatt's marches with the ROTC, Madison's kindergarten graduation, hockey games, birthday parties. We miss her."

"We only just learned of her death," Drew said. "That's why we've come. To visit her grave and pay our respects."

"So Luca told you?" Elizabeth asked.

Drew just nodded, not a lie.

"I'm glad. I've been worried about him since he didn't have any family." Elizabeth chuckled. "I always thought she'd had some sort of falling out with her family. Maybe even over Luca, since she raised him alone and to my knowledge had never been married. But of course now I know why she never said anything."

"Oh." Mirie was unsure how to respond, and she couldn't look to Drew for a cue with Elizabeth staring directly at her.

"You mean Luca, right?" Drew said.

Elizabeth shook her head excitedly, and then set the mug down as if fearful she might spill it. "Trust me when I tell you that this is big news around here. Nothing exciting ever happens around here. Trees grow and snow falls. There are only six thousand year-round residents. Half the adults in Whitefish came through Ms. Vadim's AP history classes. Even Wyatt." She stopped and exhaled sharply, and her animated expression faded. "Well, not everyone. Madison won't get to."

Elizabeth reached for her mug and sipped, covering her sudden emotion with activity. There was no missing the glint in the woman's eyes.

Now Mirie knew what to say. "I'm so sorry for your loss. It hasn't been very long. Are you and your children managing?"

Elizabeth shrugged and gave a wry smile over the rim of her mug. "We're tough. Been there, done that. They called her Graneana. Madison has been waiting to have her as her teacher ever since kindergarten. She starts middle school this year, and would have finally been in Graneana's class. It was a really big deal. It's going to be a tough year."

"I know," Mirie said softly. Even losing Bunică, who had lived a long and full life, was difficult.

Drew reached over and took her hand. Mirie knew he was playing a role, but when their gazes met, she saw the understanding in his green eyes.

"Aunt Ileana's death was unexpected," he said.

Elizabeth exhaled in disgust. "She was just crossing the street in town like she had done a thousand times before."

Drew didn't say anything, just waited.

"She always parked on the street. Unless she was biking the trail. Then she would park in unlimited parking by the train depot. But when she was just going to the bank and running errands, she parked on the street. She loved to walk." Elizabeth chuckled, a watery sound. "She used to say that parallel parking on the street made her feel as if she was back in a city."

"I'm so sorry." Elizabeth set her mug back on the coffee table. "This is your loss, too. Hit and run. Things like this don't happen in Whitefish. Well, accidents happen—" she corrected herself "—on the slopes. But people go out of their way to help each other around here. What kind of person hits someone, then takes off? It makes me so angry even thinking about it."

"They haven't found the driver yet?" Drew asked. "We're still a little sketchy on what happened. We've been emailing with Luca since his return, but he hasn't gone into detail."

"We only heard of her death from some cousins from the city after Luca came to town," Mirie added. "My mother married a Romanian engineer, so I was reared in Bucharest. We traveled to my mother's home every year. Or we did while I was growing up."

"I'm so sorry. But they haven't found the person who did it. Chief Steve absolutely refuses to close the case. He was one of Ileana's students and has made it his quest to bring the driver to justice. Such a tragic waste. Your aunt was a beautiful woman. So many people loved her."

"That in itself is a blessing." Mirie smiled. "My mother feels such sorrow to lose her, but she will feel relief knowing how much her sister was loved here. After my aunt left Ninsele, she never returned home. My mother always hoped to make this trip herself. That is why we have come. My husband was making a trip to the States for his job, so I came to pay our family's respects. I will place branches on Aunt Ileana's grave and sing her our burial song, so my mother may be at peace."

Elizabeth's expression transformed. "Oh, that is so beautiful. I can't wait to tell the kids. Madison still makes things for Graneana's grave. Flower arrangements, drawings and that sort of thing. That's our American tradition."

"What a lovely tradition," Mirie said with a smile.

"So you mentioned that you emailed with Luca?" Elizabeth asked. "I've been wondering how he's doing. He and Ileana were so close. I told him I'd deal with the house, no problem. He's got a renter in there now. Seems to be keeping the place up."

"As far as we know, he's doing all right," Drew said. "But with everything going on, he hasn't been responding to our emails regularly."

"Yeah, same here. That's why we've been following what's been going on in the media. The news doesn't cover it, but we can find stuff online. And it's been cathartic for the kids. We've lost Graneana, but we have this new part of her now. How many people can say they lived next door to a hidden prince?"

Luca of Whitefish, indeed.

Mirie forced a smile. "Not many. That's for sure."

"I didn't know she was from Ninsele." Elizabeth laughed. "All these years we thought she was Romanian. But we've learned a lot. With the war and all the political problems, I can see why she kept Luca here. She must have lived in terror thinking someone would find out about him and come after him. I mean, look at the princess who had to hide for all those years after they killed off the royal family. I guess she'll be Luca's family now. At least he'll have someone."

Mirie bristled inside. Lies and sorrow and love. What turmoil she felt. Why, oh why, would a man with such a loving mother who seemed to have cared so much for his safety and well-being go after the throne?

And was Ileana protecting Luca from someone? Is that why she came to Whitefish and never returned home?

Elizabeth's assumptions about Luca's identity made sense. Except for the question of who she might have wanted to hide her son from—*not* Mirie's father, not even if he hadn't been dead all these years.

Drew asked, "Did Luca know about his father?"

Elizabeth shrugged. "No clue. But I wondered about that myself. Ileana never once mentioned Luca's father. I could never figure out that part, and she was so closed about it, I would never have asked.

mean, she never dated, not even after Luca went off to college. But Luca must have known. Why else would he wait until she died to let everyone know who he was?"

"Who was Rob Champion?" Drew asked.

Mirie recognized the name as the man who had given the quote in the newspaper. A coworker of Ileana's.

"Oh, poor Rob. He's not doing so well," Elizabeth said, looking concerned. "In fact, the kids and I had him over for a bonfire on New Year's Eve. Poor guy. He must have lost twenty pounds since the funeral, and he was not a big guy to begin with. He was a teacher. Ileana got him a job at her school."

Drew looked at Mirie, the warning in his eyes cautioning her before he even opened his mouth. "That must be the man that Luca was with." He turned to Elizabeth. "When we got to town, we only had Aunt Ileana's address, so we went there. That's how we knew Luca had rented out her place, and about you. Jesse told us that Luca had an older man with him when he showed him the house. Must have been this Rob."

Elizabeth shook her head. "Rob is Luca's age. They're best friends. Ileana was like a mother to him, since Rob's life at home hasn't been easy. If it wasn't for Ileana, I don't think he would have made it through high school, let alone college. He even went into teaching because she had such an impact on him."

"How wonderful that she was able to help," Mirie said.

"Absolutely," Elizabeth said. "I don't know who the man was with Luca. I actually thought he might have been Luca's father when I first saw him, but that was before I found out who Luca really was and learned his father had died a long time ago."

Mirie didn't even get a chance to process that Elizabeth was referring to Mirie's father before Drew zeroed in on what was actually important.

"You saw him?" he asked, then turned to Mirie. "You don't think it was old Uncle Georghe, do you?"

"Maybe. You did think he was Luca's relation." Mirie hoped that was the right thing to say.

"I thought so. He was tall, like Luca. And something about his features seemed familiar. I might have been imagining it, though. His mom was the only family he had. Or so I thought."

"What did he look like?" Drew asked.

"Gray hair." She paused to consider, grimaced. "I really don't remember. Do you want to see him? I can show you."

"You have a photo?" Drew asked.

"Video, actually. Entirely unintentional. Luca brought him to the house the day Wyatt took his birthday present out for its very first spin. We ride the same trails that Luca did growing up, and this was the first birthday my kids could remember that Graneana wasn't here to celebrate with them. Wyatt wanted to include her, so off we went to the bluff overlooking her house. I videoed, of course. I video everything. Never even noticed I got Luca in the video until I uploaded everything to Flickr."

"Sounds like your son received quite a birthday gift," Drew said.

Elizabeth shook her head. "Oh, you're not kidding. A brand-spanking-new Arctic Cat. He's in high school now. Couldn't have been more perfect. And getting Luca in the video… Well, it was kind of like Graneana being there, too."

Mirie's heart started to race as Elizabeth shifted around on the sofa and withdrew a smartphone from the holster. Drew's face revealed nothing, but she could feel him tense beside her.

"Okay, here it is." She rolled her eyes. *Finally.* I'm such a train wreck. I take photos and videos of everything, then never erase them. I've easily got two thousand photos on this phone. It's a wonder it doesn't blow up."

She finally found what she was looking for, and held up the phone to reveal the wintry white landscape and her bundled son racing along on a snowmobile. She paused the video and expanded the image, then handed the phone to Drew.

"Is that crazy Uncle Georghe?"

There was Luca Vadim in the distant shot, walking

up the stairs to his mother's house with an older man beside him, a man Mirie did not recognize. He had been handsome once. Roguishly so, with his wavy thick hair and rugged features. He might even be considered handsome now but for the hardness about him. This was a powerful man. A man used to giving commands and expecting to have them followed.

A man who would not look kindly upon any delay.

Even Luca Vadim struck her as being overshadowed by the other man. Maybe it was the way he seemed to hang a step behind his companion that suggested reluctance? Mirie wasn't sure, but she did agree with Elizabeth. There was something about the man's features that seemed similar to Vadim's.

CHAPTER SEVENTEEN

DREW WAITED IMPATIENTLY as Mirie lingered over her goodbye, thanking their host for the generous hospitality, the warm welcome. She played her role conscientiously, careful to honor the memory of a woman who had been loved by this family, even though Mirie had never met Ileana Vadim and would likely never see her neighbor again.

He didn't mention that if Elizabeth went and spoke with her neighbor, Jesse, she'd probably hear his story about the reality TV show. Hopefully she wouldn't put two and two together and realize they'd been played. Fingers crossed. There was no point in worrying about something they couldn't change now.

This was Mirie. Drew might put a wig on her and call her by a different name, but he would never erase her concern for others, a quality so inherent to her. She cared. That was who she was. Plain and simple.

Was it any wonder he had been in love with her for so long? Despite circumstances, age and honor?

Drew only knew as he watched her with Elizabeth that Mirie could make anyone feel as if they were the most important person in the world. That was one of her gifts.

He also knew she had not realized that they'd found what they were looking for in Elizabeth's video—the *right* information.

How many hours had he and General Bogdanovich followed leads that led to dead ends? How many sleepless nights had they spent investigating the attempts against Mirie's life? How much of the NRPG's limited resources had been diverted to investigate Vadim, one of a number of opportunists through the years who had tried to lay claim to the throne to seize power of a frail Ninsele?

Mirie finally hugged the woman, wished her children well and turned toward the door.

Drew didn't say a word, afraid the two women would strike up the conversation again. So he slipped a hand onto Mirie's elbow and led her down the stairs. She looked thoughtful as they walked to the car, and she turned to wave at Elizabeth, who stood watching them from the doorway.

He got her in the car. "I can't believe that with all the work the general and I have done since the funeral we found the information we needed in the living room of a chatty soccer mom."

Mirie gasped. "You recognized that man with Vadim?"

"I've only seen a grainy surveillance shot of him, one of the very few images circulating. The general first briefed us when you came back to Briere. I'm positive it's a man named Victor Mondragon."

She frowned, clearly not recognizing the name. "Have I ever been briefed about him?"

"Mondragon is a thug who works the black market. He's on our NRPG watch list of traffickers known to have been working our borders. We've never picked up any of his people or any shipments. Or if we have, we haven't connected them back to Mondragon. Not such a surprise if he's grown his organization enough to access radioactive material."

Our watch list. *Our* borders. *We.*

This isn't your life, even if it feels like it is.

Mirie watched him intently, waiting for him to continue, and his only salvation was keeping his eyes on the road to maneuver the curves as he drove back into town. "Given what my agency is looking for, I'd be willing to bet money that if you succeed in putting a stabilization plan in place with the EC, you'll shut down one of Mondragon's primary trade routes."

She let her eyes flutter shut and left him wrestling with his own mix of conflicting emotions.

"Why else would this guy, Mondragon, be with Luca Vadim unless he was backing his bid for the throne?"

Drew shrugged. "I can't answer that. I do know they both have connections to Ninsele. Mondragon through his trafficking and Vadim through his mother's residency. How they might have connected would be pure speculation on my part."

"What do you know about him?"

"Not enough. We only ran the list whenever the border patrols made arrests. He never came up except on that list. Probably because he had enough money to pay off whoever he wanted. If this guy is transporting nuclear materials through Ninsele, he's way out of the NRPG's league. With all the work you've been doing to purge the country of the people who can be bribed, I'd also bet he considers your continued rule a threat."

She inclined her head, putting the pieces together. "You think he was behind both attempts?"

"My agency was willing to pull in NATO because whoever this trafficker is has some powerful connections. The NRPG hasn't given anyone much of an opportunity to get close to you. But the minute you were out in the open, attempts were made on your life. Put visual evidence of Mondragon in Whitefish, and it's a safe bet."

"What do we do now?"

"I have to get this intel to my agency."

She gave him a disbelieving glance. "But, Drew, if you contact them, they'll know where we are."

"We need them to connect Vadim to Mondragon. They're the only ones who can. And they can do it fast. If they can make the connections, place Mondragon behind the RDD, behind the attempts on your life, behind Vadim's bid for the throne, then they'll be able to bring him in. Hopefully before Vadim goes public. But if Mondragon is brought in, we'll be able to connect him to Vadim, and discredit Vadim until the general finds out who he paid off in the Forensic Medicine Institute."

It was the only thing to do, the only plan of action that made any sense. "There's no way we can investigate Mondragon and connect him to everything he might be involved in. We only know about two assassination attempts in Ninsele and a connection to Vadim. I promise you my agency will have more information."

"No doubt." She exhaled a sharp breath, and then turned to stare straight out the windshield.

They fell into silence. Thoughts churned in Drew's head, a jumbled mix of ways to quickly make contact with Simon, and all the possible ways they could be hauled back into Command, the ways he could be torn from Mirie. Would he even see her again before she was flown out of the United States and he was thrown in the brig?

"When will this end, Drew?"

"What?" he asked.

"The abuses against my country. Ninsele is recovering, yet still so frail, almost helpless against these terrible people. She needs the European Commission and global transparency. Others must conduct oversight until we rebuild our strength so no more terrible people with money can buy DNA testing. Or unhappy people can betray our country like terrorists to push their agendas. If not for you, I might not be alive right now. Yet after all this work, I have accomplished nothing."

She sounded so tired. She leaned back against the seat and rested her head on the headrest.

"Ninsele is on the cusp of a new era. Six years ago this would not have been possible." That was all he could say. She would dismiss any reminders of all she had done.

She needed time to heal, time to process everything that had gone on. Right now she was wounded, in a strange country with a man who wasn't the man she'd thought he was.

"Once my agency brings in this trafficker, another huge problem is out of the way. One by one the problems will be solved until Ninsele accedes to the EU and you can leave the royal compound without looking over your shoulder."

It wouldn't be him standing behind her, but some random close-protection guard. Not the man who loved her.

"There are no guarantees of that. Look at where we have just been. Tragedy cut a caring woman's life short. Elizabeth's husband was killed in a war. Yet they found each other and shared something special. I invited representatives from the EC to Ninsele for historic talks, yet we all almost wound up dead. Probably would be dead if not for you and your country. Vadim was not the first opportunist. He won't be the last."

Drew could not argue with any of what she said, but he suspected she was remembering Geta right now, her own unexpected gift during a time filled with so much terror and loss. Today had been another reminder of a lesson she already knew so well.

"I can't argue with any of that. But things can change just as fast for the good," he said. "Case in point—this visit. We got the information we needed. Not only will my agency be able to track down the trafficker who's been trying to assassinate you, but we've got something we can make public to discredit Vadim."

"When can we do this?"

"I've got to get this to my agency. I'm going to give them this information about Mondragon as a show of good faith."

"What are you going to ask for?"

"The information about whoever Mondragon and Vadim bribed in Forensic Medicine. That's the information to take public."

She gasped. "You're absolutely right. Do you think they'll give it to us?"

"Yes." Simon wasn't stupid. He had a princess to placate now. "But I need a public computer to cover our tracks."

He would send a coded email to his official address

with the NRPG. Simon would have been monitoring all transmissions since Drew had been reactivated.

Standard procedure.

He'd relay the information that he'd learned. Simon would hack into Elizabeth Van Brocklin's Flickr account and download the video that placed Vadim and Mondragon together.

When they got back to the library, Drew told Mirie, "Take our notebook computer and check out what's happening at home. The minute I send this information, my agency will be all over the IP address. They'll know we've been here, so you might as well take the chance to find out what you can. I know you're worried about what's going on."

The expression on her face nearly ripped the breath from his chest. So stoic, almost brittle, a woman who had faced so many difficulties and faced them all with that same sober expression, a mixture of determination, resignation and the peace of knowing whatever came her way, she would live through it.

Because she'd lived through so much worse.

And if she didn't survive this time… Well, she had no control over that, like so much else in her life.

He remembered her question from their drive and asked himself the same right now.

When would it end?

When would Mirie finally get a chance to balance her duty with living a real life?

Would she ever get that chance?

His only answer was that expression on her beautiful face.

MIRIE STARED AT the computer, staring at the headline splashed across the display in bold text. Activity and exhaustion had masked her anxiety about things at home she could not control. She had done what she could by instructing Georghe, asking for Carol's help, buying some time with the Crown's request for a private company to oversee Vadim's DNA testing.

Ninsele was in God's hands, and the capable hands of her staff. And the equally capable leaders—if they could stop posturing and fighting and *negotiate* for a change, which was what politicians should do. Negotiate and compromise and find solutions to overcome obstacles.

Unfortunately there were councillors—a few currently on the Crown Council—who were not doing their jobs adequately because they were stubborn. These resistant few could ground the entire political system to a halt.

Which is why the headline took her by surprise.

Council Rallies in Absence of Leader.

Mirie scanned the story. The text outlined the current session taking place in Ninsele, the very meeting that she had asked Georghe and Carol to convene.

The issues, the discussions, the questions, the debates.

According to the article, the council members were utilizing the opportunity to grill Carol on how a stabilization plan with the ultimate goal of ascendency to the EU might impact their individual factions. Mirie eagerly read the article, searched for the name of the media outlet and clicked on a link.

This next article spun the events in the royal compound differently, but the essentials were the same. The council members—from the staunchest nationalist to the most ardent socialist—were utilizing this opportunity well.

With fast keystrokes she typed different combinations of words into the browser.

Ninsele Crown Council meets with EC President.

Ninsele Crown Council talks future.

Ninsele without princess.

She found herself smiling at the display as she searched for more coverage from media outlets she trusted, and from those she did not. The germs of each story were the same. Tentatively positive. And while this might seem an unexpected miracle, Mirie knew that was not the case. Rather, the dialogue taking place was the result of years of laying a foundation, of establishing trust, of leaving a trail, so to speak. Eventually, even the most nomadic of chamois would seek out the herd.

Carol was a leader, well acquainted with Ninsele's issues and with all Mirie hoped to accomplish. Carol could answer questions and guide the council on the Crown's behalf under Georghe's guidance. Mirie would have never accomplished as much as she had without the EC's help.

If Carol could gain the ear of the extremists, then progress may be made. Maybe the factions were finally willing to listen because the bomb and NATO's appearance had driven home the reality that a divided country was a weakened country, and not everyone could get all what they wanted.

Ninsele had endured ten long years of a dictator's rule and civil strife, but compared to the heart-wrenching examples of their neighbors, ten years seemed a blessing.

Or maybe Mirie's absence made the difference. There were articles speculating on her disappearance. Conspiracy theorists who believed she had been murdered, that the palace was releasing misinformation as damage control until the Crown Council figured out how to bridge the distance between their views. That Carol Holderlin had remained in Ninsele to facilitate that process.

The theorists were not far from the mark this time. But all that mattered to Mirie was that the Crown Council behave as proud Ninselans before the president of the EC, and the world.

Whatever their motivation, the council seemed to be utilizing their opportunity productively and the media's focus was not on Vadim's claims.

She was so immersed in the news articles that

she didn't hear Drew approach and startled when he whispered, "All done. Let's cut it short here and head east."

She glanced up and searched his face. The absence of emotion revealed so much more than any expression ever could.

"East?" she asked.

He nodded. "I found a place we can stay. It'll buy us a few hours until they track us down."

Now that he had sent his message, he had given back the control to his agency. Their time together was drawing to a close.

"How long?"

"Maybe until morning."

She nodded, accepting the news with the same sort of trained detachment that she accepted all news beyond her control, when everything inside her suddenly felt urgent, as though she might weep.

Action was her only defense, so she silently helped Drew store away the laptop computer and escorted him outside. Her mood was so influenced by his.

She would be returned to a safe house, where the Americans would make her wait for news while they searched for the enemy. She could be on her way home in a few days.

Would they take away Drew before sending her home, assign her another protector while they charged him with treason?

She wanted no other protector.

"What's going on at home?" He stepped into the afternoon, so deceptively bright when it felt to her as if it should be twilight.

Home.

It was her home, but it had become his, too. She remembered Bunică's cautionary reminder in her letter. The reminder that her true purpose was *to live*. She had overlooked everything important in her life for the sake of duty.

Until she had reached out to Drew in a moment of fear, never once recognizing what her heart had known all along.

How much he cared. How much she cared.

She had been blinded for so long. And now they had squandered their time together.

"I have some very unexpected and very good news," she said, and told him about the press coverage of the Crown Council session while he drove them out of the valley and headed toward Glacier National Park.

She recounted her interpretation of the press's retelling of what was happening during the unexpected session.

"They seem to be utilizing Carol, Drew. I'm not sure whether to jump for joy or feel wounded that this happened in my absence."

"It's happening because you're absent. Nothing like a dirty bomb, an assassination attempt and NATO troops to pull people together." He sliced an amused look at her. "Seriously, Mirie. They'd all have to be idiots not to gain a little perspective. That shot you took was a public service."

She had no words, and couldn't argue his point.

"What about Vadim?" Drew asked. "Any word on him?"

"He hasn't made any move yet, or nothing that is breaking news, at any rate. There are media outlets speculating because I'm not there. The usual conspiracy theorists, and a few debates about the legitimacy of who should rule Ninsele—an illegitimate male heir or a female of the line."

"How are they leaning?"

"It doesn't really matter since we know Vadim is involved with a criminal. They're stuck with me— at least until the next opportunist makes a bid for the crown."

If her family had been alive, these sorts of attempts would never be an issue.

"How are you with all this?"

What did she even say to that? Did she admit her heart was breaking at the thought of being separated from him? Admit her feelings when he had not admitted his own? And to what end—to make them both miserable, or so that he would know he had not made this sacrifice for no reason?

She didn't get the chance to deliberate. Drew turned the car off the main road onto a narrow lane that wound along the outskirts of the national forest. She waited in the car while Drew went inside the office, a quaint wooden cabin nestled back in the woods, reminding her of the forest beyond the village gates in Alba Luncă. Isolated. Another world. How long would it take his agency to find them here? She wished the forest would swallow them up and shield them from reality for just a while longer.

He wasn't gone long, and when he returned, he handed her a key and a map. "Let's see if we can find it."

"A cabin?" she asked.

He nodded. "It'll be quiet. You must be tired. You haven't slept since the safe house."

Had it been only two days? "I slept on the bus."

"Doesn't count. You're still healing."

The cabin was nestled beneath pine boughs, icicles still clinging stubbornly to the eaves over the porch. Inside was warm and homey with red-checked curtains and a gas fireplace.

Mirie was delighted. "I'm surprised you even managed to find a vacancy while there's still snow on the slopes."

He pulled shut the door. "It's late in the season. I'll get the fire going."

With a smile, Mirie rubbed her hands together to warm them as she strolled through the cabin, checking out the small kitchen area, the breakfast nook, the view of the forest from every window.

Another world.

And the moment became surreal.

They had never been together this way. He was always there but outside the door.

Until the cave.

The thought made the bed swallow the room. She forced her gaze away from the bed, but found she couldn't drag her eyes from Drew as he got the gas fireplace working, the modern oddity adequate, but so different from Ninsele, where a wood-burning fireplace was as standard a feature as running water. In some remote mountain areas, even more of a standard.

But Mirie found herself hungry for the sight of him, those broad shoulders testing the wool of his coat, the brush of short hair at his neckline. He was so familiar, yet a stranger, too, as he knelt mere feet from the bed with its thick blankets and fluffy pillows, their surroundings so different from the last time he had built a fire for her.

"Here we go." He stood and motioned her toward him. "Come here and warm up. If I had been thinking, we could have stopped for supplies on the way in."

She went to stand beside him and held out her hands to the warmth, a mechanically generated heat that blew toward her, different yet welcomed. "We have our supplies from Philadelphia."

"I'm sure you wouldn't have minded a change of clothes."

She exhaled softly. "We probably won't be here long enough to worry about such things."

He stared down at her, and the sober truth in his expression tore at her. Extra clothing was the least of their troubles. Yet Drew had cared for her so long, and didn't seem willing to stop even at this late hour.

"There's a washer and dryer. I can do a load, so we won't have to put on dirty clothes. How does that sound?" he asked.

"Perfect. Thank you."

"Are you hungry?"

She nodded. "We still have protein bars—"

"They have a restaurant in the communal area. I'll order something. Do you want to look at the menu?"

He handed her the laminated sheet of paper, and she took it from him, watching as he prowled the room, shrugging out of his coat, then tossing it onto the coatrack beside the front door. He checked every door, every window, every lock, securing the area as she had seen him do a thousand times.

How was she supposed to go on now? Return to Ninsele and pretend everything was normal?

"See anything good?" he asked.

She shrugged. "Please just get me whatever you're having."

He knew. There was just so much between them, so many years. And now she needed a moment to collect herself. "I'm going to shower."

He watched her go, but before the door shut behind

her, she heard him say, "Hand me your clothes, Mirie. I'll put them in the washer. There's a robe in there."

She didn't reply, but did as he asked. Handing her worn denim and undergarments to him through a crack in the door. Then, with her heart breaking into a thousand pieces, she got into the shower. And only when she was standing beneath the spray did she allow her tears to fall.

CHAPTER EIGHTEEN

DREW STARED THROUGH the small glass panel in the door into the frozen night. He didn't really want to watch a perimeter team silently slip into place, could all too easily imagine being forced at gunpoint to surrender with his hands in the air. He would be handcuffed and taken back to Command either by car or by helicopter.

His only consolation was that Mirie would be with him until they got there.

After that, he would be on his own, and she would be at the mercy of Excelsior and whoever the general assigned to her protection. Someone paid to do the job. Someone dependent on the NRPG's limited resources. Someone who might hesitate that split second before placing his life before her own.

Because he didn't love her.

He could hear Mirie behind him. The whisper of her feet as she passed before the fire, the rustle of fabric as she turned down the bedding.

If he turned around he would find her in the resort's fluffy bathrobe. They had showered and eaten and washed their clothes, gone about the business of survival, pretending that everything wasn't about to blow up in their faces.

"Shall I pull out the sofa and make up the bed?" Her silken voice broke through the morose sequence of his thoughts.

"No, thank you."

There was a beat of silence. "You don't intend to sleep?"

He didn't have a night guard to replace him, and he honestly didn't think he'd sleep even if he did. How could he close his eyes and rest, knowing all it would take was one accurately aimed gunshot through a windowpane or an incendiary device placed right outside the wall to end Mirie's life?

He might never sleep again, wondering what she was doing at any given moment, what kind of trouble she may be in, whether or not she had egress. And he would be half a world away, unable to keep her safe no matter what was happening.

"No."

He heard her sigh in the quiet, broken only by the hum of air blowing from the fireplace.

The bedding rustled when she sat on the bed, and he waited for her to settle in, waited for the slowing of her breathing. She fell asleep faster than anyone he had ever met in his life. He would often lie awake for an hour before sleep came. But Mirie only had to roll over to her side and close her eyes. She would awake just as suddenly, whenever worries preyed on her mind.

Drew scanned the pools of light from the flood lamps that dotted the lane back to the resort. Each one was strategically placed to break the wintry darkness, yet not destroy the illusion that these cabins were set in the middle of the wilderness.

But Mirie didn't go to bed. Instead, she came to him and leaned against the wooden railing that separated the kitchenette from the living area. She looked up at him, searching, and he drank in the sight of her, her lean curves enveloped in plush cotton, her feet bare.

"Drew, you haven't rested since we escaped from your agency," she said in the same tone one would reason with a child. "You don't have a bodyguard to take your place. When do you plan to sleep?"

Something deep inside him responded to her concern and pushed a smile to his face. "I'll be fine. Don't worry about me."

"I know you will be fine, but I worry anyway. You won't concern yourself with your well-being because you're concerned with mine. So the task of worrying about you falls to me."

"No worrying. That's my job."

That was his life.

She shook her head decidedly. "Not tonight. We have made choices, you and I. We don't know what tomorrow will bring, if we'll even…" Her voice trailed off.

He understood.

"Everything will work out fine, Mirie." But his reassurance sounded hollow in the quiet.

She brought her chin up and stared at him with melting eyes. "I don't want your protection tonight. I want your friendship."

Reaching for his hand, she slid her cool fingers around his. "I want you to lie beside me. Let us simply enjoy being together. Whatever will come with the sunrise, will come. But this moment is ours."

How did Drew even respond to that? She placed the reality of their situation square between them, and he realized this had to be difficult for her. He felt it in her touch. He saw it in her lovely face, the shadow of impending loss.

She cared.

He had always known. He was a constant in her life, the one she could trust to protect her, and the years of his faithfulness seemed to have won out over his betrayal. She was speaking to him again, smiling at him, touching his hand.

She cared.

He was so grateful, but knowing she needed him made their inevitable parting that much harder, and giving in to her request would only complicate things further.

"The door is locked, Drew. Come to bed." She

smiled up at him, a haunted smile. "I won't make any unreasonable demands of you tonight. You need to sleep."

When she tugged at his hand, Drew knew the last thing he should do was give in. Giving in would only make the situation harder on her, and impossible on him. They would be separated by an ocean, by honor, by prison bars... And then he was being led to the bed.

The feel of her hand within his overrode all his thoughts of resisting. There was nothing reasonable about the way he felt for her. There never had been. There never would be. He had thrown his career and his future out the window to help her address an issue that Simon would not address. He would rather die than see her harmed.

Did it really matter what tomorrow brought?

She slipped beneath the blankets with her robe on, lying on her unbandaged side, and he climbed in beside her wearing his freshly laundered clothes. He wrapped his arm around her, letting her snuggle against him the way she had on the bus. There was only the glow from the fireplace to light the darkness, and the fresh scent of her hair marking his every breath.

"Isn't that better?" she asked, not giving him a chance to reply. "What are you thinking of?"

"I'm wondering what my agency is doing with the information I gave them."

That much was true.

And he was memorizing the way she smelled and the way she felt against him. The cool silk of her hair and the warm skin of her temple against his neck. The way her cheek rested on his shoulder. The way her body unfolded against his. The way her arm draped over his waist, lightly, as though she just needed the reassurance that he was there.

"Life used to be so simple." Her voice filtered through him. "I'd forgotten until now. Our days were filled with nothing more than going to the school or into the village or up to the church. Do you remember life before we went to Briere?"

He nodded, letting her talk just so he could hear her voice and be reminded of the life they had lived together. He would need those memories. They were his only defense against his future.

"No decisions to make with earth-shattering consequences. No navigating the minefields of public opinion and councillors and their many needs and views. The most important decisions I had to make were what to wear and how to squeeze in all my chores during school nights, so I could go to the lake on the weekend. Your job must have been so much simpler back then, too."

He rested his cheek against her head. "I wouldn't call chasing after you and that idiot boyfriend a challenge."

She laughed softly. "We thought we were being so clever."

"Not hardly. He wanted to get you alone. Luckily his options were pretty limited in a village the size of Alba Luncă."

"I never realized you cared so much."

For a moment, Drew sat in stunned silence, trying to make sense of what she'd said, wondering whether he was reading more into that statement than he should. "You sound sure. You know how much I care? How much I've always cared?"

"I do."

Something inside him went quiet then, felt calm in a way he hadn't felt since at the airport when he'd been reactivated and forced to leave her side.

If nothing else, no matter how she interpreted that caring, Mirie knew that he did. She would not go back to Ninsele and feel betrayed by their years together.

He would have that knowledge, that consolation, as she went back to her life without him. So he focused on the only thing that would sustain him now.

"What will you do when you can leave the compound safely and start living again?" he asked.

"What I do now isn't living?"

He arched an eyebrow. "Not from where I'm standing, and I'm usually pretty close."

She snuggled against him, and he savored the way

her body fit against his, tried to memorize the feel of her to sustain him when she was no longer with him

"I'll go to university."

"Really?"

"I know I'll be older than your typical university student, but the gaps in my education have been warranted. And people go to school at all ages nowadays."

"You're right, of course. And I don't think you'll be too old. You just surprised me. I didn't realize you were interested in continuing your schooling."

"I looked forward to university. I thought I would have to leave Ninsele, because of the war. But that was another life."

Mirie.

He remembered that woman so well, and wondered when the dust settled, when the chaos finally ended, who would Mirie be then? "If you weren't a princess, what would you be? Do you have any idea?"

"I do, actually. There was a time when I thought I would have to hide my identity forever." She laughed softly. "I had grand plans for my life."

Drew would bet some of those plans had involved a wedding. "What were your plans?"

"I wanted to teach. To be a professor at a prestigious university like Oxford in the United Kingdom or Karolinska Institute in Sweden."

"What would you teach?"

"Political science. I find the subject fascinating."

She sounded thoughtful. "I used to love debating with my tutors. We would debate issues for hours upon hours. I used my debating skills to drive my schoolteachers crazy."

"I know."

She laughed softly. "I never realized you were paying such close attention."

"So you want to get your degree."

She tipped her head back to glance up into his face, their close proximity making her skin appear to glow in the shadows. "Then I want to get married and make babies. I want a very large family. Lots of children and dogs. I always planned to be like Queen Elizabeth with her corgis."

Another unexpected revelation. "You want corgis?"

"No. I want German dachshunds. The small ones like the ones Margarethe Visnoi had when I attended that activities camp that summer. Do you remember?"

"How could I forget?" He rolled his eyes. "You overcame your fear of heights. I nearly lost my mind every time you jumped from the ridge into the lake."

Her mouth formed the most perfect O. "I had forgotten."

"I won't. Not ever. I don't even have to close my eyes to see what you would look like if you had lost your footing and crashed into the rocky gorge on the way down."

"Oh, my poor Drew." She laughed. "I never realized what a worrier you were."

He gave a snort. "I almost killed that idiot Samuel for goading you into trying it the first time."

"If I had known, I wouldn't have tried to escape you so often. Please understand I was young. I didn't properly understand how my actions could impact those around me. I had a bodyguard when normal people my age were just going about living their lives. No one knew who I really was, and I longed to fit in."

He couldn't resist tightening his arms around her.

"I'm not complaining," she said. "Or making excuses. But I am sorry I made your task so much more difficult. I was selfish."

"You don't know the meaning of selfish. And I have been honored to chase you around."

He had not meant to be so serious, but the finality in his words brought the present crashing in on the warm darkness.

And Mirie responded to it, never one to shy away from the truth.

"I never considered that the day would come when you wouldn't be there, Drew," she said softly. "I thought you would be with me always. No matter where life took me. I counted on you."

"I know."

Their words faded into silence. Then she lifted her hand to his cheek, traced his jaw with light fingers as though she, too, wanted to memorize the feel of him to take with her.

"Make love with me," she whispered. "Not because I'm asking you to, but because you want me. As a woman."

Drew supposed he had known ever since she had led him to this bed that they would wind up here, facing this choice. He shouldn't give in. Not if he needed to let her go.

But he couldn't deny this woman he loved, couldn't face his own future when he would no longer share her life.

And he couldn't let her leave without showing her how much he cared. He may never speak the words, but he would love her until she knew beyond a doubt that she was his life.

Did tomorrow matter while they still had tonight?

MIRIE WAITED IN an office alone. She wasn't sure for whom—the director, most likely. But with each passing minute, her anxiety intensified. She knew better than to sit; she'd been sitting the whole time on the flight from Montana back to Washington, D.C.

Their apprehension had been civilized. Drew told her his agency would give him the chance to be apprehended with dignity, and they had. A car had arrived, so they didn't attract any unwanted attention.

The director hadn't met them on the plane. Apparently a rebellious princess hadn't warranted any special attention. Not even Violet had shown up. But they had kept Mirie with Drew up until they brought her into this room. She didn't know if he had been taken to prison. He assured her he wouldn't be executed.

The door opened. She spun away from the window that opened to a gray day in an ugly city.

"Welcome back, Your Royal Highness." The director didn't smile.

Circling the desk, he set down a folder and sat. "Please, make yourself comfortable."

She sat across from him and waited, refusing to show her nerves. She wouldn't react until she received the information she needed to formulate her position so she could negotiate with strength.

"I'm glad to see you are well," he said.

"Very well, thank you."

"Your injuries?"

"Are healing."

He inclined his head, then rested folded hands in front of him. He looked stoic as he met her gaze. She sensed he was summing her up the same way she was him.

She resisted the urge to fill the silence.

"Thank you for sending me the lead from Whitefish, rather than taking the information to the media."

Mirie shouldn't have been surprised by the man's civility. Drew hadn't been clapped in irons and dragged to a cell. Or executed, to her knowledge.

She decided to be all business. They had nego-
tiated before. She had already proven she would
negotiate in good faith, but would also gamble to
be treated fairly. A lesson in nuances that she had
learned from her stubborn councillors.

"Sending the information to you was Drew's idea,"
she admitted. "He understood both our needs and our
limitations. He believed you would be able to plant a
trail for our enemy and had the resources to pursue
the information he uncovered to catch the guy. He
courageously risked his reputation and his future to
do his part. I have done my part by allowing myself
to be used as bait and by not going to the press with
the information. Have you done your part?"

The director's eyes widened, a show of emotion
Mirie suspected was rare for this man.

"I have, Your Royal Highness. I just received word
that my team succeeded in taking Victor Mondragon
into custody."

Mirie inhaled sharply. This was news she had not
been expecting. It had been only twenty-four hours
since they had sat in Elizabeth's living room, drinking cocoa.

"So, he is the man you have been looking for,"
she said. "Do you know for a fact that he's funding
Vadim and is behind the assassination attempts?"

The director didn't reply. He held her gaze, and
she knew he was annoyed that she was asking him
to tip his hand.

"I'm sorry if I caused you to worry," she said, extending an olive branch in exchange for information. "I appreciate everything the Americans have done for Ninsele, but I didn't feel I had any other choice. Drew explained you were limited with your choices, too. But my duty is to my people, and I couldn't allow them to be misled when there is still so much unrest. I hope you will understand and excuse me."

There was something in this man's expression that made Mirie suspect her boldness had amused him.

His icy eyes glittered when he admitted, "Had anything happened to you while you were on the run in this country with Drew, I would have had a great deal of explaining to do."

She spread her hands. "Apparently I am tough to kill."

That made him smile, a look that transformed his expression.

"I would not argue that, Your Royal Highness, which is fortunate for you." He lifted open the cover of the folder and said, "Here is the information my people have uncovered about our trafficker since we received Drew's intel."

He explained the connections that proved Mondragon was indeed the financier behind the attempt on her life in Alba Luncă as well as the bomb in the airport.

"Mondragon recruited your men through their connection to a socialist extremist organization. Inidentally, he used the same tactic to find an appointed executive at the Forensic Medicine Institute. A different organization and a different cause, but Mondragon appears adept at manipulating people to his purpose."

"Who was it, please? There is a very small administration in that institute."

The director shuffled through some papers. "A man named Anton Dobos."

Mirie inclined her head in acknowledgment. She knew the man. Unassuming and thorough, he had been with the institute for a long time and had been directly involved with the exhumation of her father to prove her own claim of paternity. Had he opposed her rule all along or had he only now become willing to be purchased for a price?

"You will provide me with proof, so I may instruct my military to remove this man from his post and arrange for a trial?"

The director nodded. "By bringing in Mondragon, we will shut down the most dangerous trafficker in our country. That is no guarantee others won't attempt to replace him until you strengthen your borders. You must understand the United States is the primary destination for just about everything sold on the global black market. And we're generally a target, too, so we have a calculated interest in who controls your region."

"This is what my country is working toward with

the European Commission. We don't want to be
abused by criminals." Or by opportunists. "What
did you learn about Vadim? Why did Mondragon
choose this man to place on the throne? We learned
much about his life in Whitefish, and by all accounts
he seems to be an unlikely candidate."

"Yes, and no," the director surprised her by saying. "Once we ID'd Mondragon, we were easily able
to trace the connection between him and Vadim."

"Which is?"

"Ileana Vadim was an envoy to the consul when
the honorary consulate was established here in the
United States. At that time Victor Mondragon was
a businessman, traveling between our countries. We
believe his work at the time was a cover for his illegitimate dealings, but we haven't proven that yet.
I've got people working on it."

"Are you saying Ileana Vadim was involved with
a criminal?"

"For quite a while, in fact. I don't have all the details in place yet, but I have documentation from a
domestic abuse program that became involved in her
situation. Apparently, they helped her relocate safely
when she became pregnant."

"Victor Mondragon is Luca Vadim's father." Miri
gasped. Elizabeth and the tenant had both been right.

The director inclined his head. "Apparently, Mondragon had been generous with Ileana Vadim finan-
cially, so she was able to get a fresh start with her

child. I don't know yet how Mondragon learned he had a son after all this time, but until I do, we can discuss how to effectively spin this development to the press."

Obviously they would keep the American agency out of the media. The director wanted to unravel Mondragon's organization entirely and pointed out that revealing Mondragon would be counterproductive, as it would drive his associates underground.

"We can serve Ninsele's needs simply by revealing that Vadim paid off Anton Dobos for fraudulent results," Mirie said quickly. Drew had been genius. "Dobos may tell his tale in court before a judge. That will take time. A long time if necessary."

The director appeared pleased with the concession. "Will you bring charges against Vadim?"

Mirie frowned. "I haven't decided yet."

"I would caution you to consider the extenuating circumstances. Vadim is guilty as charged, but he is not a willing accomplice. He has been manipulated by Mondragon into believing he really is your father's illegitimate son. Once he learns who his father really is and how his mother died, I believe he will own up to his actions."

Mirie shut her eyes tight against the wave of sorrow and surprise at that revelation. "You know for a fact that Mondragon was behind the hit and run?"

"Yes."

Mirie exhaled heavily. All the resentment over

Vadim's bid for her throne, the damaging media reports, the slurs against her father's honor, were forgotten. Vadim had lost his family in a brutal way. She understood how that felt.

There was no need for justice. Mirie had heard of a woman who so fiercely loved her son she would hide him away from his powerful father to give him a good life. A son who, by all accounts, had loved his mother as much. That son would learn he had a killer for a father. There was no need for forgiveness, when all there could be was compassion, and empathy.

"Then we are agreed," Mirie said soberly. "We will arrest Dobos and deport Vadim. I'll instruct the military to release him into your custody?"

The director nodded. "Agreed."

Mirie inhaled deeply, troubles being cleared away. "Which leaves us only with one more item of business."

"That is?"

"Your promise to an old man."

The director leaned back in his chair and considered her thoughtfully. "You don't believe fifteen years of service honored that promise?"

"Yes, and no," she said. "You had an agenda."

"This is about Drew." She nodded.

"I'm sure Your Royal Highness understands the gravity of the choice he made. I am also sure you understand and respect the need for a chain of command and loyalty to one's country."

"Like you, I also understand extenuating circumstances."

The director shut the folder, never taking his gaze from hers. "The only extenuating circumstance I see is that my operative went rogue with a monarch from a foreign country. He risked an international incident that would have not only placed the United States in an extremely embarrassing position, but directly risked exposing this agency."

"*You* exposed your agency to me. Not Drew. And who am I going to tell, really?" She raised her hands, a gesture of profound helplessness. "I can't even get my country recognized by the EU. Random men make attempts for my throne, and I am the one who must defend my claim. If I scheduled a press conference tomorrow and announced your agency to the world, the media would create a fiction to fuel the conspiracy theorists. One-third of my own people might believe me."

An exaggeration, perhaps, but based on simple, frustrating truths. Not a commentary on Mirie's ability to rule, but on the aftereffects of a system damaged by a dictator's abuses and a people forced to struggle for survival. And circumstance.

Mirie was a princess, not a queen.

That she could not change.

"What is it you want, Your Royal Highness?"

"I want to know what your intentions are. Will you continue to honor your promise to my father's bodyguard?"

"Fifteen years wasn't long enough? You're grown, and you have your country back."

"I want Drew."

The director narrowed his gaze.

"I want him to be my bodyguard."

"How does that benefit me when he is loyal to you?"

That brought a smile to her face, although humility in the face of the director's annoyance would have served her better. "He will honor your promise to my father's friend, but you will no longer have to keep him on your payroll. He will see to my safety, yet cost you nothing. You would still have to feed and clothe him in a prison. This is mutually beneficial."

"He went rogue from this agency."

"He gathered the information *you* wanted to apprehend a criminal with access to nuclear devices who was trying to murder the woman you vowed to protect."

The director positively scowled, such a dark expression that Mirie suspected the man was not used to having to explain himself to many people. A king in his own right.

"Drew had a mission," the director said. "And he changed the parameters to serve your needs, not this agency's."

"He had no choice. You and I were not effective at our negotiations. Had Drew not taken action, you would not have identified Mondragon and Vadim might now be sitting on my throne."

"He violated orders."

"Drew has done everything you have asked of him for fifteen years. He has been working for you still since we arrived in America. He has kept me alive, and he has given you Victor Mondragon. At great risk to his life, I might add. How can you possibly ignore these honorable deeds?"

Mirie swallowed back a caution that rulers who acted based on a challenge to their authority were dictators, not leaders.

The director steepled his fingers before him and considered her for a long, long time. Mirie held her breath and his gaze, refusing to show weakness, even though her heart was pounding, and everything important to her lay stretched between them. She did not know what the future held for her and Drew, but she didn't want to return home without the man she loved.

"Off my payroll?" One question that proved the sternness the director wore like armor masked a man who bore a great deal of responsibility and was often forced to make hard choices.

She understood. "I will offer Drew the job and a raise."

"I'll consider your offer." The director slid his

chair back and collected the folder. "That's all I will promise. I'm sure you'll want to make the arrangements for Vadim and Dobos. I'll provide you an office and staff. If you need anything else, just let them know. But before I go, let me ask you a question, Your Royal Highness."

"Please."

He eyed her curiously. "You're sure Drew will accept? What if he wasn't facing prison, but a return to active duty?"

After the night she had spent in Drew's arms... Mirie's breath caught in her throat when she said, "I'm sure."

CHAPTER NINETEEN

MIRIE DIDN'T KNOW how long the director would make her wait to know if he would accept her offer, but she suspected a time of penance would be built in to the careful consideration.

She accepted his timing graciously and put herself to good use. Telephone calls needed to be made to assuage worries since she hadn't been in contact with her people in several days. There was a press release to prepare. A criminal to arrest. An imposter to deport.

General Bogdanovich would see to the latter tasks, but she needed to brief him first. Mirie needed to speak with Georghe before she set any of these tasks in motion.

She needed to hear his voice, needed to know all was well in Briere. She was eager, too, to hear how the talks today had gone, since she had no chance to check for herself.

Glancing at the clock on the wall of the office, she knew the time difference meant she should catch Georghe settling into his suite for the night.

The routine felt familiar. He was her family. Like

Drew and Helena, they all had their lives in the royal palace, separate yet together, alone yet en masse, work and life bleeding into each other.

Mirie thought of her glittering eggshell and realized she hadn't missed the home of her childhood. She hadn't realized how much of herself she had shut down to exist in the place where she could still hear the screams of her family.

She didn't hear them often anymore, and didn't think about that night much at all, yet the memory was always there, underlying every second of her days.

She simply hadn't realized until leaving. Now in America, she clearly recognized how imprisoned she felt by her memories because she was freed of them when she was away.

Not that she forgot. Ever. Her loss was a part of her. As her loved ones would always be a part of her. But the memory did not cover her mind like a shroud when she left Briere.

She set aside the thought. Moving to sit behind the desk, she decided to make her telephone calls before involving the director's staff in her work. She lifted the receiver and spoke English to the young man on the other end of the line.

"I want to call Georghe Nemirich in the royal compound in Briere. The palace switchboard will connect you to him."

There was silence until Georghe said, "Thanks be to God. I had almost forsaken you."

Mirie melted at the sound of his voice, she'd been so starved for contact with her people. "How goes the running of our country, my friend?"

"Eventful, as always. But no talk of work yet. How are you? Are your injuries healing? When are you coming home? We were all worried sick, then no phone calls for days." He scolded her until she felt terrible. "We had despaired of you. You might have died, and we had no way to reach you."

"Drei would have let you know if there had been any trouble." The name felt strange in her mouth, a name she had spoken most of her life.

But not the name of the man who had her heart.

"No worries, Georghe, I am well. The doctor will be removing the stitches soon, and I will come home. Lest you think I have been lounging around while my skin knits and you work, I have been working, too, and have much to share."

"Good news, I hope."

"Indeed, my friend. Good news."

She explained the truth about Vadim's identity and the evidence of bribes to Anton Dobos, making no mention of Mondragon. She allowed Georghe to continue to believe she had been working with NATO, and that the organization had a lead on the people responsible for funding the assassination attempts.

"Hopefully, they will have the answers soon," she

said. "But we are free to act. Vadim's claim must be publicly disproved and Dobos questioned. I will have everything the general will need sent within the hour."

"You don't know how to rest, do you?" Georghe asked with a laugh. "You squandered your vacation."

"I had to be shot to get away and kept under guard to be safe? This does not sound like much of a vacation."

But it was a commentary on her life.

Would she ever get to stay in a cabin, nestled beneath a snowy mountain, wrapped in the arms of the man she loved when she wasn't hiding from some threat?

Would she ever see all the different American beaches Drew had spoken of?

With every Mondragon who was stopped, every Vadim who was circumvented, every Dobos who was replaced, Mirie took a step closer to a life where a vacation was possible.

Yet there was still so much to be done.

"Tell me how the session has gone," she said. "I was able to read coverage yesterday, but haven't seen any yet today."

"Anton Dobos treated us all to a rant on the moral degradation any future with the EU would have on Ninsele," Georghe spat. "I will personally accompany the general to apprehend this traitor, just for provoking people with his scare tactics during an otherwise productive and positive session."

"Ah, Georghe. I've missed you." And she had. "Now tell me what miracles you and Carol are working there. What I've read in the press sounds extraordinary."

"Carol went at the council with no mercy as soon as she walked through the door. She brought up the assassination attempts, the terror attack, the dirty bomb. She demanded to know if this was the future the council wanted for our country." Georghe chuckled at the retelling.

"You should have heard her, Your Royal Highness," he continued. "She told everyone that she didn't care one way or the other whether Ninsele attempted to join the European Union. But the fact that we would not even be considered candidates should tell them something about the state of affairs in Ninsele and the efficacy of their council."

Mirie sank back in the chair and gasped. "She did not."

"She did. She swept their knees out from beneath them and then went on to put each one of them on the spot. In the process she earned their respect, if for no reason other than how knowledgeable she proved herself to be with regard to our country. That's why we're still in session. We've yet to reach an impasse."

"I'm amazed."

"You're in good company. This session has become like a papal conclave. People turn on their televisions at the end of each day to await the smoke. An Orthodox conclave."

Mirie laughed. She had no trouble envisioning Carol with her bright tailored suits presiding over sixty councillors and telling everyone exactly what she thought of their tactics. "Carol's worked extremely hard on finding a way to bring unity to our country."

"She said the same thing about you," Georghe said. There was a small part of Mirie that felt hurt that she hadn't been able to achieve similar cooperation after all her efforts.

But that was *Mirie speaking,* not Ninsele's leader. She understood this was not about her, personally, even when it felt that way. This was all about the people and their beliefs and their dreams and their wounds.

Of which there were many.

"So where does that leave us on the issue?" she asked. "Any hope of gaining middle ground?"

"Are you sitting down? You've been injured. I don't want to cause you more harm if you faint and hit your head on the floor."

"You'll cause harm by keeping me in suspense. Holding my breath makes my ribs ache."

More laughter, and that alone told Mirie that Georghe's news had lifted his spirits greatly. "Remember the draft we prepared to present to the representatives?"

"Of course. What about it?"

"We're almost there."

For one throbbing heartbeat, Mirie could only sit there, and stare. She shook her head, tried to clear it.

"You're not dreaming," Georghe said into the silence.

She heard what he said, but she knew these councillors intimately. Knew how they fought for the interests of those they represented, those who wanted no monarchy and all state and those who wanted all monarchy and no state.

"How is this possible?"

"Carol gave the dissenters a swift kick in their pants. She told them the situation will never change until they learn to work out their issues, and they're the only ones who can do that."

"They agreed to accept you as appointed prime minister, Georghe?" That was her intractable condition.

"Two terms, not four. Then a general election."

Mirie sat up to ease the ache in her chest and allowed herself to draw a strong breath. This man who had fought so hard for their country, who had endured so much beneath Ninsele's dictatorship, who had stepped aside humbly to bring back the monarchy, was the man best suited to serve their people during the transition to democracy.

"Two terms is acceptable." That gave them eight years to transform the system of government with the man best suited to the job.

After two terms, the rule of the government would be in the peoples' hands, where it belonged.

"Thank you, Your Royal Highness, for all your faith in me. You know I will do my best."

"I have been so lucky to have you."

There was silence, and Mirie could practically see the embarrassment creeping into Georghe's cheeks. He hated when she got sentimental. But he wouldn't argue with her. Not while she was away.

"All right, Georghe, we may get back to business, so long as you know how much you're appreciated."

There was a short silence, and then Georghe said, "We're still hammering away at an issue or two."

"Which ones?"

Another beat of silence. "The role of the monarchy. Someone put Britain on the table as a compromise."

"A symbolic monarchy. Hmm." Mirie knew the days of an absolute monarchy had ended and hoped to share responsibility with a prime minister elected by the people: a balance of power. She had always intended to be a part of Ninsele's political process, not simply a figurative head of state.

Was a dramatic change best for her people?

"If the time has come for me to consider compromise, then I will consider it," she said. "I've set the example of values I have preached for six years. Hear what the people have to say."

A symbolic monarchy would be one way to safeguard the throne against more imposters.

"We'll listen to what is discussed, Your Royal Highness. One thing is for sure, we know your mind. No worries there."

"Ha! Is that your diplomatic way of saying I've pounded my wants like a board over your thick head?"

There was a chuckle on the other end of the line. "You do sound well, which means you will be home soon. You're missed. We can celebrate with a picnic." He laughed.

Mirie felt longing for home then, and she asked about Georghe's grandchildren and caught up on Helena and the others in the compound. By the time she set the receiver back into its cradle, she was filled with rioting emotions.

Perhaps the events of the past weeks had finally caught up with her. Staring out the window at the city, she thought of all that needed to be done and suddenly felt like doing none of it. Everything was changing. The distraction of activity would no longer shield her from that truth.

In the time since Bunică had died, so many things had spun out of her control.

Once long ago, Mirie had considered a life that had not involved ruling Ninsele, but a symbolic monarchy? To be head of state while an elected parliament did the actual work? To visit charities and support causes and carry on with tradition?

It was a noble life, but was it *her* future?

Mirie only knew how she felt right now.

Alone.

DREW DIDN'T REGRET a single decision he'd made. He didn't care that he faced life inside a cell that would probably look a lot like this one. Gray concrete floor. Gray concrete walls. He could walk *eight* steps in every direction. A perfect square. Perimeter equals side one plus side two plus side three plus side four. Area equals width times length. He knew the area. He knew the perimeter. He had been pacing this cell for almost three days. When he wasn't exercising to work off the adrenaline, he was pacing this cell.

But he also remembered the way Mirie had felt in his arms. He remembered how her wet skin felt in the shower, the morning after they had made love all night. The way her long legs had felt wrapped around his when they had made love in the warm bed.

Drew could do this. He'd had fifteen years with her. If he relived every one of those moments, every one of the memories, he could survive happily until he lost his mind.

And he would. Alzheimer's ran in his family. Drew sighed.

Pacing a cell would be better than trying to live a normal life without Mirie. Knowing she was a plane flight away. Watching her go on with her life, whatever she chose to do with it.

Where was she now? Had Simon sent her back to Ninsele? Had their last minutes together truly been their last? Was she already working with a new close-protection guard, mopping up the mess left over from the murder attempts, the bribery of a government official and an imposter?

Had Simon brought in Mondragon yet?

Questions looped in Drew's head, one sparking another.

Had Excelsior solidly connected Mondragon to the assassinations yet? The dirty bomb? Had Drew passed along Mondragon's identity in time to stop Vadim from going to the press? Would the *poliţie* press charges against him? Had they discovered who had been bought at the Forensic Medicine Institute? Had that person been charged?

How was he supposed to go on without knowing if Mirie was okay?

The questions came so fast that Drew was about to drop to the floor and start with the push-ups again.

Then grinding metal echoed in the hollow silence. He turned to watch a meal tray appear through the door, but the lock clicked instead. His pulse accelerated as he faced the opening door. Would he finally get some answers?

Mirie.

Not a figment of his imagination. *Not* a memory. Alive. Her smile relieved. Her hair falling in soft waves around her beautiful face, her freckles only just visible in the yellow overhead light.

Drew went stupid at the sight of her, just stood there in his orange jumpsuit, a prisoner, every worry of the past three days suddenly engulfing him like a tsunami.

Her gaze raked over him as if she took in everything at once, her expression pained as she surveyed the cell.

"Drew." His name slid from her lips in a sigh. She rushed to him, life sweeping into this dead cell with her.

Then she was in his arms, her warm curves pressed close, the familiar scent of her hair in his nose, assaulting his senses after days of deprivation.

For a stunned instant, his only reply was the heartbeat hammering inside his chest, the pulse throbbing in his ears, the arms that locked her tightly against him.

Then he came to his senses. Their mouths came together, hungrily searching, as if the past three days had been a lifetime. He drank in the taste of her, the way her lips parted beneath his. They shared their breaths greedily, as if they might inhale each other, become a part of each other.

He hadn't known. He had only loved her from afar. Loved her when she had needed him. Loved her when they had both wanted.

A flame could never be recognized in the light of the sun, only in the darkness. It was an old Ninselan saying.

He had not realized how they had become one during their years together. He only realized now when they had been separated, forced to face a future alone.

So he held her and kissed her. He ran his fingers over her cheeks and along her jaw. He grasped at this chance to make another memory to carry him through the rest of his life.

"Drew." His name broke on a breath. "Oh, Drew."

He tried to stop kissing her, couldn't, and pressed his mouth over her face. He could taste her smile beneath his lips and nibbled along the sensitive place behind her ear.

She trembled in his arms, and only his worry for her made him stop.

"Are you all right?" he asked. "Have you seen the doctor? What about the stitches? When are they removing them?"

So many questions.

She smiled up at him. "I'm fine. How about you?"

"Good, now that I see you. Have you come to say goodbye?"

To his surprise she leaned back in his arms and waved an impatient hand. "I can't believe you're here. He wouldn't tell me where you were."

He was presumably Simon, and there was definitely attitude in her tone.

"Where else would I be?" Drew asked.

"Where else indeed? Your director has a disturbing penchant for treating the people who work for him like criminals."

"I am a criminal."

Mirie scowled, and Drew captured her expression in his memory. Only this woman, with her full pout and freckles, could make scowling look adorable.

"No, you are not," she said. "You are a man who made the choice to act in difficult circumstances. Had you sat back and followed the rules, we may not have accomplished all we have."

She made his actions sound noble. He had wanted to be her hero. "I haven't been briefed."

"We have accomplished everything, Drew. *Everything.*" She squeezed him tightly, and laughed. It was a sound that had once rung through flower-covered fields, echoed in steep mountain gorges. "You risked yourself for me and your agency. You demonstrated such courage, and we have accomplished all we hoped to."

Her admission soothed the fury of the questions

inside him, and he dared to breathe. "The director brought in Mondragon?"

She nodded eagerly, caught his chin with her fingers and coaxed his face down for a quick kiss. "And Vadim is being deported." Another kiss. "And Anton Dobos of the Forensic Medicine Institute is being questioned by the general."

Drew caught her kiss this time and shared a breath. "Mission accomplished, then."

"Yes. Thanks to you."

"Thanks to the agency. We just pointed them in the right direction."

She broke away from him, scowling again. "No humility. Not with me. Not with him. He already knows."

"He?"

"Your director."

"What does he know?"

"That your courage made everything possible."

Courage? More like *insubordination*.

Drew folded his arms over his chest and watched her. She was enjoying this. "My director said that?"

She nodded. "That is why I am here. It's all done. We've worked out everything, and he was very agreeable. He knows he owes you a debt of gratitude."

Drew had no reply for *that,* not when her excitement was beginning to infect him, giving him hope he couldn't afford right now. "What have you worked out?"

"I'm here to negotiate. I have a proposition for you.'
He waited, not daring to breathe.

Whatever she saw in his face made her expression
melt. Returning to him on light steps, she rested her
hands over his arms. "My proposition involves giving up your life. I need a protector, and there is only
one man I would have for that job."

"What about the decade or two I'll be spending in
a federal penitentiary?"

She waved an impatient hand. "There will be no
prisons or punishment. You broke rules, but there
were extenuating circumstances. It's all forgotten."
She snuggled against him, forcing him to wrap her
in his arms. Then she tipped her face to his and
smiled a smile of such peace he was reminded of
the young woman who had once danced through
the meadows of Alba Luncă without a care in the
world.

The woman he had fallen in love with.

"I am a skilled negotiator, Drew, very accomplished at getting my way. You should know this.
I want you."

He had no worthy reply, no words to convey, when
what he saw in her beautiful face was the realization
of every hope he had never admitted.

"I would only trust my life to the man who loves
me. The man I love with all my heart."

And his life was already hers. It always had been.

One year later

SUMMER IN CHARLOTTE, North Carolina, was so lush and green Mirie knew she'd found the most beautiful place in America. There were arbors everywhere, dripping with the largest, most colorful blooms, so perfect they didn't look real.

She stood beside Drew on the steps of his family home, a large house he called an antebellum plantation. His arm was around her waist, and she leaned into him, so content with the day she could only sigh.

"May I introduce Drew and Mirie Canady," Drew's brother announced from his place on the wraparound porch.

Jay was a younger version of his big brother, and he stood with his wife beside him, their toddler daughter between them, a beautiful blonde girl with her uncle's green eyes.

Their guests cheered, and Mirie glanced up at Drew to find him smiling at her. Rising up on tiptoes, she kissed her husband again, setting off another round of applause. They joined hands and took off down the stairs, waving as they passed through the crowd, greeting friends on their way to the celebration, which was taking place on the grounds by the lake, surrounded by all those gorgeous flowers. She could already hear the music on the warm summer air.

There was no media. No palace guard. No pomp one might expect from the wedding of a princess.

There were friends and loved ones. There was Georghe and Helena and Carol and the general, and people from Drew's family she'd only just met.

There was her beloved new husband.

This dear man who had given many years of his life in service to his country, and had been discharged honorably. She smiled up at him, still not quite believing they would finally be together.

She'd given many years to her country, as well. And she would continue to do so, but only on her terms, under the newly restructured government system. She would define the role of symbolic royalty to suit her and the people.

And she had already begun.

She had told her staff that she would be away on an extended vacation and had not told anyone where she would be.

Only her wedding guests. They would enjoy a few days together after the wedding, touring this area, and then they would depart, for they couldn't be away from their work for long.

Mirie and Drew, though, had other plans.

She didn't even tell Georghe when she would return to Ninsele after her honeymoon travels. She didn't know yet.

Because the first items on Mirie's new agenda were to love, and *to live*.

* * * * *

LARGER-PRINT BOOKS!
GET 2 FREE LARGER-PRINT NOVELS PLUS
2 FREE GIFTS!

HARLEQUIN®

super romance®

More Story...More Romance

YES! Please send me 2 FREE LARGER-PRINT Harlequin® Superromance® novels and my 2 FREE gifts (gifts are worth about $10). After receiving them, if I don't wish to receive any more books, I can return the shipping statement marked "cancel." If I don't cancel, I will receive 6 brand-new novels every month and be billed just $5.69 per book in the U.S. or $5.99 per book in Canada. That's a savings of at least 16% off the cover price! It's quite a bargain! Shipping and handling is just 50¢ per book in the U.S. or 75¢ per book in Canada.* I understand that accepting the 2 free books and gifts places me under no obligation to buy anything. I can always return a shipment and cancel at any time. Even if I never buy another book, the two free books and gifts are mine to keep forever.

139/339 HDN F46Y

Name _____ (PLEASE PRINT) _____

Address _____ Apt. # _____

City _____ State/Prov. _____ Zip/Postal Code _____

Signature (if under 18, a parent or guardian must sign)

Mail to the **Harlequin® Reader Service:**
IN U.S.A.: P.O. Box 1867, Buffalo, NY 14240-1867
IN CANADA: P.O. Box 609, Fort Erie, Ontario L2A 5X3

Are you a current subscriber to Harlequin Superromance books and want to receive the larger-print edition?
Call 1-800-873-8635 today or visit www.ReaderService.com.

* Terms and prices subject to change without notice. Prices do not include applicable taxes. Sales tax applicable in N.Y. Canadian residents will be charged applicable taxes. Offer not valid in Quebec. This offer is limited to one order per household. Not valid for current subscribers to Harlequin Superromance Larger-Print books. All orders subject to credit approval. Credit or debit balances in a customer's account(s) may be offset by any other outstanding balance owed by or to the customer. Please allow 4 to 6 weeks for delivery. Offer available while quantities last.

Your Privacy—The Harlequin® Reader Service is committed to protecting your privacy. Our Privacy Policy is available online at www.ReaderService.com or upon request from the Harlequin Reader Service.

We make a portion of our mailing list available to reputable third parties that offer products we believe may interest you. If you prefer that we not exchange your name with third parties, or if you wish to clarify or modify your communication preferences, please visit us at www.ReaderService.com/consumerschoice or write to us at Harlequin Reader Service Preference Service, P.O. Box 9062, Buffalo, NY 14269. Include your complete name and address.

HSRLP13R